P9-AQN-435

the thin game

the thin game

by **Edwin Bayrd**

in consultation with
Clifford F. Gastineau, M.D. and Edwin Bayrd, M.D.

NEWSWEEK BOOKS, New York

 For information address Newsweek, Inc., 444 Madison Avenue, New York, New York 10022.

Published simultaneously in Canada by Thomas Nelson & Sons, Ltd., Toronto.

First Edition

Library of Congress Cataloging in Publication Data
Bayrd, Edwin
The Thin Game
Includes index
1. Reducing 2. Reducing Diets I. Title
RM 222.2.B39 613.25 77-99204
ISBN: 0-88225-255-0

Book Design: Mary Ann Joulwan

For A.G.

CONTENTS

1

Why Diet?

Imprisoned in every fat man a thin one is wildly signaling to be let out.
Cyril Connolly

The war of the waistline—a battle that ultimately engages three out of four adult Americans—is an unremitting struggle against two potent forces. The first of these is simple hedonism, born of our widely held conviction that the pursuit of personal happiness is one of life's inalienable rights. Eating is a private joy, and dining is one of mankind's most civilized public rituals. Consequently, any attempt to restrict the pleasures of the table is likely to be regarded as an unwarranted infringement on one of the most basic of human rights—the right to overeat.

The second of these forces is force of habit. Our reasons for finding eating pleasurable have their roots in cultural practices that have existed for centuries, family customs that are generations old, and personal preferences that date back to earliest infancy. Singly, these are formidable obstacles to successful weight loss; together, they overwhelm all but the most determined dieters and sabotage nine out of ten serious diets.

Plainly, overweight Americans need an ally in the war of the waistline—and they have one in *The Thin Game.* It explains, clearly and concisely, the causes of obesity, the fraudulence of fad diets, the benefits of sound nutrition, the merits of simple exercise, and the value of behavior modification. And it concludes with a fifty-page Master Plan for Weight Control that should enable any well-motivated adult to achieve significant *permanent* weight loss.

* * *

Our culture is weight-conscious to a degree that is without precedent in human history, and we have translated that obsessive concern into something approaching a national mania for dieting. Recent statistics indicate that at least 79 million Americans are significantly overweight and that, at any given time, 52 million of them are either dieting or contemplating a diet. We are, in short, a nation of compulsive dieters, given to periodic bouts of systematic fasting and punishing self-denial aimed at achieving—and then maintaining—significant weight loss. That few of us succeed in doing so is a fact to which anyone who has ever attempted to lose weight can attest; that many of us try, despite past failures, is evidenced by the fact that the diet industry has become a multibillion-dollar business.

To achieve a consequential reduction in body weight, a dieter must do battle with his own body's remarkable capacity for maintaining body weight at a steady level. So precise are the human body's regulatory mechanisms that the difference between caloric intake and energy expenditure rarely varies more than 0.05 per cent, regardless of whether the person is lean or fat, young or old, at work or at rest. Tipping that delicate balance in favor of weight gain—either by eating more or exercising less—is relatively easy. It has been estimated, for example, that the average adult gains four pounds a year for every ten minutes of daily exercise dropped from his or her daily regimen. And it has been calculated that eating a single slice of chocolate layer cake more than your body needs each day will cause you to gain as much as *forty* pounds in a year. Few obese Americans would care to consume quite so much chocolate cake, but many do eat in excess of their caloric needs and exercise less than they should. And too late they discover that the body's metabolic balance, so easily tipped in favor of weight gain, is stubbornly resistant to attempts to achieve weight loss. As caloric intake declines, so does energy expenditure, making dieting an arduous, unpleasant, and all too frequently unrewarding chore.

Dr. A. W. Pennington took note of this phenomenon in the 1950's, at a time when he was actively promoting the virtues of the high-protein, low-carbohydrate diet now more frequently associated with Drs. Stillman and Atkins. "In the obese person of constant weight," Pennington wrote, "as in the lean, the appetite is balanced to the energy output with fine precision." He then added this sobering conclusion: "Caloric evaluations cannot match, nor conscious willpower rival, the exactness and the persistence of this biological adjustment." Which is, of course, precisely why fad diets similar to Pennington's are foredoomed to failure.

It was also Pennington, a curiously pessimistic prophet of quick weight loss, who ruefully observed that "of low-calorie diets, there are many; of patients who have solved the problem of obesity, there are few." Few indeed, if the results of a study conducted recently at a small Midwestern college are any indication. The subjects of that study were grossly obese male students, all of whom lost a considerable amount of weight during the first phase of the experiment and several of whom lost more than one hundred pounds. These results naturally gratified the clinicians who had devised the overweight students' diet—and had the experiment concluded with phase one, it might have been regarded as an unqualified success. Unhappily for everyone involved, the study included a second phase, an eighteen-month follow-up. It revealed that every student participating in the program had regained the bulk of the weight he had lost.

This pattern of significant weight loss followed by equally dramatic weight gain is not merely common, it is the rule—as millions of Americans know from bitter personal experience. Few cases are as dramatic as the one reported by Dr. Hilde

Bruch, a professor of psychology at Baylor Medical College, who observed a young female patient lose, regain, lose, and regain a total of 500 pounds between her fourteenth and seventeenth birthdays. But millions of cases repeat this discouraging and ultimately dangerous pattern on a more modest scale.

Consider, for instance, the not atypical case, reported recently by the *Washington Post*, of a forty-eight-year-old Philadelphia woman who had been on diets of one sort or another since she was eleven. In those thirty-seven years her weight had never exceeded 183 pounds, and in the last decade or so it had twice dropped to 124 pounds. By her own estimate the woman had lost an aggregate of 375 pounds at a total cost of $14,288—or $38 per pound. At the time she was interviewed, she had broken a twenty-seven-year-long dependency on amphetamine-based diet pills and had lost twenty-eight pounds on a protein-sparing modified fast. She was, she said, beginning to regain the weight she had lost on this most recent fad diet, her twentieth in approximately as many years.

Some 40 million Americans—two-thirds of them past forty and most of them women—are seriously overweight. The average overweight American embarks upon three serious diets every two years, each one lasting two to three months. This amounts to fifteen major diets between the ages of twenty and fifty, and it means that overweight Americans are eating unappealing, unpalatable, and, all too frequently, unnourishing food for at least a quarter of their adult lives. Clearly, if the first of these diets proved a success, the next fourteen would be unnecessary. The fact that they are necessary—that many Americans are dieting at more or less regular intervals from adolescence through late middle age—is in itself a condemnation not only of national eating habits but also of modern medicine's ability to cope effectively with what is now recognized as the country's number-one health problem.

Few experts in the field of diet and nutrition would disagree with Dr. Albert J. Stunkard's assessment of the problem: "Most obese persons will not remain in treatment. Of those who do remain in treatment, most will not lose much weight, and of those who do lose weight, most will regain it promptly." In the face of such a resoundingly pessimistic prognosis, proffered by one of the acknowledged experts in the field, it seems reasonable to question the wisdom of any attempt to lose weight. Does any diet really work? Does anyone really manage to take weight off and keep it off, permanently? The answer to both questions is a qualified but emphatic yes.

Any program of systematic weight loss, if it is to be effective, must be undertaken with a clear idea of how the body functions, both under normal circumstances and under the additional physiological and psychological stresses imposed by dieting. The risks as well as the benefits of dieting should be understood, and the limits of what one can reasonably expect from a diet, if one is to lose weight and *not* regain it, should be defined. But with all of that clarified, weight reduction becomes not only possible but desirable for all overweight people, regardless of age or sex. The exceptions—persons with certain psychiatric or somatic problems such as those suffering from tuberculosis and chronic ulcerative colitis—are sufficiently uncommon that they need not be mentioned here except in passing. Such people are invariably under a physician's care anyway, and where weight reduction is indicated it can usually be achieved gradually. For the rest of us it is overweight, not weight loss, that presents the real threat to our well-being.

The dangers of obesity are legion, and many are genuinely life-threatening. More Americans die of heart and circulatory system diseases each year than of anything else, and the preponderance of these deaths is directly attributable to atherosclerosis, or hardening of the arteries. Reflecting on the number of fatal cases of cardiovascular disease that occurs annually in the United States—the figure now exceeds 1 million per year—Jean Mayer, the dean of American nutritionists, observed, "The development of cardiovascular diseases has essentially nullified in the past twenty years our advances in medicine and our advances in social and health sciences to the point where we have made almost no gain in the life expectancy of adult men"—this despite the fact that annual medical expenditures in the

United States have risen from $12 billion to $106 billion in the past two decades.

Where they do not kill, atherosclerosis and obesity contribute to a number of other incapacitating cardiovascular problems, among them congestive heart failure, angina pectoris, hypertension, cardiac enlargement, varicose veins, and polycythemia, a blood disorder that may abnormally enhance the possibility of blood clots. In addition, excess weight on the chest wall makes breathing less effective. As a result, some overweight men and women may have cold hands and feet because their lungs cannot keep their bodies properly oxygenated—and therefore warm. Obesity is also directly linked to diabetes, to certain gallbladder disorders, to a number of endocrine gland and metabolic disturbances, and to osteoarthritis, an inflammation of the weight-bearing joints. In pregnant women, obesity can lead to toxemia, complications in surgery and delivery, and stillbirths.

Even from this partial catalog it is clear that, from a health standpoint alone, anyone with a significant weight problem should reduce. Add to this the knowledge that with some of the aforementioned diseases moderate obesity may have almost as adverse an effect as severe obesity, and it is clear that anyone with a weight problem of any sort should reduce. But how do you know if you actually are overweight? Most doctors define clinical obesity as weight exceeding the norm for one's height and build by 10 per cent. What they have more trouble defining is just what normal is.

For a large-boned woman of medium height, for instance, 146 pounds is considered the tolerable upper limit of the normal range, yet one would be hard-pressed to find a large-boned woman of medium height who was happy at that weight. Professional athletes represent the other extreme; many of them are technically overweight without being the least bit fat. (Readers may recall what happened to the members of the 1941 Green Bay Packers football team when they tried to enlist in the Navy on the day after Pearl Harbor was attacked: they were rejected to a man as being overweight.)

The question of what constitutes excess body weight, then,

can be highly subjective. Some overweight people carry their extra pounds well, both in physical and in emotional terms, while others, with no apparent weight problems at all, succumb to an emotional disorder known as anorexia nervosa and literally starve themselves to death. There are a number of methods of determining how closely your own weight approximates the ideal for your age, sex, and body type; these will be discussed in a later chapter. A competent physician can assist you in this diagnosis, but you should be aware that he cannot mandate weight loss. That decision rests with the individual.

If the decision is to lose weight, there are several other questions that you must ask youself. The first question, which requires some understanding of diet and nutrition, is: Can I diet successfully? And the answer here is that anyone can, but some are destined to have a much rougher time of it than others. Jean Mayer, who headed Harvard University's School of Public Health before becoming president of Tufts, likes to say that girls with long, skinny fingers will never get fat. This is demonstrably so, but Mayer offers it not for its face value but to underscore the role that heredity plays in obesity. In his estimation it is critical to discover when the onset of obesity occurred, for "persons who were obese as youngsters are much more likely to be obsessively concerned with self-image and to view their obesity as a badge of shame rather than as a medical problem which can be attacked by rather simple means." Also, of course, they are much more likely to have failed repeatedly to control their weight in the past, and failures have a way of anticipating failure.

All the evidence seems to suggest that Mayer is right: the longer you have been overweight, the more difficulty you will have in taking weight off—and those who have been fat since childhood will have the most trouble of all. Fully one-third of all overweight adults were overweight as children, and more than 80 per cent of the children reared by obese parents grow up to be obese themselves. (This is true for a number of reasons—some physical, some psychological, and some purely circumstantial, as we shall discover in an ensuing chapter.) So bleak does Mayer consider the prospects for significant weight loss among the chronically obese that he states flatly that "Diets and willpower are useless prescriptions for those millions of Americans who have been obese since infancy."

What makes fat children fat—what makes anyone fat—is adipose tissue, better known as fat cells. These cells serve a number of extremely vital bodily functions, no matter what your weight. They cushion the body; they insulate the internal organs and conserve heat; they perform highly complex metabolic interconversions between proteins, carbohydrates, and fat; and they both store and burn reserve energy in the form of fat. The problem in cases of obesity is twofold. First, most overweight individuals, particularly those who have been too heavy since childhood or adolescence, have a superabundance of fat cells—sometimes three times as many as their lean contemporaries. And second, all overweight individuals have fat cells that are themselves too fat, gorged with stored energy that the body will never conceivably use. A man who is a hundred pounds heavier than his theoretical ideal weight, for instance, is carrying a third of a *million* unburned calories around with him.

Whether this excess of adipose tissue is the result of heredity or environment, or a combination of the two, is not altogether clear, but it does appear that adipose tissue is formed during infancy and early childhood, and that once fat cells have been created they are there forever. Any subsequent weight loss merely shrinks the existing cells; it does not diminish their number. There is even some evidence to suggest that the fat cells themselves generate fat, with bigger cells obviously generating more fat than smaller ones.

Plainly, then, the problem begins at a very tender age—and it often persists throughout life. More than 80 per cent of all fat five-year-olds grow up to be fat adults. Their bodies contain two or three times as much fat as do those of their peers, in part because they often have three times as many adipose cells, in part because those cells are one and a half times as large as normal. In trying to cope with their obesity in later life, former obese children often find themselves doubly cursed. According to Dr. Bruch, the very mothers who encourage overeating tend to discourage exercise. This means that obese children often grow up with two critical deficiencies: an inability to control their intake of food and a failure to enjoy exercise.

Food is the most abundant and least expensive mood-altering drug on the market, and it is hardly surprising that nutritionally ignorant mothers all too frequently use food as a means of modifying and controlling their offspring's behavior. Used initially to silence a crying child—whose tantrums are as often provoked by physical discomfort, emotional distress, or simply a need for "mothering" as by hunger pangs—food soon becomes a device for securing correct behavior. Going without dinner is the supreme punishment; an extra dessert, the ultimate reward.

Thus conditioned from infancy, overweight children mature into obese adults who respond socially rather than physiologically to food. They eat at mealtimes, whether their stomachs are full or not, having lost the perception of hunger as an internal stimulus. And deprived of the "euphoriant effect" that ordinarily accompanies exercise, they are deprived of the other vital component of any weight-loss program—physical exertion. An active man or woman with a modest weight problem is often able to achieve half of his daily caloric deficit—the crux of any diet—by exercising rather than by restriction of food intake alone. The passive, obese individual rarely exercises this option.

We know, then, that the roots of adult obesity lie in the eating habits and patterns of socialization established in early childhood, habits practiced with such regularity over a long period of time that they become, for all intents and purposes, autonomic and reflexive—that is, performed below the level of consciousness. Knowing this, we may be able to save the current generation of overweight infants from chronic, lifelong obesity. It is the American Medical Association's contention that the only real cure for obesity is prevention, the affliction itself being so stubbornly resistant to correction after its onset.

This is all well and good where the present generation of fat babies is concerned, but it is no help at all to the millions of overweight adults who developed their pernicious eating habits and their engorged adipose tissue decades ago, the chronically obese individuals whom Dr. Mayer has written off as virtually beyond salvation. They put on their pounds long before medicine produced its ounces of prevention, which makes their problem that much more resistant to treatment—but far still from hopeless. There are a number of solutions to the problem of adult obesity. Unfortunately, not all of them are equally attractive, and none is guaranteed.

From the physician's point of view, the easiest way to induce weight loss is to encourage a heightened level of physical activity while prescribing a nutritionally balanced diet that yields a daily caloric deficit. Even the most intractable excess poundage ultimately responds to this sort of regimen, if only the patient can be persuaded to follow it long enough. Unhappily, the universal experience of the medical profession is that most overweight individuals abandon their professionally supervised diets before those regimens can have their full effect, and an even larger number soon resume the uncontrolled eating habits that made them fat to begin with. In short, doctors find that it is extremely difficult to get a corpulent patient to stick to even the most modest regimen, and it is nearly impossible to get that patient to exercise.

The physician's task in this regard is complicated by the durability of the erroneous belief—probably fostered by the indolent overweight themselves—that exercise only increases appetite. In truth, exercise does not increase the voluntary intake of food until it has reached a certain critical point of intensity and duration—a matter of concern to marathon runners, but not to Sunday joggers. Up to that critical point the caloric expenditure actually increases with the intensity of the exercise—and it increases proportionally to body weight, which means that overweight individuals use more calories to do the same amount of work, no matter what the task. The great pity is that they don't work as hard as their lean counterparts.

Studies show, for example, that overweight housewives walk half as far in the course of their daily chores as thin housewives do, although both are performing essentially the same duties. They also spend an extra half hour in bed each night and 15 per cent less time on their feet during the day—additional proof of what Dr. Mayer calls the obese individual's almost preternatural capacity for conserving his or her energy reserves—and with them, of course, the body's stored fat.

Part of the problem with assessing the value of exercise has to do with the obsolescence of the scientific nomenclature that is used to describe it. When the German physiologist Karl von Voit devised his four standard classifications of personality by activity—very active, active, moderately active, and sedentary—he was basing his descriptions on nineteenth-century models. His sedentary type, for instance, was a clerk. But in those days a clerk was someone who got up at first light, split wood or hauled coal for an hour, walked an hour to work, worked standing up at a scrivener's desk for ten hours, walked home, and did his evening chores. He did this six days a week. On the seventh day, his day of rest, he took his family on a three- or four-hour walk in the country. As Mayer says, "There isn't any city dweller in the United States who expends as much energy as did that sedentary man of 1890." This explains, in part, why we eat less than our turn-of-the-century ancestors did but weigh more.

Much the same can be said for most exercise charts, which tend to give caloric equivalents for what are, in this day and age, irrelevant expenditures of energy. It hardly benefits Professor Mayer's city dweller to learn that it takes seven hours of log-splitting to shed a single pound; few American males spend that much time chopping wood in their entire lives. But it would have been highly relevant information for Herr Voit's archetypal clerk of the 1890's who spent half an hour each day in his woodshed. To the modern urbanite, who does not know how to sharpen an axe, let alone wield it, such a statistic is meaningless. To Voit's "sedentary" clerk, who stood to lose twenty-six pounds a year through such exercise if he could not make up the caloric deficit at the dinner table, it would have been pertinent indeed.

What all overweight Americans need to know is the true value of all forms of exercise. A man who plays tennis, squash, or handball twice a week can take off sixteen pounds a year, and a woman who takes a brisk twenty-minute walk each morning after the children have left for school can lose ten. Exercise is, in Mayer's words, "the great variable in energy expenditure" and therefore in weight loss. It is also, by and large, the neglected variable. So valuable is exercise—the subject of Chapter 6 of this book—that no serious exponent of sensible weight reduction could fail to stress its importance. As we shall see, neither sex nor age is a barrier to this most efficacious method of girth control.

The second alternative open to anyone who wishes to lose weight is to opt for a calorically restricted diet. In order to shed one pound of body fat, the average adult must cut his calorie intake by 3,500 units. Physicians generally recommend a calorie cutback of roughly 500 units per day, which in theory permits the conscientious dieter to drop a pound a week for as long as he or she chooses to adhere to the diet. There are a number of reasons why this theory does not translate so neatly into practice. One is the sheer difficulty of devising a diet that provides all the necessary nutrients except calories, that is inexpensive and uncomplicated to prepare, and that is also palatable.

The situation is further complicated by the fact that individual caloric needs vary greatly, with active males sometimes requiring twice the caloric intake of more sedentary females. Moreover, active, ambulatory men and women cannot easily tolerate a diet that contains fewer than 1,000 calories per day for an extended period of time without becoming listless and irritable. Mayer considers it "very unwise for people, except under extreme circumstances and almost under hospitalization, to have a deficit of more than 1,000 calories for any length of time."

To combat the body's reluctance to accommodate itself to such change, medical science and the diet industry have developed a plethora of diet aids designed to suppress or simply confound the body's normal responses to food. Foremost among these are the so-called diet pills—mixtures of amphetamines, barbiturates, stimulants, and sedatives that have a powerful, if temporary, impact on the hypothalamus, the satiety center of the brain, creating a pharmacologic sense of fullness in the absence of real food. As we will later see, the short-term effect of these diet pills can be impressive. They do produce immediate and dramatic weight loss in most cases. They also create an excess of tension and generate both cardiovascular and gastroenterological disturbances. Used regularly for a month to six weeks, they can induce hallucinations and paranoid delusions. For reasons not clearly understood, they also lose their effectiveness within a six-week period, and the pill user not infrequently regains all the weight he or she has dropped.

The liquid diet—once Metrecal, now liquid protein—is another means of achieving a rapid drop in body weight. It shares all of the virtues of the amphetamine-regulated diet—it is essentially passive, it obviates self-control as a factor, and it produces immediate and dramatic results. As it happens, in its latter form it shares the vices associated with diet pills, namely that it is potentially life-threatening and should properly be undertaken only with competent medical supervision. Not incidentally, it also shares the basic failing of all "quick weight-loss" diets, namely that it in no way alters the subject's basic eating habits—and that in itself makes regression virtually a foregone conclusion.

One step beyond this regimen is the total fast, generally supplemented by vitamins and essential salts dissolved in water. Within forty-eight hours most fasting patients lose all sensations of hunger, and thereafter they can often tolerate the fast for up to a full month. (Dr. C.C. Sturgis, a professor of internal medicine at the University of Michigan, insisted that it is possible for a person to live for four or five months on nothing but water and roughly one hundred pounds of his own fatty tissue.) During the course of the fast the liver is gradually depleted of stored glycogen, a starchy substance that is rapidly converted to glucose, the body's principal source of energy. Unfortunately, muscle protein as well as body fat is depleted during the fast, and ketone bodies are produced. Ketones, powerful appetite suppressants, account for the loss of hunger that occurs during the second day of any rigorous fast.

So-called ketogenic, or ketone-producing, diets have been around for better than a century. An English surgeon by the name of William Harvey first began experimenting with high-protein, low-carbohydrate, ketone-generating diets in the mid-1800's, and the regimen he developed is generally known as the Banting Diet, after an early patient of Harvey's who was so delighted by the effects of the good doctor's weight-loss program that he published a broadside in praise of it. Since that time versions of the Banting Diet, with minor modifications, have cropped up at regular intervals: as the Pennington or Dupont Diet in 1953, the Air Force Diet in 1960, as the Drinking Man's Diet in 1965, and as the Stillman and Atkins diets in the 1970's.

Although these diets differ a bit in specifics, they all generate short-term weight loss by inducing ketosis. The long-term results of this gross disturbance of the body's metabolic function are irritability, lethargy, decreased productivity, and changes in mental activity. The short-term results of such diets, on the other hand, are undeniably impressive: with rare exception all those who faithfully follow a ketogenic diet manage to register consequential weight losses for as long as they can endure the diet and sustain their bodies in a ketonic state. What must be stressed, therefore, is that the initial weight loss achieved by disciples of Pennington, Stillman, and Atkins is *illusory*.

During the first few days of a ketogenic diet the kidneys, unable to conserve salt and water, shed a portion of the body's water weight through diuresis, or copious urination. There is no loss of body mass at this point, and the weight loss that occurs later on comes as a result of *total* caloric restriction imposed by the ketone bodies, not as a direct result of any particular combination of proteins and fats. The result is a pattern of rapid weight loss, lasting precisely as long as the patient can endure the diet, followed by rapid weight gain at approximately the same rate.

The first sign of a rising intolerance to ketogenic diets is pathologically low blood pressure, often followed by a generalized sense of fatigue, and two months seems very nearly the outside limit of endurance on such a regime. There are other, less noticeable but equally pernicious side effects of such diets, a principal one being that the ketogenic diet is high in fats, which not only increase blood lipids and cholesterol levels, but accelerate the development of atherosclerosis. Over the long term, it would seem, there is nothing to recommend such extreme diets over a calorically restricted, nutritionally balanced diet—and much to recommend against them.

One alternative to strenuous exercise—which most obese people will not tolerate—and extreme diets—which many of them cannot tolerate—is a group like Weight Watchers, Diet Workshop, or TOPS, all of which stress group therapy over serious fasting. According to Dr. Bruch, who has studied such groups extensively, they are for the most part composed of middle-class, middle-aged women who feel culturally or emotionally isolated. They are, of course, of no value whatsoever to chronically obese people with deep-rooted personality disorders, for such individuals are beyond responding to the cheery socializing that is the weight-loss club's stock-in-trade. But for the thousands who belong to these clubs, the combination of public humiliation and private encouragement is an effective spur to continued weight reduction, at least as long as the member remains with the club.

Perhaps the single most significant development in the dietary field in the past century is what is known as behavior modification. Based on the theory that obesity is an addictive behavior disorder akin to alcoholism or drug addiction—and both complex and difficult to change for precisely that reason—behavior modification programs attempt to alter how you eat rather than what you eat. The results are sometimes startling. Conventional methods of weight reduction rarely produce more than one dieter in four who can lose twenty pounds—and less than 5 per cent ever lose more than forty. The leading behavior modification specialists, on the other hand, report that a whopping 80 per cent of their patients achieve the first goal and fully 30 per cent achieve the second.

The exact nature of behavior modification programs will be dealt with at greater length in a separate chapter. For the moment let it suffice to observe that behavior modification is of immense value in treating the group that Dr. Bruch identifies as "the 50 million middle-aged Americans who are overweight and eat too much because it is there." Those people, as it happens, also respond well to programs like Weight Watchers and do well under the care of a physician. What behavior modification cannot do is reach people who have severe personality problems, and this group includes those who most need to lose weight, either from the point of view of their health or that of their emotional well-being.

If both body and temperament resist weight loss, if sedentary Americans resist the notion of diet or exercise even when their lives depend upon it, and if the currently popular diets offer little more than what Jean Mayer calls the "rhythm method of girth control"—loss followed by like gain in an endless cycle—then what answer is there for the millions of Americans who must lose weight? There is indeed an answer, one that the internationally renowned Mayo Clinic has long espoused—even as it has steadfastly denied authorship of the succession of fad diets that bear its name. The purpose of this book is to provide that answer. It is contained in the Master Plan, a sensible, easy-to-follow program for gradual, long-term, *permanent* weight loss—a program accessible to anyone who wants to reduce, regardless of age, sex, or past experience with diets.

2

The Mechanics of Fat

Ascribing overweight to overeating is hardly more illuminating than ascribing alcoholism to overdrinking.

Jean Mayer

Of all creatures on earth, only humans—and some, but not all, of the animals man has domesticated—become fat. They do so because they are regularly consuming more food than their bodies need or can utilize and because the body, with an efficiency superior to that of any machine, rapidly converts that excess food to stored fat. The short-term result of such behavior is an increase in adipose tissue; the long-term result is chronic obesity. There is no disputing this fact; if obesity can properly be labeled a disease, then it has a universally acknowledged etiology—gluttony—and a stipulated cure—fasting. But as Dr. Mayer observes, ascribing obesity to overeating tells us nothing we do not already know, and we desperately need to know more about the nature of obesity and the mechanics of fat if we are to rescue ourselves from a national eating binge that has, in the past half century, made obesity the most prevalent physical abnormality in America.

Obesity itself is at least as old as settled society and probably a great deal older. The famous Neolithic Venus figurines, with their pendulous breasts, protuberant abdomens, and fleshy limbs, may have represented idealized female somotypes, but they were almost certainly based on actual models. Gross obesity was a prized attribute in Paleolithic females for several reasons. It was directly associated with fecundity—which often meant the difference between survival and extinction 25,000 years ago—and it was indirectly linked to mortality. It has been estimated that less than half of all Paleolithic peoples lived as long as twenty years, and only 12 per cent reached the then considerable age of forty. There were no females at all in this latter group, and studies of Ice Age skeletons indicate that the women of this period never lived beyond thirty. Under such daunting conditions, each extra pound of reserve energy that a woman carried materially increased her chances of surviving the vagaries of a bitter climate and uncertain diet, the depredations of predators, both animal and human, and the rigors of pregnancy and childbirth.

It is interesting to note in this regard that fat people are found in the greatest numbers in climates where the food supply is seasonal; in the Arctic as at the equator, climate is constant and so is genotype. This would seem to suggest that, over the centuries, peoples living in regions where the food supply was unpredictable or variable developed a greater capacity for fat storage against prospective famine—what geneticist James Neel calls "thrifty" genotypes. The Paleolithic Venuses belong to this group, which is characterized by large bones, long torsos, barrel chests, and short limbs. It is, in short, a frame well adapted to conserving body heat, for the surface area is small relative to the body's bulk, and the vital organs are thoroughly insulated.

It is also, more often than not, a short frame as well, and it is not mere happenstance that the Lapps, who live within the Arctic Circle, are among the shortest of peoples, the men averaging slightly over five feet in height. Here the adaptation is to cold rather than fluctuating food supply, of course, and it should be noted that the Lapps, like the Eskimos, are rarely obese. Neither, for that matter, are the Pygmies of the African rain forests, whose diminutive stature is probably a response to humidity rather than temperature. Their Nilotic neighbors, the Masai, who inhabit one of the most arid regions on earth, are the world's tallest people, with male tribesmen regularly exceeding six feet in height. Here the adaptation is to implacable heat: long limbs increase the evaporative surface area of the body, and this helps stabilize internal temperature.

Obesity, once vital to survival in a hostile and precarious world, became maladaptive as soon as men settled in cities, where the fluctuations of food supply were minimized and the physiological drawbacks of overweight became of greater concern than the prospect of famine. It was the advent of the city that permitted the first real division of labor, allowing some men to become shopkeepers while others tilled the fields. The latter, the Bible's hewers of wood and toters of water, remained lean; the former became increasingly sedentary—and increasingly overweight.

One need only look at the wooden statue of the portly Sheikh el-Beled, an ancient Egyptian official who lived almost five thousand years ago, to appreciate how long corpulence has been the curse of the sedentary class. Until very recent times, of course, that class has been extremely small, so small that significant overweight has traditionally been associated with great wealth and at least until World War II it was both customary and logical to speak of bankers and businessmen who wore their success around their middles.

What is most startling about the pandemic of obesity that has swept the United States and Western Europe in the latter half of this century is that it obeys no historical rules and observes no social class distinctions. If anything, the old order is reversed. A noteworthy study conducted in New York City in 1974 showed obesity to be *seven times* more prevalent among members of the lowest socio-economic order than among members of the highest. Overweight, it would seem, is an all-but-universal dilemma in an affluent society, but it is not necessarily the special problem of that society's most affluent members.

If American society is indeed the first in history in which mass obesity has manifested itelf, then it must follow that overeating is the nation's number-one health problem. A recent report issued by the Department of Health, Education and Welfare maintains that the average American male is eighteen pounds overweight and the average female, twenty-one pounds. In fact, Americans as a nation are eating so much and so well that the diseases medicine associates with undernourished, primitive societies—rickets, pellagra, scurvy—have been virtually eliminated, only to be replaced by a host of obesity-related disorders.

To appreciate the profound impact that postwar affluence has had on the nation's health, we need only look at the dramatic increase in diagnosed cases of diabetes, an affliction commonly aggravated by overeating. In 1950 there were 1.2 million known diabetics in the United States; today there are 5 million, and 40 per cent of them are severely overweight. As Dr. Richard F. Spark of Harvard Medical School has ruefully noted, "We are in a chronic state of caloric surfeit, and it is our own fault. We have demanded and constructed a society that has made it hard to stay thin . . . Our daily routine could not be more perfectly designed to promote obesity."

Fatness is certainly a personal catastrophe, but it is also a social problem and a medical dilemma. Its underlying causes are psychological and circumstantial as well as physiological—which is why it is both insufficient and inaccurate to say simply that overeating causes overweight. Overweight is also due, in differing degrees in different cases, to hereditary factors, endocrine disturbances, poor nutritional and dietary habits, and psychological disorders. Because its cause is so complex, varying not only from individual to individual but, within each individual, from year to year and even month to month, obesity is remarkably resistant to treatment. Knowing this, and knowing that some 95 per cent of all diets ultimately fail to produce permanent weight loss, many physicians are reluctant to prescribe even the most modest of low-calorie balanced diets for their overweight patients, reckoning that the stress and anxiety that are induced by dieting may more than counterbalance the benefits that are derived from a small temporary weight loss.

Sadly, this professional pessimism comes at a time when the need for sound counseling on the subjects of weight loss and weight control is as great as it has ever been. According to Dr. Clifford F. Gastineau, a Mayo Clinic physician who has long been interested in the problems associated with the treatment of obesity, statistics suggest that modern medicine is rapidly approaching a point of diminishing returns in terms of curing the diseases that afflict mankind. Even redoubled efforts on the part of the medical community may reduce the death rate only slightly, he believes, unless more attention is paid to solving the problem of obesity, which has been called preventive medicine's greatest failure.

Dr. Gastineau, the co-author of a book on obesity, is convinced that "great improvement in the health of the nation is possible to achieve by means of the correction and prevention of obesity." Doing so, he says, will require that doctors across the country recognize the perils of excess weight, appreciate that while the disease of obesity can never be cured the symptoms of fatness can be alleviated, and "develop something of the missionary spirit and zeal in correcting obesity." Failure to do so would be particularly unfortunate, Gastineau concludes, precisely because reducing "may be the very best chance to lengthen the life and diminish the future illnesses of the patient."

With the exception of emphysema (which is exacerbated by, not caused by, obesity and which is irreversible), all the diseases that become more life-threatening with each pound an obese person gains become less so with each pound lost, and some disappear altogether. As we have already noted, the correlation between corpulence and obesity-related diseases is not linear, with the risks increasing in direct proportion to the excess poundage the individual carries; some afflictions are as common in the moderately overweight as in the morbidly obese. What does seem to correlate is the relationship between weight *loss* and life expectancy: the mortality rates for men who have successfully lost weight after having been obese are approximately the same as those for men who were never obese.

This is true in large part because our major health problems today are those associated with the so-called degenerative diseases, particularly cardiovascular disease, and gross obesity accelerates the process of degeneration. Smallpox and measles, scarlet fever and influenza, tuberculosis and typhus, cholera and yellow fever, dysentery, polio and bacterial infection—the great plagues and epidemic contagions of the previous century—no longer pose a serious health hazard in contemporary America. And because we no longer die in infancy of fevers, pox, or mumps—or later in life of infectious diseases borne in our food and drinking water—we die instead of degenerative diseases or from cancer.

According to Ancel Keys, onetime director of the Laboratory of Physiological Hygiene at the University of Minnesota, there is good reason to believe that the incidence of degenerative diseases in the general population is strongly influenced by habitual diet. In a later chapter we will review the evidence that suggests a causal relationship between high-fat, high-cholesterol diets and cardiovascular disease, and between low-fiber diets and colo-rectal cancers. These facts and figures will only serve to confirm the widespread belief that overeating causes the vast preponderance of modern health problems—and that eating correctly helps to eliminate many of them. Faced with such evidence, one must concur with Dr. Gastineau that the time has come for a concerted, coordinated assault on the nation's leading health hazard, one conducted with missionary spirit and zeal.

At whom should this assault be directed? At the nation's 79 million overweight citizens, of course; but also at "fat doctors" who promote expensive, short-term weight-loss programs as a substitute for sensible regimens and dietary reeducation. And at the multimillion-dollar exercise industry, which peddles unneeded and sometimes downright dangerous paraphernalia to gullible buyers whose immediate need is to shed excess weight not build muscle bulk. And at the multibillion-dollar diet food industry, which foists hundreds of additive-laden, saccharin-laced, possibly potentially carcinogenic products upon a nutritionally ignorant public that responds to the illusion of sugar in sugar-free drinks, desserts, and snacks and ignores the potential dangers. (These dangers are psychological as well as physiological, for although the carcinogenic properties of cyclamates and saccharin in the human diet have not been conclusively established, the detrimental effects of excessive sugar consumption have. It is the nurturing of the nation's collective "sweet tooth" that is the real evil, and sweeteners add to this dietary problem even as they eliminate actual calories from the diet.)

Our assault should also be aimed at the manufacturers and distributors of sugar-saturated "convenience" foods, which account for 60 per cent of the typical American diet and provide the consumer with nutritionally empty calories that add nothing to the diet but taste—and rot the teeth of the taster. And it might as well include food faddists, health food hucksters, promoters of dietary supplements and weight-reducing pills, and even those members of the medical profession who may mislead and misinform their overweight patients. In sum, the list is so comprehensive that there are very few soldiers left over to launch Gastineau's campaign. As Walt Kelly's Pogo so rightly observed: "I have seen the enemy and they are us."

Who is fat? Not all of us, surely, although if the Department of Health, Education and Welfare's figures are even roughly correct—if the average American male is eighteen pounds overweight and the average female is twenty-one pounds overweight—then more than half of us are indisputably fat. And since most current definitions of "average" weight are generous in their allowances—and since most physicians do not regard patients as medically obese unless they weigh at least 10 per cent more than the upper limit for "average" in their age and height category—it can reasonably be assumed that the actual number of seriously overweight Americans is higher than any official estimates. And those estimates range upwards from 30 per cent of all adult Americans—which means that there are a minimum of 50 to 60 million overweight men and women in this country. Add to this number millions of adult Americans—the recently graduated, the recently wed, the recently pregnant, the recently divorced, the recently bereaved—who have gained ten, fifteen, or even twenty unwanted pounds, and you understand the justification for Anne Scott Beller's declaration in *Fat and Thin, A Natural History of Obesity,* that weight loss is a daily preoccupation for 70 per cent of the United States population.

Who is fat? Children born to fat parents are fat. Some 40 per cent of those children born to one overweight parent are themselves overweight, and a staggering 80 per cent of those with two overweight parents are obese. Certainly there is no more pitiful figure in all the data on obesity, for these fat babies invariably grow up to be fat adults. Fewer than one in five manages to avoid lifelong obesity, and those who do are often condemned to a lifetime of strenuous dieting. As Dr. Mayer has noted, "People *can* control their weight, and they don't necessarily let their genotype blossom." But the price that these formerly fat children—these fat men imprisoned in thin bodies, signaling wildly to be let out—must pay is a terrible one indeed, for they have been doomed, perhaps from the moment of conception, to a perpetual fast, a never-ending struggle against their genotype.

Three principal factors contribute to childhood obesity, and the first of these—heredity—is both the most disputed and the most immutable. Dr. Mayer has long held that genetics plays a key role in determining who is fat, and he backs up his assertion with the results of his studies of identical twins, who generally remain within four pounds of each other in weight throughout their lives. Siblings of the same sex, on the other hand, often outweigh one another by ten pounds or more. To some extent, of course, this can be attributed to the mere fact that twins are twins, raised in the same household and fed the same food. But Dr. Mayer has also studied sets of identical twins who have been raised separately, and he has found that their weights do not vary more than 4 per cent, even when the environments in which they have been raised differ considerably.

Studies conducted by Dr. Stanley M. Garn of the Center for Human Growth and Development in Ann Arbor, Michigan, flatly contradict Mayer on this last point. It is Garn's contention that "fatness in families shows evidence of being learned, and not simply gene-determined." In a sense this is good news for the overweight, who need no longer regard themselves as foredoomed to fatness. But in another sense it may be very bad news, for the grip of habit is very nearly as powerful as the vise of heredity, and if Garn is right, then the thin man who fails to break through the prison walls of his own fat cannot blame his genes for that failure.

The single most consequential genetic factor in obesity is, of course, sex. Girl babies are generally smaller than boy babies, but they are always fatter. A greater percentage of their total body weight is adipose tissue, and the disparity grows more pronounced with each passing year. Men, for the most part, tend to reach their maximum weight while in their thirties or early forties, whereas women go on depositing fat for as long as two decades thereafter. In both, muscle tissue stops proliferating in the late teens and early twenties, which means that whatever weight is added thereafter is fat. And because the female body is "thriftier" than the male, women can maintain their excess fat on roughly 10 per cent fewer calories than those consumed by males of the same age, weight, height, and level of physical activity. The relationship of sex to weight is not quite as simple as it may sound, for statistics show that while black women are generally fatter than white, black men are thinner than white men.

The second factor contributing to childhood obesity is diet, and most experts now agree that the modern mother's feeding practices are outmoded and out of phase with the times, better suited to the active life of nineteenth-century America than to the sedentary life of the twentieth century. Modern feeding practices, which include the early introduction of solid foods, early weaning, and a shift from breast- to bottle-feeding, all encourage overfeeding. Increasingly it is the mother, rather than the infant, who determines hunger and satiety, by feeding on schedule rather than on demand and by feeding by unit—one bottle, one bowl, one cup—rather than by need. The result of this well-intentioned force-feeding, prompted by motherly devotion and administered out of false conviction that a fat baby is a healthy baby, is the unchecked production of superfluous fat cells during the first years of a child's life.

These same women, responding to another, equally erroneous maxim—"You're pregnant; you're eating for two"—overeat during the last stages of their confinement. In doing so, they not only gain weight they themselves do not need, weight that they will have great difficulty shedding after delivery, they also promote the development of fat cells in their unborn children, who develop much of their adipose tissue during the last trimester in utero. (It is known, for example, that the excess fat that distinguishes girl babies is acquired during the two or three weeks immediately prior to delivery.) Thus the best-intentioned mother-to-be sometimes jeopardizes the health of her unborn child by striving too hard to ensure it. And the child who is born fat, and who is consciously and conscientiously fattened from birth, may lose his chance for a lean adulthood before he is old enough to walk. By the age of two an obese child may already have developed half the fat cells found in a normal adult—and by the age of six or seven he may have two or three times as many fat cells as the average adult.

It should be noted in passing that pregnancy is universally lipogenic, or fat-producing, and the vogue for keeping pregnant women on a strict diet, one that restricts their weight gain to fifteen to eighteen pounds (the estimated combined weight of the fetus, placenta, and amniotic fluid), is now generally recommended only for women who are obese at the onset of pregnancy. Among other things, such strenuous dieting may possibly lead to impaired brain development in the fetus—and to abnormally small spleen, liver, and adrenal glands. The "normal" weight gain during pregnancy ranges from zero to fifty pounds, with the average somewhere between twenty-three and twenty-five pounds. The function of this seemingly superfluous fat is to protect the mother during delivery and immediately thereafter—a holdover from Paleolithic times, when many an expectant mother delivered on the trail and then proceeded alone to rejoin her tribe.

It is the conclusion of Drs. Jules Hirsch and Jerome Knittle of Rockefeller University that all individuals who have been fat since childhood have an abnormally large number of fat cells, and that the earlier in life this obesity begins, the greater the number of these cells. By contrast, people who become overweight later in life do not have an excessive number of fat cells; their existing adipose cells are merely enlarged. This is a very real difference, and it has profound impact on an individual's ability to successfully control his weight after adolescence. Since all a diet can ever hope to achieve, no matter how protracted or strenuous it is, is a gradual shrinking of the body's fat cells, those cells remain a potent threat even when a lower, more desirable weight has been reached. They never vanish, and their number determines the speed with which weight is regained once the diet has been abandoned.

This phenomenon is graphically demonstrated by the case of a female patient who went to a famous clinic some years ago. Among other things, she was suffering from morbid obesity. Her doctors at the clinic put her on a nutritionally balanced, 1,000-calorie-per-day diet, and by adhering to it she managed to lose more than 150 pounds over a period of several years. At the end of that time she returned to the clinic, this time demanding that her doctors do something about the apron of flab that now drooped from her midsection—all that remained of her once considerable abdomen. Surgeons subsequently performed a lipectomy, excising the now shrunken adipose tissue and drawing the women's badly stretched abdominal skin taut at the waistline. Had the patient been able to maintain her new weight, her problems—both physiological and cosmetic—would have been solved. But she could not do so, and when she ballooned up to her former weight, it was the remaining adipose cells—in her thighs and upper arms—that filled with stored fat. While once she had been fat but proportionately so, now she was disproportionate—no longer merely obese, but grotesque.

The third factor in childhood obesity, and certainly the most mutable, is purely circumstantial. Dr. Hilde Bruch has found that the mothers of overweight children tend to respond to their infants' distress, no matter what its actual cause, with food. Hunger is life's first producer of tension, and that tension is most easily assuaged with food. But mere hunger is not the only source of infant distress, and when all displays of unhappiness are met with the same response—feeding to end the crying—an invidious pattern is established, one with lifelong implications. Small wonder that many overweight adults readily confess to eating whenever they feel angry, or sad, or disappointed, or sexually frustrated. After all, they have been meeting those stresses with that response since the cradle.

Significantly, the mothers cited by Dr. Bruch for treating food as a panacea for all behavioral problems are also the ones who discourage exercise in their offspring—thus exacerbating an already dangerous self-perpetuating pattern among obese children, who tire more easily when they do exercise and therefore tend to exercise less. Overweight children and adolescents have, as Mayer observes, a truly remarkable capacity for conserving energy, often moving about one-third as frequently as their thin counterparts while engaged in essentially the same activity. Their failure to exercise, and to burn off calories by doing so, allows them to grow even more obese, and having grown more ponderous they find themselves even less inclined to engage in strenuous activity. This explains why obese children and adolescents are able to gain weight while eating essentially the same amounts of food as their thin compatriots. It also explains, at least in part, why 45 per cent of all adult Americans engage in no physical activity solely for the sake of exercising: the habit has been discouraged, actually or implicitly, since early childhood.

Unkind as it may seem to lay so much of the blame for adult obesity upon the tender ministrations of well-intentioned mothers, the blame does not seem misplaced. A recently completed ten-year survey of childhood obesity, the most comprehensive nutritional study of the subject ever undertaken, indicates that close to three-quarters of all mothers of small children fret if their offspring are not hungry at mealtime. A quarter of these women use food itself—generally candy or a sugar-loaded dessert—as a reward for good behavior and an incentive for further eating. And a minuscule 3 per cent worry that their children may be overeating. The same study indicates that roughly one out of every five American youngsters is seriously overweight—which means that millions of American mothers are asking themselves the wrong questions at mealtime.

There are a number of reasons for this. One is the sheer availability of modern convenience foods, all of them high in calories and many of them low in other nutritional value. Another is purely social and perhaps uniquely American: in a heterogeneous society composed largely of immigrants and their offspring, it is perhaps logical that the fear of hunger remained strong among the country's recent arrivals long after the actual threat of another crop failure or another potato famine had vanished. The result is that immigrant parents, themselves thin, fatten up their offspring. Upwardly mobile lower-middle-class families, on the other hand, encourage their children to stay thin, recognizing leanness as an upper-class trait.

Who, then, is fat? Children. And fat children grown into fat adults. And pubescent girls, whose adolescent "growth spurt" is mostly fat and occurs at the same time that teenage boys are adding a significant amount of lean body mass to their frames. Before puberty, girls have 10 to 15 per cent more body fat than boys; afterwards, they have 20 to 30 per cent more. This may in part account for the remarkable record that females have posted in swimming the gelid English Channel; they are simply better insulated.

Fatter from birth—and significantly fatter after they achieve sexual maturity—women find weight control an almost universal dilemma. Their role in buying, preparing, seasoning, and serving thousands and thousands of meals in their adult lives makes them especially prone to the creeping overweight of middle age, and the recent proliferation of "labor-saving" household appliances also works to their collective disadvantage. In 1929 the average housewife spent fifty-one hours a week doing household chores. Today she spends seventy-seven hours a week doing the same chores—but her actual energy expenditure is smaller. She has no servants to assist her, as her mother and grandmother may have, but she has a battery of servomechanisms to make her task easier—ranging from self-cleaning ovens, frostless refrigerators, and washer-dryer combinations to one-step floor waxes and foaming antiseptic cleansers. The fat she once burned—scrubbing floors, beating rugs, kneading bread, weeding the garden, wringing laundry—is now stored.

Who else is fat? Nonsmokers and former smokers, among others. The latter because they gain an average of seven pounds apiece when they stop smoking, the former because they do not enjoy the dubious benefits of impaired taste and smell associated with heavy smoking. (Both groups can take comfort from the fact that heavy smoking is roughly equivalent to carrying *one hundred pounds* of excess body weight in terms of its impact on personal health.) Regular drinkers, even those who classify themselves as moderate or "social" drinkers, are also inclined to be overweight. Dr. Gastineau's calculations indicate that the daily consumption of two highballs before supper and one at bedtime adds about 400 calories to the diet—roughly 20 per cent of most individuals' daily caloric needs. As Gastineau also notes, alcohol tends to be ketogenic when consumed in sufficient quantities and in the absence of carbohydrates—which explains the success of the so-called Drinking Man's Diet.

Who else is fat? Whites are fatter than blacks, which may have less to do with diet and more to do with the Nilotic origins of most American blacks than is generally acknowledged. And Eastern Europeans are heavier than Western Europeans, with the Slavs and Russians heading the first group and the British and Irish bringing up the last. Among all peoples, those of Mongol ancestry are the least fat. They also exhibit the smallest physiological differences between males and females, both sexes having developed their short-limbed, barrel-chested, cold-adapted physiques in Paleolithic time.

Irrespective of race or sex, old people are fatter than young people. For one thing, the human metabolism rate falls one-half of one per cent per year after the age of twenty, which means that an adult must *decrease* his caloric intake by 5 per cent per decade in order to maintain a constant weight. Few achieve this objective, which is why the average American adult adds a pound of excess body weight each year after the age of twenty-five.

It is also possible to identify the obese members of society sociologically. They are more often unemployed, for instance. Fat people find themselves systematically discriminated against in the job market: they are hired less readily, promoted less frequently, are fired fastest. Some 8.4 million Americans are simply too fat to hold any sort of steady job, and even those who do work are more likely to be single, separated, divorced, or widowed—and consequently subject to the emotional stress that loneliness induces. They are also likely to be lower middle class, where obesity is *four times* more prevalent than it is among members of the upper middle and upper classes. To know who is fat, however, it is not really necessary to divide the population according to the weight/height scales employed by insurance companies or the nomograms devised by the medical profession. It is enough to say that anyone who looks fat or feels fat probably is fat—although, as Dr. Mayer would doubtless observe, that is not particularly illuminating. The real question is not *who* is fat, but *why* they are fat.

There is no simple explanation for obesity, just as there are no simple solutions. "For most of the chronically overweight," Anne Scott Beller observes, "eating too much is only the last and possibly the least link in a long chain of causal connections between the food they eat and the flesh they end up carrying around." Many theories have been proposed over the years to explain obesity, and in general those that have seemed the simplest and gone the farthest to exculpate the individual have held the most appeal. That they have also ranged from the highly implausible to the grossly inaccurate has done little to dim their appeal, and overweight Americans still regularly excuse their overindulgence by insisting that they have a thyroid condition, or a glandular problem, or hypoglycemia. All are metabolic disorders that have been used, by doctors and patients alike, to explain away excess weight that the medical profession could not induce the patient to shed or that the patient could not shed on his own. The truth is that only one seriously obese person in a thousand has any kind of glandular problem, and more often than not these metabolic irregularities are a consequence of, rather than a cause of, obesity. Indeed, Dr. Gastineau is willing to assert from his experience that "there is no known endocrine condition that will give you obesity if you do not overeat."

The inescapable fact, Gastineau continues, is that the obese person must eat more than the average person in order to remain obese. Anyone who claims otherwise is deluding himself and deceiving his doctor. "Fat," Gastineau affirms, "comes only from food, and obesity results only from eating more than is required to meet the energy requirements of the body." It has been suggested that some obese individuals have a mechanism for conserving energy—for storing fat more efficiently and burning it more slowly than normal people—but the presence of such a mechanism, if it exists, has never been adequately demonstrated.

It seems rather clear, then, that the mechanism that controls appetite, rather than the one that governs metabolism, is the key factor in determining whether an individual is overweight or not. For a long time it was thought that the hypothalamus, a tiny portion of the brain identified as its "hunger center," was the mechanism that dictated appetite, and there seems to be no question that an important center of normal appetite regulation does reside there. It can be conclusively demonstrated with laboratory animals, for example, that destruction of the hypothalamus produces concomitant changes in appetite, sometimes resulting in gross obesity.

It has long been Dr. Mayer's contention that the hypothalamus functions much like a furnace thermostat by monitoring fluctuations in the body's blood sugar levels. Whenever there is a significant drop in blood sugar, this "glucostat" responds by increasing the appetite. Then, as food is consumed and glucose levels build up again, the glucostat signals satiety. To demonstrate that the hypothalamus is more a satiety center than a hunger center, Mayer has fed mice a special chemical compound, gold thioglucose, which is composed of a molecule of glucose, an atom of harmless sulphur, and an atom of lethal gold. What Mayer found was that the hypothalamus was so powerfully programmed to annex glucose that it would do so even when glucose was bonded to a deadly poison. And once the gold had destroyed the hypothalamuses of Mayer's laboratory animals, they lost all sense of satiety and ate themselves into a state of gross obesity.

Human beings are not laboratory animals, however, and their responses to food are far more complex and subtle than those of even the most highly evolved primates. In man, as in no other animal, the higher learning centers of the brain, located in the cerebral cortex, may simply override the more primitive and automatic centers of appetite control. This is particularly true in the case of obese individuals, many of whom seem to have lost their capacity for responding to the more primitive sensations of hunger and respond instead to external cues—sight, odor, and even the memory of food or the knowledge that mealtime is approaching—rather than to hunger itself.

In such cases the mind is dissociating hunger—which is a generally unpleasant sensation of physiological origin—from appetite—which is a generally pleasant sensation of psychological origin—and responding only to the latter. This may, in fact, be a principal cause of obesity, for it robs the overweight individual of the only sure clue to his body's needs, his sense of hunger. Unable to tell when his body needs nourishment, the overweight individual responds instead to the dictates of his appetite, which are all too often at odds with his body's actual needs. It is for this reason that obesity is often labeled America's most widespread form of malnutrition—a reflection of the belief that modern man has largely lost the ability to balance his diet, as all nondomesticated animals do, by responding instinctively to his body's need for salt, or roughage, or protein.

Hunger, which once controlled when man ate and also what he ate, is often associated with the gastric contractions of an empty stomach—hunger pangs. If this were the sole source of appetite stimulus, it might be possible to control overeating simply by deadening the sensation of hunger that accompanies gastric contractions, but this is not the case. Laboratory animals that have been deprived of all sensation in their stomachs retain their appetites, and pills and potions designed to coat the stomach and reduce gastric activity in humans have proven of little use in curbing appetite.

It is Dr. Gastineau's contention that hunger—by which he means appetite as well—depends on the integration of a large number of sensory impulses. The complex mechanism by which it is aroused varies from one person to the next, and even, from time to time, in the same individual. In its simplest form, obesity is the result of a derangement of the normal mechanisms governing our sensations of hunger and satiety. It is, in addition, a compulsive, addictive behavior disorder not unlike alcoholism or drug addiction. Because it is complex in nature, it is refractory to treatment; because it is rooted in patterns of behavior that often antedate one's earliest childhood memories, it is resistant to hypnosis, psychoanalysis, and numerous other forms of behavior modification.

According to Dr. Gastineau, there is no apparent difference between the corrected basal metabolism rates of obese and normal individuals. Significantly overweight subjects have a higher metabolic rate, but they also have a larger body surface area, the basis for establishing basal metabolism rates in the first place. They are merely stoking a bigger fire, and their obesity cannot be attributed to "slow metabolism," no matter how tempting that explanation may seem to patient and physician alike. Harvard's Richard F. Spark concurs. Less than 1 per cent of all people have metabolic problems even when they are obese, he notes, but upwards of 50 per cent of all dieters develop metabolic problems. He sees no correlation between hypoglycemia and obesity, and he concludes that "increased hunger in the obese is not due to abnormalities in the hunger and satiety centers, or to metabolic alterations." In order to understand what does cause obesity—if it's not a thyroid condition, or a glandular problem, or hypoglycemia—it is first necessary to understand something about the mechanics of fat.

Perhaps the most startling thing about fat is how vital it is to our well-being, no matter what we weigh. Fat, which makes up roughly 20 per cent of normal body weight—and up to 60 per cent of an obese person's weight—serves two classical functions, not only in man but in all animals. First, it is stored energy in readily available form, and, like the camel's hump, it can be drawn upon during periods of reduced caloric intake. (It is believed by some scientists that man once had, and has gradually lost, a far greater capacity for depositing fat. In prehistoric times man was obliged to subsist for long periods of time on a semistarvation diet, and during those periods of involuntary fasting, individuals with excess fat doubtless stood a better chance of survival. There is even some thought that steatopygia, the excessive concentration of fatty tissue on the buttocks that is a morphological feature of certain African tribes, may be the anthropomorphic equivalent of the camel's hump.) Second, fat both cushions the body's major internal organs against shock and insulates them against sudden changes in temperature.

Fats must therefore be considered desirable constituents of any diet, however strict, and any regimen of high nutritional value should contain from 20 to 40 per cent fat. The actual fat content of the diet may vary widely from day to day and week to week, however, without appreciably altering the diet's value. In any significant amount, animal and vegetable fats serve as a source of essential fatty acids and, under more specialized conditions, of fat-soluble vitamins. Not incidentally, they also contribute markedly to the tastiness of any diet.

Fat deposited in adipose tissue remains there until it is broken down into water and carbon dioxide, and the end effect of any serious diet is to achieve precisely that while disturbing the rest of the body's delicate chemistry as little as possible. The next chapter, on fad diets, will examine the ways in which men have sought to accelerate this process of conversion, and the perils inherent in doing so. For now it is sufficient to say that all diets are undertaken at some risk, and the risk grows with the severity of the diet.

In addition to fats, two other fuel-producing foodstuffs are stored in the body. These are proteins and carbohydrates, and an excessive intake of any or all of the three will lead to the buildup of fat in adipose tissue. When there is excessive ingestion of protein—as there is in the recurrently popular high-protein, low-carbohydrate "quick weight-loss" diet most recently promoted by Drs. Stillman and Atkins—part is utilized and part is converted to fat. And when such diets are abandoned, as they so often are, in favor of a diet high in previously forbidden carbohydrates, the body's glycogen reservoirs are refilled—and whatever remains after fuel needs are satisfied is converted to fat.

Animal and vegetable fats account for nearly half the calories in the average American diet; most of the rest comes from refined sugar. Last year meat consumption in the United States averaged 155 pounds per person, an all-time record. At the same time the per capita consumption of grains and fiber dropped to 142 pounds annually—less than *half* as much as the average American consumed in 1909, the year the Department of Agriculture began to collect statistics on our national eating habits. Moreover, most of those 142 pounds were refined grains, stripped of their outer husk, and it is that husk which is our most readily available source of roughage. Roughage has no actual nutritional value, but it is necessary to a balanced diet nonetheless, and its increasing absence from our tables is linked to the increase in numerous digestive diseases, foremost among them cancers of the colon and rectum.

In addition, average Americans now consume an estimated 126 pounds of sugar each year, ten pounds of it in the form of cornstarch and most of the rest of it as refined sugar. In either form these are nutritionally empty calories. Our steadily increasing consumption of refined sugar presents enough of a threat to our health that it has led one respected nutritionist to declare before a Senate select committee that "if the food industry were to propose the introduction of refined sugar as a new rather than an existing food additive, it would surely be enjoined from doing so."

In sum, the question "Why am I fat?" has a number of answers, any or all of which may apply in a given case. In most instances heredity is a large part of the answer: obese parents are likely to rear obese children, and whether this is chiefly attributable to genetics or upbringing does not really matter, for the net effect is the same. For a tiny minority, serious endocrine system disturbances may also be a contributory factor. For all, poor eating habits—too commonly inculcated during infancy and childhood and too frequently combined with a poorly balanced diet—are a significant factor. Tension, stress, anxiety—and a broad range of psychological disorders, both mild and severe—can be contributory as well, although emotional problems are only very rarely the sole cause of obesity. And, finally, obesity itself is a cause of further obesity. As we have seen, there is increasing medical evidence that fat people lose their ability to respond to their own bodies' internal appetite and weight-regulation mechanisms while simultaneously developing an enhanced capacity for converting glucose to stored fat.

For centuries the problem of overweight was rather easily solved—one simply ate a bit less at each meal until a lower and more desirable weight level was reached. This is still the safest and surest way to take off excess weight and keep it off, but the problem of dieting is vastly more complicated today than it was even three decades ago, for according to experts the caloric level recommended for sedentary, nondieting Americans has already reached the lowest possible level. Further reductions seriously interfere with the energy level an individual must sustain just to breathe, eat, and sleep. This means, in short, that for some there is no longer much margin left for diet. Many obese Americans are currently maintaining or gaining weight on diets that contain few calories above recommended daily maintenance levels, which means that any sort of low-calorie diet they undertake will prove extremely difficult to sustain.

Devising a sane diet for the seventies thus poses preventive medicine its greatest challenge. And fad diets, the subject of the next chapter, pose the treatment of obesity its greatest threat.

3

The Puzzle of Obesity

Overweight, like offshore oil, is a natural resource that adds to the GNP.
Jean Mayer

Ten billion dollars. That is what overweight Americans invested in the diet industry last year. By all accounts they would have been better off putting their money into sow-belly futures or South American real estate, so dismal were the returns on their collective investment. According to the American Society of Bariatrics, a professional association whose members specialize in weight problems, only 12 out of every 100 dieters actually succeed in losing an appreciable amount of weight, even on the most rigid of regimens—and only 2 of those 12 manage to maintain their new weight. What this means is that 98 per cent of the money spent on diet foods and diet aids is misspent. Or, to put it another way, that millions of Americans pay out billions of dollars each year for small, temporary, and often illusory weight losses.

The actual annual cost of the Great American Diet is all but impossible to calculate, for it must properly be reckoned not only in dollars spent but in pregnancies terminated, skeletons overburdened, cardiovascular systems weakened—even lives lost. Heart attacks, to which the obese are especially prone, cost American industry 132 million man-days a year, and each year some 100,000 middle-aged men—those considered most valuable to their employers—die of cardiovascular diseases. It is probably fortunate that no such tally can be kept, for it would serve little purpose save to underscore a truth that is already self-evident: where diet is concerned, we are paying far too much for far too little. We do so because we want to, and we frequently do so in the face of incontrovertible evidence that the fad diet we are following is not only worthless but potentially hazardous.

In a very real sense, then, the key component of the Great American Diet is our own seemingly limitless capacity for self-delusion. We have heard the words of Dr. Gastineau and his colleagues—*Fat comes only from food, and obesity results only from eating more than is required to meet the energy requirements of the body*—and we are determined to disbelieve them. So great is our desire to disbelieve and so strong our conviction that obesity is nothing more than a puzzle awaiting solution—in the form of a new pill, a new fad diet, a new combination of vitamins and exercise—that we willingly subscribe to one patently bogus weight-reducing program after another.

Consider, for example, the storm of controversy that greeted the Food and Drug Administration's decision to impose a partial ban on saccharin, the suspected carcinogen that is the sweetening agent in diet soft drinks. Had the F.D.A. announced that an additive in dry dog food was suspected of causing cancer in rats, one wonders, would the American public have been quite so vociferous in demanding that the suspect product be kept on supermarket shelves? Americans are notoriously solicitous toward their pets, many of are so corpulent from a steady diet of table scraps that they must be put on periodic weight-loss programs themselves. (The dog-food industry, which has achieved phenomenal growth in the last decade by marketing high-protein, fat-saturated pet "dinners" of dubious nutritional value, recently introduced a line of diet dog foods for housebound, overfed, overweight pets.) It is hard to imagine animal lovers of any sort deliberately feeding pets a diet loaded with potential carcinogens, yet those same consumers—and millions of others as well—seem perfectly willing to take such risks with their own health, rather than sacrifice the illusion of refined sugar in their sugar-free drinks.

Consider, too, the fact that a recently published diet book—billed as "revolutionary" although its essential recommendations are a century old—sold a million hardback copies in seven months despite public denunciation by numerous nutritionists and by the American Medical Association. Or the fact that thousands of presumably intelligent people were taken in by a mail-order promotion for a "European miracle reducing liquid" that promised the hapless consumer a weight loss of *sixty* pounds—more than all but the most dedicated dieters are able to lose in an entire year—after five fifteen-minute baths in the miracle liquid. Such examples of dieting folly are legion, and in their ubiquity and persistence they are a source of grave concern to physicians and nutritionists alike, a concern perhaps best expressed by Dr. Norman D. Gross in his testimony before a Senate subcommittee on antitrust and monopoly. "It is my medical opinion," said Dr. Gross, "that the obese person of our nation is in far greater danger from improper weight-control methods and the use of potent combination drugs than from the inherent dangers of being overweight."

Ignoring the best advice of the medical profession, the accumulated wisdom of the scientific community, and the dictates of common sense, the overweight American invests billions of dollars every year in a losing war against his own waistline. Some $90 million is spent in chain drugstores alone, on diet aids that can be purchased without prescription, and another $54 million is spent on prescription drugs, principally appetite suppressants. (These are chiefly amphetamines, sold legally under stringent governmental regulation as anorexic agents and illegally as "speed." There is no accurate way of determining how many units of amphetamine-type drugs are marketed sub rosa each year, although most estimates speak in terms of billions. But that is not really a matter of concern here. The licit use of amphetamines *is,* however, and it will be discussed at greater length in the next chapter.) Billions of additional dollars are spent on dietary foods, whose manufacturers spend further millions advertising the nutritional claims, real or spurious, of their products.

But diet foods and diet pills are only part of the picture. There are also health spas, gymnasiums, and reducing salons, most offering a wide range of diet and exercise programs for the sedentary, the slack, and the frankly flabby—and, incidentally, netting $220 million each year in membership fees and related sales. For those who cannot get to a gym, or who want to supplement their supervised exercise periods with a private program of calisthenics, there is a bewildering array of exercise equipment to choose from—barbells and benchpresses, weighted belts and isometric toners, slant boards and medicine balls—and these account for another $100 million in annual sales.

And finally—for those who have tried and, for various reasons, abandoned appetite suppressants, health spas, diet charts, exercise devices, and all the rest—there are an estimated 2,000 physicians in this country who deal exclusively with obese patients and perhaps another 5,000 who maintain a limited general practice but concentrate on the problems of obesity. The more active among them call themselves bariatricians, from the Greek word for weight, *baros.* Theirs is not a recognized medical specialty, however, and they are more generally known, by both medical men and laymen, as "fat doctors."

By and large, bariatricians profit handsomely from their work. One recent convert, an erstwhile general practitioner with an income of $55,000 a year, cheerfully reported to the *Wall Street Journal* that by confining his practice exclusively to overweight patients he had cut his workweek by eighteen hours and his house calls to zero—while boosting his income to $225,000. The problem is that only the fat doctors appear to be profiting from their practice; in most cases the patients fare no better under medical supervision than they do on self-imposed diets, and the recidivism rates are virtually identical. As we observed earlier, it is not unreasonable to call obesity preventive medicine's greatest failure.

With modern science seemingly stymied by the problem of obesity, and modern medicine unable to offer any easy solutions to the nation's millions of overweight men, women, and children, it is small wonder that so many obese Americans turn to the prophets of quick weight loss each year, hoping against hope that this time, unlike all the other times, someone has succeeded in solving the puzzle of obesity for them. Nourished by an unflagging optimism that has survived dozens of fad diets and fanciful formulas in the past, they subscribe to each innovation in turn. They buy the sugar-free dessert mixes and the sauna pants, the European miracle reducing liquids and the hormone shots. But above all else they buy the books, millions and millions of them every year.

At any given moment there are roughly 200 diet-related books in print. After the Bible they may well be the most widely distributed literature of our time, and their popularity is undisputed. Even the most modestly conceived volumes sell well, and those that capture the public imagination often become publishing phenomena. At one time, for example, demand for *Dr. Atkins' Diet Revolution* was so great that five separate presses were being used to supply the eager market. Too often these books are triumphs of style over substance—a catchy new title for a timeworn and nutritionally unsound reducing program—and more often than not they fail what Dr. Fredrick Stare, chairman of the nutrition department at Harvard University, calls the two tests of trustworthiness in any diet book.

According to Dr. Stare, any serious approach to the problems of obesity will mention that "adequate nutrition requires a balanced intake of nutrients: protein, carbohydrates, fats, minerals, vitamins, and water. Any diet that recommends disrupting that balance for longer than a few weeks is dangerous." A book on diet, he adds, will also indicate that "the only sound way to lose weight is gradually." But fad diets are by nature unbalanced, and quick weight loss is by definition rapid, not gradual, so most of these books are predestined to fail Dr. Stare's test.

The granddaddy of all diet books is Joe Bonomo's *Calorie Counter and Control Guide*, a pocket-sized, eminently practical little volume that cost only a quarter when it was first published in 1951 and has subsequently sold more than 20 million copies at a profit in excess of $5 million. It has been followed, in increasingly rapid succession, by a host of others: Herman Taller's *Calories Don't Count; The Air Force Diet Book* (which was, incidentally, neither developed nor endorsed by the United States Air Force); *The Drinking Man's Diet;* Irwin Stillman's *Doctor's Quick Weight Loss Diet* and its companion volume, *Doctor's Inches-Off Diet;* and *Dr. Atkins' Diet Revolution.*

The above books, and dozens of other less popular contemporary publications, have two things in common. The first is that they have been astounding commercial successes, each selling more copies than the one before it. It took six years, for instance, for Stillman's first book to sell 5 million paperback copies, whereas *Dr. Atkins' Diet Revolution* sold 1 million copies in seven months—in hardback at $6.95. The second, as any alert reader already knows, is that with the lone exception of Bonomo's *Calorie Counter,* they are essentially the same book. Differing only in style, format, and particulars, they all offer versions of a high-protein, low-carbohydrate diet that first became popular more than a century ago.

Over the decades this durable diet has been known by many names. In the 1950's it was revived and assiduously promoted by Dr. Alfred W. Pennington, medical director of the Dupont Company, and consequently it was known then as either the Pennington or the Dupont diet. It recurs regularly as the Mayo diet, obliging the Mayo Clinic to dissociate itself from the diet at equally regular intervals. In this permutation it generally features an excess of grapefruit, which is touted as a natural catabolic, or catalyst in the metabolizing of other foods. Unhappily, grapefruit is no such thing. As Jean Mayer has noted, "grapefruit does contain citric acid, which is necessary for the breakdown of food, but no one has a deficiency of citric acid." But the diet—and the myth of its origin at the world-famous Mayo Clinic—remains curiously resistant to official efforts to set the record straight, and a recent count yielded fifty-one versions of the grapefruit-and-egg "Mayo" diet.

By any name this diet has two principal attractions. In all its various manifestations it is nutritionally unbalanced and lacking in sufficient carbohydrates for normal body function—but in all its manifestations it works, at least for a time. More important, it works rapidly, thus avoiding the tedium and monotony that are inevitable by-products of all medically sound, long-term weight-loss programs. No other diet ever devised, whether balanced or unbalanced, medically sound or utterly foolhardy, has achieved such immediate, tangible results, and for fully a century there has been no arguing with the diet's success. It has not seemed to matter that this high-protein, low-carbohydrate regimen produces dehydration during the first week and tissue loss thereafter—with little, if any, concomitant wasting of actual body fat. What has mattered, at least since 1862, is that the diet works.

Significantly, the original high-protein, low-carbohydrate diet is named not for the man who invented it but for the patient on whom he first tried it. William Banting, the patient, had been corpulent all his life, and by 1862, the sixth decade of his life, he had tried every known method of weight control—except, of course, eating and drinking less. He had essayed short-term starvation diets, steam closets, leeching and purging—even exercise—and he had visited the great spas of Western Europe, all to no avail. He stood five and a half feet tall, he weighed better than 200 pounds, and, by his own admission, he had grown too gross to tie his own shoelaces or descend the narrow stairway in his London shop without turning sideways and sucking in his considerable stomach. His business was prospering—he made coffins for a well-heeled clientele that included, at the appropriate time, the Duke of Wellington—but he was miserable. Then, in 1862, he developed a persistent earache, and for that reason and no other he consulted William Harvey, a physician who had recently heard the illustrious French physiologist Claude Bernard lecture on the liver's role in body chemistry.

It was Harvey's notion that excess fat might be impinging on Banting's inner ear, and he attempted to alleviate his patient's suffering by placing him on a diet that was high in saturated fats and low in sugars and carbohydrates. On this regimen Banting was permitted five ounces of lean meat or poultry at every meal—two ounces more than what is today considered an adequate portion at lunch or dinner, and two and a half times what the average adult consumes in a day. In addition, he was encouraged to eat three or four ounces of fiber, in the form of leafy vegetables and bran, and one or two ounces of fresh fruit. He was to wash down all this with two or three glasses of claret or sherry and unlimited quantities of unsweetened tea. All starches and sugars were forbidden, as were beers, ales, and fortified wines. In sum, Banting was on a carbohydrate-free diet of roughly 1,200 calories per day, similar in general outline, if not in specifics, to all the diets mentioned above.

To William Banting's unbounded delight, he lost weight on this new diet: twenty pounds in the first four months and fifty pounds by the end of the first year. Eager to share his good fortune with others—and to honor the man who had made it possible—Banting wrote, and in 1864 published at his own expense, a pamphlet entitled "A Letter on Corpulence Addressed to the Public." In it he outlined his own unhappy history of chronic obesity, including the details of his lifelong search for a cure to his affliction, and then set forth the details of Harvey's miraculous new weight-loss program.

The new diet caused a minor sensation in England and on the Continent, as women who had long depended upon whalebone corsets to maintain their hourglass figures turned to "banting" instead. The number of overweight men who followed Banting's example is not known, so it is impossible to gauge the diet's impact on either Dr. Harvey's profession or Mr. Banting's. But it is clear that these first practitioners had not yet learned the first bitter rule of dieting—which is that the faster the weight comes off the greater the likelihood that the dieter will be unable to keep it off for any significant length of time.

Half a century after the publication of Banting's letter on corpulence, proponents of the high-protein, low-carbohydrate diet were to receive reassurance of its efficacy from an entirely unexpected quarter. That endorsement came in 1910, and it came from above the Arctic Circle, where a young anthropology instructor from Harvard by the name of Viljalmur Stefansson had spent a year among the Eskimos. Stefansson's sojourn in the Arctic was quite unintentional. He had journeyed northward in 1909 to join the Leffingwell-Mikkelson expedition but had somehow gone astray, missed the rendezvous point, and been obliged to spend the winter living with the natives.

Having no other option, Stefansson subsisted through the winter on his hosts' primitive diet, which consisted exclusively of fish and blubber washed down with water in which gobbets of fish had been briefly boiled. Here was a Banting-type diet in its purest form—all protein and no carbohydrates whatsoever—and although the fare so nauseated Stefansson initially that it was all he could do to gag it down, he found that he suffered no ill effects from it. Indeed, when Stefansson was sent back to the Arctic some years later by the American Museum of Natural History, he and his companions elected to eschew the nutritionally balanced rations provided for the expedition and live instead on the "hunter's diet" of the Eskimo.

Stefansson's second expedition was scheduled to last twelve months. It lasted four years, by which time Stefansson had established himself as one the giants of Arctic exploration and the "hunter's diet" had established itself as an idée fixe in the anthropologist's mind. So enthusiastic was Stefansson about the high-protein, low-carbohydrate diet that he actively proselytized on its behalf upon his return to the United States, even going so far as to undertake, in 1928, a year-long, medically supervised, Banting-style diet at Bellevue Hospital in New York.

Latter-day proponents of high-protein diets have taken pains to cite Stefansson's experience as historical evidence of the merits of such a regimen. By quoting extensively from Stefansson's journals, they have further blurred the distinction between Stefansson the accomplished explorer and Stefansson the amateur nutritionist. (In fairness, of course, it should be observed that this is a confusion first engendered by Stefansson himself, and that he is hardly the first public figure to use the public forum provided by prominence in one field to broadcast unsubstantiated claims in another.) The truth is that Stefansson's experiences in the Arctic prove nothing more than the possibility of survival for years in the frozen reaches of the north on nothing other than what the Eskimos eat. Which is something we knew anyway, since the Eskimos have been doing it for centuries.

Interestingly enough, Stefansson's much-touted year-long diet at Bellevue, which was conducted by Dr. Eugene F. DuBois, then the medical director of the Russell Sage Foundation and later chief physician at New York Hospital and professor of physiology at Cornell Medical College, would seem to suggest that a Banting-style regimen is contraindicated for anyone trying to lose weight, for the famed explorer lost less than two pounds on the diet in an entire year—no more than he might have been expected to lose by fasting for several days before his end-of-the-year weigh-in.

Nor had Stefansson lost an appreciable amount of weight during his expeditions to the Arctic; he had merely subsisted, which is scarcely the same thing. And by subsisting he had merely proved that it was possible to do so, and not that the hunter's diet was inherently superior to our own. What Stefansson did succeed in doing was to color civilized man's thinking about the Eskimo diet so completely that when subsequent expeditions made a thoroughgoing medical evaluation of the Arctic tribes—and found them to be suffering from pellagra and scurvy—those findings were attributed not to vitamin deficiencies in the hunter's diet but to the pernicious influence of the white man, who, by introducing elements of his own diet into the "pure" diet of the Arctic huntsman, had corrupted the latter.

Modern medicine now understands that the concept of a "balanced" diet is an extremely flexible one. Meals need not be balanced on a daily—or even a weekly or monthly—basis. So long as all the proper nutrients are available in the diet at large, the individual will eventually balance his own diet, and there is scarcely a habitable corner of the planet where it is not possible for him to do so. Studies of concentration camp survivors corroborate this point. Inhabitants of the Nazi internment camps, fed on a thin soup made of cabbage and potatoes, showed no marked vitamin deficiencies at the war's end, while Japanese prisoners of war, obliged to subsist on rice and water, often contracted vitamin-deficiency-related illnesses. However small the traces of essential vitamins and minerals in the concentration camp soups, they were sufficient to prevent the onset of beriberi, scurvy, and the like. Rice, which lacks the vitamin content of cabbage and the mineral content of potatoes, was not.

The real issue, of course, is not whether it is feasible to survive in the Arctic—or elsewhere—on Arctic fare, but whether it is prudent to do so. And recent studies on the etiology of obesity and the mechanics of fat synthesis suggest most emphatically that it is not. Any diet that is out of balance, whether it favors protein, saturated fats, or carbohydrates, is inherently dangerous, and the more radically imbalanced the diet is, the more perilous to the dieter's health. As nutritionist G.J. Muscante has observed, "If a diet is nutritious and maintains a caloric deficit, it matters little in terms of weight loss whether the diet emphasizes cottage cheese, grapefruit, or anything else; the dieter will lose weight." The key words here are *nutritious*—which means balanced—and *caloric deficit*—which means that the body's energy output is exceeding its energy intake, and consequently fat is being burned. Neither term applies to a Banting-style diet, which is unbalanced in favor of protein and fats and which, in many cases, tolerates a caloric surfeit.

As Jean Mayer has stated with particular emphasis, "There is at present no evidence available which would support the idea that some of the more extreme diets recently popularized have any advantage over a calorically restricted, balanced diet." Yet the idea persists. It was resurrected in 1944 by a New York physician named Blake F. Donaldson who treated his severely obese patients by putting them on a carbohydrate-free regimen that included up to two full pounds of meat per day, but it got its most spectacular boost in the early 1960's from a Romanian-born gynecologist and obstetrician named Herman Taller, who served up the same old diet with an all-new tag line: "Calories don't count."

Herman Taller, it seemed, had made the most significant dietary breakthrough in almost a century, and it had nothing to do with metabolism; he had learned to tell his obese patients what they wanted to hear rather than what the medical profession at large believed to be true. In their eyes, at least, he was more messiah than medical man, inveighing against "that prize of all fallacies, the low-calorie diet" and promising the faithful that "there have been no failures, nor can there be any" where the principles of his diet were properly applied. They would all lose on Dr. Taller's diet, and so they would all win.

In his book, *Calories Don't Count,* which was to become the first runaway best-seller among diet books, Taller informed his readers that "all calories are not the same" and then proceeded to divide all foodstuffs into two groups—the first "good," regardless of caloric content, the other "bad," no matter how small the caloric value. "You do not have to count calories," he then admonished the reader, "but do not eat *any* of the foods that are not permitted." What followed was a list of "foods that are not permitted," a list that included all carbohydrates and refined sugars. Taller's diet was, in essence, Dr. Harvey's diet for Mr. Banting, updated in the light of almost a century of medical advances and distinguished by a bizarre refinement. Not content to restrict carbohydrate intake and encourage the consumption of saturated fats, Taller urged his readers to supplement their already severely unbalanced regimen with doses of safflower oil, which had the effect of accelerating the process of dehydration that is the salient aspect of any Banting-type diet.

"When you eat large quantities of unsaturated fats," Taller suggested, "you set in motion a happy cycle. You *stimulate* body production of certain hormones which work to release fats stored around the body. You *limit* the production of insulin, a substance which seems to prevent the release of stored fat. And you change the character of your fat. The hard, tough fat, difficult for the body to utilize, softens." All this sounded so plausible to the layman that few recognized it for what it was—sheer nonsense. "There is hardly a word of sense in the whole book," observed Harvard's Fredrick Stare, but his characterization of Taller's volume as "trash" did not stop two million gullible dieters from buying *Calories Don't Count.* Stare was telling them something that they didn't want to hear—that this solution to the puzzle of obesity was no solution at all, and Taller, by contrast, was telling them precisely what they had been waiting years to hear. "You can visit people," he enthused, "go out to the best restaurants, live a full life and not gain weight. You will never have to tell people you are on a diet. Best of all, you will never *feel* that you are on a diet, and yet you will lose weight."

For all the scientific wrongheadedness of Taller's advice, he might have gotten away with it if his own desire to "live a full life" had not occasioned an excess of greed. The good doctor not only recommended that his readers take diuretic pills (to stimulate water-weight loss) and thyroid pills (to elevate the body's basal metabolism), he also encouraged them to ingest safflower oil in capsule form. He even provided the reader with the name and address of the manufacturer of those capsules. The Food and Drug Administration, convinced that Taller's book was nothing more nor less than an elaborate and deceptive means of promoting the sale of safflower-oil capsules, impounded the unsold copies of *Calories Don't Count.*

The manufacturer of the capsules promptly sued Taller's publishers, who countersued with equal alacrity. In the course of the ensuing trial, Taller's cozy relationship with the capsule manufacturer came under close scrutiny. It seemed Taller was recommending that his readers take a grand total of eighty-four safflower-oil capsules per day, rather than drink three ounces of bottled safflower oil. The price, not surprisingly, was astronomically higher for the oil in capsule form, and the profits, for both the manufacturer and Taller, were consequently greater. The doctor and his colleagues were eventually convicted of mail fraud, conspiracy, and violation of federal drug regulations.

There were, it appeared, three important lessons to be learned from Dr. Taller's experience. The first was that a diet high in fat produced an even more rapid weight loss than a diet high in protein; Taller's "calories don't count" regimen worked because the dieter gave up 1,500 calories of carbohydrates for 900 calories of fat. The 600-calorie deficit was itself consequential, although not nearly as significant as the impact of a diet that was 65 per cent fat and only 5 per cent carbohydrate.

The second lesson was that calories *do* count, as more responsible medical men would soon prove in an experiment at Baltimore's Johns Hopkins Medical School. There, over a period of many weeks, student volunteers were fed a balanced diet that was calculated to supply each student with precisely the number of calories he needed to maintain his body weight. Then, over a period of time, the proportion of carbohydrates, fats, and proteins was altered. Significantly, each of the students maintained his old weight, regardless of the proportions of his diet—indicating that no one kind of nutrient is any more or less fattening, per calorie, than any other.

The third lesson to be learned from Taller's case was to market the idea but not the product, and subsequent promoters of Banting-type diets have been careful to avoid that legal pitfall. Among them is Dr. Irwin Stillman, who has made a fortune from two books promoting his version of Harvey's high-protein, low-carbohydrate diet—a version most notable for its sheer eccentricity. Stillman's basic diet is lean meat, poultry, fish, eggs, cottage cheese, and water—eight full glasses of water per day. For variety, Stillman offers sixty-four supplemental "quick weight-loss" diets from which to chose. All are variations on the same theme, and all recognize one of the truisms of dieting. It is that if you offer an obese person a highly restricted diet but allow him to indulge his appetite for one item—say, bananas, or grapefruit, or yogurt—he will do just that, for a time. After which he will find it impossible to contemplate another banana, let alone eat one, and will voluntarily restrict his intake to those items on the approved list.

What distinguishes the Stillman diet is its fluid component. It obliges the dieter to consume a greater than normal quantity of water and it offers no plan for replacing the salt that is lost through copious urination. The net effect is to leach salts and more water out of body tissue, causing rapid and severe dehydration. The human body being almost 60 per cent water, it is naturally possible to force fluids out of the system and achieve a significant temporary weight loss. The problem is, of course, that only water and some lean-tissue mass are lost in this manner—not fat. And as soon as the Stillman diet is abandoned, the body replenishes its lowered fluid reservoirs.

A simple exercise in arithmetic reveals the truth about Stillman's diet, on which certain model patients were said to have lost as much as twenty-five pounds in their first week of dieting. Begin by imagining a man so grossly corpulent that he actually needs 5,000 calories of food each day to balance his body's energy output. This man will weigh very close to 300 pounds. Now imagine that he eats *nothing at all* for an entire week. His total caloric deficit would be 35,000 calories, roughly equivalent to ten pounds of body fat. The rest of the weight loss—another fifteen pounds—would have to come from somewhere else; and since Stillman does not advocate prolonged strenuous exercise as a component of his diet, the additional weight loss must come from water and lean tissue. Few of Stillman's patients managed to lose twenty-five pounds on his regimen, of course, but then few of them weighed 300 pounds, either, which means that their fat loss was just as illusory as that of our hypothetical 300-pound man.

Small wonder, then, that the A.M.A.'s Philip White should have inveighed against the Stillman diet when it first appeared. "This diet is an intentional nutritional imbalance," he warned. "Anyone with kidney trouble, or with a proclivity for gout, diabetes, or any medical problem in which nitrogen, ketone bodies, or electrolyte balance are poorly handled, would be a candidate for sensational trouble."

Stillman's successor is Dr. Robert C. Atkins, a cardiologist whose variation on the century-old Banting diet has the distinction of being simultaneously the most widely criticized and the most wildly successful quick weight-loss regimen of all time. Atkins's "diet revolution" is in fact no revolution at all; rather it is the distillation of all that has been discovered about high-protein diets since William Banting issued his letter on corpulence in 1864. First and foremost, it recognizes the central role that the physiological process known as ketosis plays in any unbalanced, fat-saturated diet. Second, it recognizes the tedium factor in most diets, including Stillman's, and therefore urges the reader to indulge himself or herself on approved luxury foods—lobster, caviar, lump crabmeat, imported cheeses—and sniffs at the so-called "rabbit food" that is the staple of all nutritionally balanced low-calorie diets. Overweight, Atkins recognizes, is a disease of affluent societies; his cure is a diet that only the affluent can afford.

Atkins's theory is that fat people respond to carbohydrates by producing too much insulin, which in turn lowers their blood sugar level and makes them feel tired, irritable—and hungry. "Hunger," he says, "is the reason behind the unpopularity of low-carbohydrate diets." Of course. Eating less, and consequently feeling less than sated, is the first principle of weight reduction. And when he suggests that it is possible to lose weight *without* going hungry, Atkins appeals to the weak-willed glutton that lurks within everyone who is overweight. By encouraging his readers to eat fatty foods, which have a high satiety value, and by inducing ketosis, which among many other things has the effect of depressing the appetite, Atkins is indeed able to get people to lose weight without suffering hunger pangs.

Most authorities argue with Atkins's hypothesis—Jules Hirsch of Rockefeller University going so far as to say flatly that "there is absolutely no evidence that most overweight people suffer from low blood sugar"—but few can argue with his results. Atkins's followers do lose weight, just as William Banting did, just as Herman Taller's patients did—and it is often hard for them to understand that they are losing the *wrong kind* of weight.

Hirsch asserts that Atkins's diet works only because it totally eliminates carbohydrates and therefore induces ketosis—and not because it redresses any insulin deficit. Many specialists, aware of the debilitating side effects of ketosis—which include nausea, vomiting, weakness, apathy, dehydration, calcium depletion, kidney failure in susceptible individuals, cardiac irregularity, and a tendency to feel giddy or faint—caution against any diet that is more than mildly ketogenic.

Not Atkins, who asks his readers to supply themselves with Ketostix—commercially produced plastic wands that turn purple when dipped in the urine of a ketogenic dieter—in order to ensure that they remain in a state of ketosis. Ketostix, which had been manufactured by Miles Laboratories for twenty years before Atkins's book was published, were developed to enable diabetics to detect insulin imbalance. When sales of Ketostix rose dramatically following the publication of *Dr. Atkins' Diet Revolution,* a spokesman for Miles Laboratories, perhaps mindful of the *Calories Don't Count* scandal, felt compelled to say: "I should underscore that we don't recommend the diet. We have nutritionists on our board of directors. They think the diet is dangerous."

Miles Laboratories' directors were not alone in their opinion that Atkins's diet was dangerous. The American Medical Association's Council on Foods branded the diet "a bizarre regimen ... neither new nor revolutionary [and] without scientific merit." "If such diets are truly successful," the council asked rhetorically, "why, then do they fade into obscurity within a relatively short period, only to be resurrected some years later in slightly different guise and under new sponsorship?" The Mayo Clinic's Dr. Charles Roland pointed out that "despite Atkins's sweeping generalizations and exuberant confidence, his thesis rests largely upon unproven assumptions, among them that overweight results from the inability to metabolize carbohydrates properly." And Dr. Neil Simon, himself the author of several diet books, declared that in his opinion only protein, and not fat, is broken down to sugar when blood sugar levels drop.

Atkins's response to the A.M.A.—which labeled his regimen "grossly balanced" and "unlikely" to produce a practicable basis for long-term weight reduction—was to assert, without documentation, that 90 per cent of his patients had achieved a substantive weight loss. He accused the A.M.A. of faulting his diet without producing supporting documentation. Atkins also locked horns with Dr. Philip White, secretry of the A.M.A.'s Council on Food, by asserting that during ketosis unmetabolized fats are "sneaked" out of the body in the urine and on the breath.

White argued that Atkins had grossly overestimated the number of calories excreted during ketosis, and he was supported in his views on Atkins's diet by the New York County Medical Society, whose public attack on *Dr. Atkins' Diet Revolution* was without precedence in the society's history.

Other medical men fretted publicly about the wisdom of recommending any form of high-fat—and therefore high-cholesterol—diet to overweight, middle-aged American men, who already suffer one of the world's highest rates of serious cardiac disease, much of it believed attributable to a fat-saturated, high-protein diet. And Atkins himself withdrew his recommendation that pregnant women adhere to his diet when confronted with evidence that a zero-carbohydrate diet can jeopardize the intellectual and neurological development of the fetus. He was, he said, "very sorry" that he had repeatedly recommended the diet to expectant mothers.

In March of 1973 Atkins was also to find himself very sorry, at least temporarily, for having recommended his diet to middle-aged men, for one of them, a 66-year-old actor who also happened to have a law degree, sued him for $7.5 million, claiming that adherence to Atkins's high-cholesterol diet had caused his heart attack. Had the court found against Atkins in this instance—which it did not—he might soon have found himself wishing that he hadn't recommended his diet to anyone. Instead, Atkins weathered the critical storm stirred by his colleagues, withstood court tests, and ultimately sold a million hardback copies of his book.

What exactly was Atkins selling? In part, of course, he was selling self-indulgence. Caviar instead of carrot sticks, and weight loss without hunger pangs. In part he was selling precisely what the public has always wanted to buy—a solution, however temporary, to the puzzle of obesity. And partly he was selling an old notion—rapid weight loss through induced ketosis—in a slightly different guise.

And what exactly is ketosis? It is the inevitable result of carbohydrate deprivation, which is the crux of any Banting-type diet. The human body needs carbohydrates for two principal reasons—because our muscles work most efficiently while burning carbohydrates, and becuase our brains burn nothing but carbohydrates in the form of glucose. Dr. George F. Cahill, working at Harvard in the late 1960's, discovered that during dieting of any sort the liver converts stored fat to partially oxidized fatty acids known as ketone bodies, which the brain uses as a substitute source of energy in the absence of glucose.

Previously, high-protein, low-carbohydrate diets had been faulted for their failure to provide adequate "brain food." Now it was clear that the human body had already made provision for periods of carbohydrate deprivation by providing an alternate system for supplying energy to the brain. Moreover, it was evident that the liver could produce as many ketones as the brain required, even in the total absence of carbohydrates.

This, then, was the key to the success of the Banting diet and its numerous progeny: carbohydrate deprivation leads to ketosis, and ketosis leads to a natural reduction in appetite. As long as a ketogenic state is sustained, the dieter will not feel hungry and consequently he will not eat as much as he once did. *What* he eats, as long as he keeps his body in a carbohydrate-starved state, is of little consequence—which is why both Drs. Stillman and Atkins permit their followers to "cheat" up to forty grams of carbohydrates per day after ketosis is induced, knowing that the quantity is insufficient to supply the body's need and break the embargo on glucose.

Cahill, it seemed, had discovered the secret of the Banting diet, but he had not supplied a satisfactory answer to the puzzle of obesity, for it was soon discovered that ketogenic diets produced the wrong sort of weight loss. The first result of any true ketogenic diet is a dramatic loss of water weight through prodigious diuresis and copious urination. During this period there is no loss of body mass, although, depending on the severity of the diet, the dieter may lose another three to eight pounds of solid wastes. These, of course, are replaced as soon as normal eating habits are resumed, but they do contribute a significant portion of the eight to ten pounds that the dieter is able to lose during the first week of a ketogenic diet.

All subsequent weight loss, once ketosis has occurred, comes as a result of *total* caloric restriction imposed by the ketone bodies, and not as a result of any specific mixture of fats and proteins. This regimen yields a steady weight loss for as long as the dieter can endure the diet, but it is always accompanied by a significant and, to medical eyes, unacceptable loss of lean body mass. A well-balanced diet, by contrast, permits only minimal loss of lean tissue and results in weight loss that is almost entirely in the form of fat.

Another undesirable aspect of ketosis is that the gradual depletion of lean tissue stockpiles leads to a lower basal metabolism rate, which means that after several months on a ketogenic diet the body is burning far fewer calories than it once did to maintain itself, for it is now maintaining a diminished tissue mass. And this in turn means that as soon as the dieter returns to his normal eating habits, he gains weight faster than ever before because he is burning calories at a slower rate.

There are other worrisome side effects of ketosis, a number of which came to light quite accidentally during World War II. The Canadian Army, searching for an adequate emergency ration for its field troops, issued pemmican, a dried meat and suet preparation devoid of carbohydrates, to a group of volunteers. After four days on pemmican and water, those troops were fatigued, listless, dehydrated, nauseated, vomiting—in short, anything but battle-ready. To this list of pernicious side effects of the ketogenic diet most doctors would now add pathologically low blood pressure, constipation or diarrhea, and dramatic increases in the level of lipids and cholesterol in the blood.

With all that is now known about the dangers inherent in all high-protein, low-carbohydrate diets, it would be logical to assume that researchers are looking elsewhere for the solution to the puzzle of obesity. What we find instead is the Banting diet in an altogether new guise. In this most recent—and, by some accounts, most dangerous—incarnation it is known as the liquid-protein diet, or, more properly, as the "protein-sparing modified fast." This diet, which was developed by Dr. George Blackburn, an associate professor of surgery at Harvard Medical School and director of the Nutrition Support Service at Boston's New England Deaconess Hospital, was intended for the supplemental feeding of critically ill patients. Blackburn demonstrated that small amounts of dietary protein "spared" body protein stores in fasting patients better than small amounts of carbohydrate. His enthusiasm for the protein-sparing modified fast ended there; it was a Pennsylvania osteopath named Robert Linn who popularized the use of liquid protein in treating obese but otherwise healthy patients.

In its strictest form the liquid-protein diet consists of ingesting *nothing* except sugar-free fluids (water, unsweetened iced tea, or diet soft drinks) and four to six ounces—roughly 300 calories at a cost of three dollars a day—of a syrupy, fruit-flavored formula made from the fibrous protein found in animal tissues, amino acids, and collagen. According to the Food and Drug Administration, most of these products are gelatin-based substances of "extremely low nutritional quality." Some are fortified with a limited number of essential amino acids, vitamins, and minerals, but most are nutritionally incomplete. They are also expensive. Gelatin in bulk form sells for two dollars per pound; liquid protein, with its minimal additives, sells for three times as much.

Linn claims that it is possible to lose up to ten pounds a week on this diet, and there is little reason to doubt him. Because the liquid-protein formula contains no carbohydrates whatsoever, the regimen is strongly ketogenic, producing the sort of immediate water-weight loss and loss of lean body mass with which we are already familiar. And because it restricts the dieter to 300 calories per day, well below the 800-1,000 calorie per day minimum level recommended by most nutritionists, it quite naturally produces the adipose tissue loss associated with near-starvation diets. The worst, in short, of both worlds—and the deleterious side effects of both as well.

Under close medical supervision, such as that which George Blackburn was able to provide his patients at New England Deaconess, such a diet supplement might have considerable value in the clinical treatment of morbid obesity. It is safer than the total fast, which Stunkard and many others recommend as the only effective way to reduce the intransigent corpulence in patients with life-threatening obesity, and it achieves nearly the same results. It is emphatically unsafe when undertaken without adequate medical supervision, however, and because the Food and Drug Administration has ruled that liquid protein is a food rather than a drug, it is available without prescription and is currently being used without proper caution by an estimated 2 million dieters. As Blackburn has repeatedly warned, there is a severe possiblity of acute mineral loss on this diet—mineral loss that can cause both renal and coronary disease.

The key to success on the liquid-protein diet, according to Blackburn, is ensuring that the patient receives adequate doses of necessary minerals, chiefly potassium. When an individual is deprived of potassium, he may collapse. And when that happens, Blackburn notes, "we don't know what to do. It's like treating Legionnaires' disease." Unfortunately, there is no way to adequately gauge an average adult's daily dosage of potassium; what is surfeit for some is insufficient for others. The upshot of which is that the F.D.A. is currently investigating the deaths of some forty women, ranging in age from twenty-five to forty-four, who succumbed while on the liquid-protein diet or shortly after abandoning it. One of them, the forty-four-year-old wife of a Minnesota physician, died of apparent heart failure after seven weeks on a protein-sparing fast. She left eight small children.

Under sharp questioning by a House subcommittee on health and the environment, Dr. Linn has insisted that these deaths are "mere coincidence." Experts at the Federal Center for Disease Control in Atlanta, Georgia, are not so certain that coincidence alone can account for all forty deaths. After a careful, case-by-case study in which they eliminated those victims with histories of heart disease or diabetes—either of which might otherwise have been a contributing factor—they found fifteen cases in which there was but one common factor: the protein-sparing liquid fast. The center tentatively links all fifteen of these deaths to the diet, and researchers there suggest a number of possible causes. The first of these may be simple starvation, for at 300 calories per day many of the women involved were receiving less nourishment than the most deprived concentration camp inmates. All had been on the diet for anywhere from two to eight months—long enough, for example, for severe depletion of heart tissue to have occurred. Significantly, the F.D.A. reports that the syndrome seen in these fifteen cases is rarely, if ever, associated with simple starvation.

Another possibility, one that Blackburn warned of when he first proposed the diet for in-hospital use, is some sort of interruption of the heart's rhythm due to chronic electrolyte deficit. This is most often cited as the fatal flaw in the liquid-protein diet, but there are two other possible causes that deserve consideration. The first of these is that the protein supplement itself contains an as yet unidentified toxic substance that accrues in the body over a period of weeks—something added to the diet, something lethal. Or it may be that there is something missing from the diet, some essential nutrient that the body demands and that medical science has thus far failed to recognize. A Mayo Clinic physician, cautioning against the indiscriminate use of vitamin supplements as substitutes for a nutritionally balanced diet, warned that "if you take vitamin pills, you get only the vitamins that have been discovered." The same may be said of liquid protein, which even in its most fortified form, contains only the nutrients that have been discovered.

In any case, the F.D.A. is sufficiently concerned about the rash of deaths linked to the protein-sparing modified fast that it has proposed a mandatory warning label to be placed on all protein products intended for use in weight reduction. It would read:

> WARNING: Very low calorie protein diets may cause serious illness or death. DO NOT USE FOR WEIGHT REDUCTION OR MAINTENANCE WITHOUT MEDICAL SUPERVISION. Do not use for any purpose without medical advice if you are taking any medication. Not for use by infants, children, or pregnant or nursing women.

Fortunately, such labels may never be necessary, for the liquid-protein vogue seems to have run its course: since the F.D.A. announced its findings, sales of liquid protein have fallen almost 95 per cent and a reversal of this trend seems unlikely.

Undaunted by these developments, Linn continues to promote what he calls the "single most significant advance in the control of obesity in the last forty years." He claims an 80 per cent success rate with his patients—in a field known for 95 per cent recidivism—but like Dr. Atkins, he has produced no figures to back up his claims. This had led at least one disgruntled colleague to observe that "the key ingredient of Linn's diet is not protein but hype." More cautious critics of the protein-sparing fast, noting that it produces severe muscle weakness, changes in the menstrual cycle, nausea and vomiting, hair loss, excessive skin dryness, demineralization of bones, kidney stones, gout, and mental disturbances, conclude that only physicians schooled in the metabolics of starvation should attempt to administer it.

The drawback to the Banting diet, whatever its form, is that ultimate failure is built into the regimen itself. It cannot be sustained indefinitely, and as soon as it is abandoned the most significant component of the total weight loss, that due to dehydration, is immediately redressed. Just as importantly, it contains no provision for any sort of long-term adjustment of the dieter's eating habits—an absolute prerequisite for achieving and maintaining a consequential reduction in total body fat.

In cases of modest obesity, the restructuring of eating habits is probably more important than actual caloric restriction in determining the success or failure of a given diet—an aspect of weight reduction that we shall inspect more closely in a later chapter. In cases of morbid obesity, however, where medical men are dealing with patients who weigh *twice* what they should, the inclination is to abandon all thoughts of dietary reeducation in favor of more radical approaches to weight reduction. The oldest and most widely favored of these is the total fast.

Voluntary starvation, even under constant medical supervision, is extremely risky; for starvation, whether total or partial, depletes the body of lean tissue and essential electrolytes as well as stored fat. The loss of tissue is enervating, and the loss of vital trace minerals is downright dangerous. (Just how dangerous is pointed up by the case of a 215-pound woman who died recently in a New Jersey diet clinic after her fourth day on a 500-calorie-per-day regimen—presumably of cardiac arrhythmia provoked by a deficiency in the blood minerals needed to sustain the heart's electrical activity.) Mayer notes that duodenal ulcers, gout, and severe psychological disorders are also common in fasting patients.

To offset the mineral imbalance produced by fasting, weight-reduction experts recommend careful monitoring of the dieting patient's electrolyte levels and supplemental doses of vitamins and water-soluble salts. This done—and the threat of cardiac arrest at least theoretically eliminated—the total fast proves a highly effective way of achieving a dramatic, if temporary, drop in body weight. Initially at least, fasting is less stressful than dieting, for most of the familiar hunger cues are absent from the fasting patient's environment.

In addition, the severe ketosis that ensues within forty-eight hours of the cessation of eating reduces sensations of hunger almost completely, which helps explain why the obese patient often has an increased sense of well-being during the first weeks of a starvation diet. This is not the case when lean individuals starve, according to Dr. Gastineau. In such instances heat production diminishes rapidly, physical exertion of any kind becomes increasingly difficult, and depression, anxiety, and emotional instability often occur.

Happy for the fat man, then, that fasting makes him feel healthier, for it is he who needs the fast. Most overweight individuals have what Gastineau calls "good fasting tolerance"—they can sustain a total fast for up to thirty days with little apparent difficulty, losing as much as fifty pounds in the process. As a safety precaution, however, Stanford University's Albert J. Stunkard recommends an in-hospital fast of no longer than ten days to two weeks to his overweight patients who must lose fifteen to twenty pounds. The cost of such a course of treatment is considerable, needless to say, and its long-range effectiveness, if it is not coupled with a lifelong maintenance diet that is nutritionally balanced and calorically restricted, is often nil.

Costly as fasting may be, it does not begin to approach the cost of medicine's most radical solution to the problem of uncontrolled gluttony, the so-called jejuno-ilial shunt or intestinal bypass operation. The purpose of this surgical technique is to reduce the functional length of the small intestine from twenty feet to two—and to cut nutrient absorption proportionately. In theory, this procedure permits the grossly obese patient to eat unrestricted quantities of high-calorie foods and still achieve a steady weight loss, since most of those foods are passing through the system faster than their caloric value can be extracted. In practice, these people are simply malabsorptive, and they have all the problems associated with inadequate digestive systems: abdominal pain, gastrointestinal disorders, and acute diarrhea. They also develop the "fatty" liver associated with fasting, a condition that cannot be corrected with vitamin supplements, suggesting that it is caused by an amino acid imbalance that will last until the bypass is surgically reversed.

Postoperative complications are only one reason for opposing bypass surgery in all but the most stubborn cases of morbid obesity. Another is the fact that this "cure" presupposes the patient's inability to understand his own dietary problems or participate in their resolution—which, Gastineau says, is very rarely the case. (The Mayo Clinic has performed only two bypass operations in its history, and both of those occurred under extenuating circumstances.) In short, the cure is often more dreadful than the affliction, a situation which has led the esteemed British medical journal *Lancet* to liken the jejuno-ilial shunt to cutting off the hands of a heavy smoker.

In any case, bypass surgery is a last resort for those with a life-threatening weight problem. It is of limited efficacy in a handful of those cases, and it is hardly applicable to the situation in which millions of moderately overweight Americans find themselves after years of inactivity and incautious eating. For them, neither radical surgery nor "revolutionary" quick weight-loss diets holds the solution to the puzzle of obesity.

4

Exploiting the Overweight

The overweight consumer is the most unprotected consumer of all.
George McGovern

For as long as anyone could remember, the prevailing wisdom with regard to dieting was that the only effective way to lose weight was to take something *out* of one's diet. That made eminent sense, after all—eat less and eventually you will weigh less. And besides, it was the only counsel being offered by reputable members of the medical community. And so uncounted millions of overweight men and women, following the vogue of the moment, gave up desserts, or alcohol, or starchy foods, or dairy products. In time the most desperate would even try giving up everything—and that, of course, worked best of all: take away all food and you must inevitably take away whatever is making you fat.

To aid morbidly obese patients with uncontrollable appetites, resourceful surgeons developed a procedure for wiring the jaw shut, and this, quite naturally, proved a highly effective means of weight reduction—as long as the wires remained in place. The hitch was that as soon as the patient's jaw became functional and old eating habits were resumed, the old problem resurfaced. It was not enough to take certain foods out of the diet for months at a time; it was not even enough to take all food out of the diet for a time. What was needed was a means of taking some foods—or some portion of all foods—out of the diet forever, and here again the perceived need was met by a new mode of surgery, the intestinal bypass. The trouble here was that a number of patients did not survive bypass surgery, and those who did often developed complications more inherently life-threatening than mere obesity. The surgeons had provided a kind of solution, one that was as attractive in theory as it was unworkable in practice, but they had not succeeded in providing *the* solution to the puzzle of obesity.

What had become abundantly clear from these accumulated experiences was this: the more taken *out* of the diet, the greater the likelihood that the dieter would succeed in liberating the thin man inside himself, the one wildly signaling to be let out. It was clear, too, that the more taken out of the diet, the greater the risk to the dieter's health. So great that many experts on obesity could only concur with Dr. Philip White, director of the American Medical Association's Department of Food and Nutrition, when he observed that "the trauma in such reduction is so great and the success so limited that it is better to let them stay fat."

Under the circumstances it was inevitable that men should begin to think in terms of what could be *added* to the diet, rather than subtracted from it, in order to produce a permanent drop in body weight. A low-calorie food that bulked up in the intestine and caused a sensation of satiety, for example; or a potion that would coat the lining of the stomach and eliminate hunger pangs. A drug that would double or triple the basal metabolism rate and cause the body to burn off its stored fat; or a drug that would interfere with the functioning of the hypothalamus, the "hunger center" of the brain, and deaden all desire for food. A machine that would massage the abdomen, hips, and buttocks until the adipose tissue concentrated there melted into the bloodstream. A pill, a hormone, a liquid formula; a potion, a lotion, a salve. It hardly mattered what, as long as it worked.

Where there is a market, a product will appear—and it is no surprise that the long, dismal history of man's war against his own waistline is replete with bogus diet aids, each heralded as the final solution to the puzzle of obesity, each promising subtraction through addition. Pills, hormones, formulas; potions, lotions, salves—all have been foisted upon the overweight at one time or another. And a gullible and desperate public has managed, time after time, to swallow its common sense along with the newest "miracle reducing aid"—and in so doing has made nutrition quackery the biggest racket in the health field.

The bewildering array of diet aids available to the unprotected overweight consumer is directly attributable to the fact that the promoters of reducing devices, unlike the manufacturers of prescription drugs, are not obliged to prove the safety and effectiveness of their products before putting them on the market. But the commercial success of those diet aids must be attributed to what was earlier referred to as our own seemingly limitless capacity for self-delusion where diet is concerned. How else to explain why thousands of sensible Americans rushed to buy a distillation, made from West African berries, that was said to give a sweetening effect to low-calorie foodstuffs if held in the mouth for two minutes prior to every meal. And how else to explain the brief but considerable popularity of "Rosicrucian wine," a potion purportedly derived from a secret formula known only to select members of that venerable mystical order. It sounds anything but plausible, yet its promoter got some of Western Europe's leading socialites to down quantities of the liquid at his Swiss spa by promising them a painless 75 per cent reduction in appetite.

The con, it would seem, is very nearly as old as the problem of overweight itself. Diet aids have long outsold aphrodisiacs, perhaps because impotence and frigidity are less universal than obesity, but certainly not because the case made for reducing products is more compelling. What makes the con work—and what makes even the most patently worthless diet aids sell—is that the overweight individual, having experimented fruitlessly with taking things *out* of his diet, sees little harm in putting something novel *in*, on the outside chance that the manufacturer's sweeping claims for the product in question are even partially true.

At worst, this too will prove to be a waste of time—and the fat American, who is conditioned to failure where weight control is concerned, is also reconciled to wasting time. He recognizes the arrant hyperbole, for instance, in Victor Lindlahr's preface to his *Calorie Countdown*, one of dozens of diet books on the American Medical Association's "not recommended" list—"In the next ninety days you will get back the figure you used to have and it will be yours for keeps. That's the Countdown promise to you." But time and time again the dieter permits a curious admixture of unquenchable optimism and increasing desperation to color his judgment. Wanting to believe, he finds belief easy; and the more subtle the con, the readier his acquiescence.

Few diet scams in history have matched the subtlety—or the sheer audacity and cynical calculation—of the one that John Andreadis perpetrated on the American public in the 1950's—and consequently few have matched its success, either. Andreadis, or John Andre as he styled himself, did not invent the diet scam any more than Henry Ford invented the automobile; like Ford, he merely turned someone else's idea into Big Business. Andre's career as the nation's leading impresario of weight loss reached its apogee—or, depending on your outlook, its nadir—on the East Coast in the late 1950's. It had actually begun on the West Coast a decade earlier.

What Andre was marketing in 1948 was something called "Hollywood Beauty Cream," which accompanying circulars claimed could melt away up to fifteen pounds in thirty days. The U.S. Post Office did not agree, and it issued a fraud order barring further mail-order sales of Andre's beauty cream. This did not prohibit retail sales of the product, of course, nor did it prevent the enterprising young Greek from repackaging his product—which the Post Office said contained nothing but Vaseline, wintergreen, and water, doubtless soothing to the skin but otherwise valueless—and selling it under another name in other states. The exact nature of the product changed from time to time, and the subtlety and sophistication of Andre's sales pitch grew apace, but the essential pattern remained unchanged. With the exception of Man-Tan—a skin dye he marketed with astonishing success in the late 1950's, selling $20 million worth of the "indoor tanning" preparation in six months—Andre confined himself to promoting bogus diet aids that combined essentially inert ingredients with wildly extravagant promotional claims. These included a vitamin preparation, an arthritis "remedy," and Propex, an appetite suppressant of dubious value unless used in combination with the "recommended" 1,000-calorie-per-day diet that accompanied it.

Propex eventually ran afoul of the Post Office's Division of Inspection, whose wheels grind slowly but exceeding small, and it went the way of Andre's "Hollywood Beauty Cream"—but not before it gave the indefatigable entrepreneur the idea for a new sort of pill, one that would confound the Post Office and gull the public more completely than any diet aid before or since. The new product was Regimen, and for years it was the nation's most widely popular nonprescription reducing drug, netting upwards of $6.5 million in sales annually before the Post Office's Division of Inspection and the National Better Business Bureau closed in on Andre's latest brainchild.

Like all great propagandists—and he was nothing if not a brilliant propagandist—John Andre appreciated the peculiar power of the printed word, the authority that is automatically conferred on ideas when they are set into type. Only academics and natural-born skeptics are disciplined to doubt; the rest of us read for information, accepting what is written as accurate simply because it *is* written. We are often ill-equipped to challenge the work of a self-styled authority, particularly if his remarks are cloaked in pseudoscientific jargon; and we are generally disinclined by long habit to do so anyway. And when that voice of authority is speaking with apparent conviction—and is saying what the listener wants to hear—credulity subsumes common sense. It was precisely that combination of factors that rendered Andre's hyperbolic claims on behalf of

Regimen plausible to millions of readers. It is easy to recognize the calculated appeal and the sheer fabrication that are mixed in nearly equal portions in this excerpt from a typical Regimen ad:

> ***AMAZING NEW MEDICAL RELEASE*** (Available Now Without Doctor's Prescription) ***NO-DIET REDUCING*** with New Wonder Drug for Fat People ***CAUSES YOUR BODY TO LOSE WEIGHT THE FASTEST ACTING WAY***!
> No diet, no special eating, no giving up the kinds of food you like to eat—yet new wonder drug acts directly on the cause of your overweight—It's safe . . . automatic. ***YOU MUST REDUCE UP TO*** 6 ***POUNDS IN*** 3 ***DAYS*** . . . ***UP TO*** 10 ***POUNDS THE FIRST WEEK*** . . . ***OR YOU PAY NOTHING***!

Whoever first said "You can't cheat an honest man" had obviously never met the promotional genius behind the Regimen campaign, which was without question the most artfully conceived, elaborately contrived, and brazenly executed diet scam of all time. It began with printed endorsements from professionals and concluded with televised public endorsements from ordinary citizens—and from start to finish it was a complete fiction.

The doctors who supplied the initial endorsements and provided the weight-loss charts that were an early feature of the Regimen campaign—charts purporting to show dramatic, across-the-board weight losses in users of Andre's wonder-tablets—were all in Andre's pay. Their statistics were heavily fudged or, in some cases, wholly invented: existing patients achieved fictional weight losses, and nonexistent patients (who naturally showed even more remarkable progress on the Regimen regimen) further skewed the charts in favor of the new pills. Andre—who understood perfectly the selling power of professional endorsements, the magic inherent in the phrase "Recommended by physicians"—also understood that it was not impossible to find medical men and women, down on their luck or deeply in debt, who might be willing to compromise their Hippocratic

Oath for what amounted to the right cash consideration.

What Andre also understood to an almost uncanny degree, and at a very early stage in the medium's growth, was the awesome power of television as a marketing tool. Fraudulent professional endorsements launched Regimen, but it was television that kept the product afloat. Readers may remember the succession of young to middle-aged women, most of them housewives and all of them overweight, who appeared with host Dave Garroway on the "Today" show in 1959. These women were participants in what was perhaps the most public diet in history, for it included a weekly weigh-in before a live television audience of millions. Who could question the efficacy of such a diet when the results were a matter of public record? Here were ordinary women from ordinary households, fighting the ordinary housewife's age-old battle—and winning, thanks to an extraordinary new diet aid. They were, by their own account, eating what they liked to eat—no extreme or restrictive diets—and yet they were losing weight at a steady rate. The difference, as each woman took pains to point out at each weigh-in, was Regimen, which had reduced her craving for food without producing any unpleasant side effects.

By 1959 Andre was spending close to $4 million a year advertising his various health and diet aids, but no amount of money could have bought him the sort of air time that Garroway and his colleagues on the "Today" show were providing for free, nor could he have bought a professional endorsement more valuable than theirs. What Garroway and his staff did not know, of course, was that Andre's "average housewives" were professional actresses, and that the dramatic weight losses that they were achieving had nothing to do with Regimen and everything to do with the fact that they had voluntarily put themselves on near-starvation diets. Their apparent high spirits and glowing good health, like their tributes to the miraculous powers of Regimen, were a theatrical illusion—one produced and directed by John Andre.

To recruit his regiment of Regimen women, Andre placed the same small advertisement in a number of show-business publications: "Fat girl wanted, who was once thin, to lose weight." A number of the women who responded were not actresses at all, although all met Andre's first qualification. Several were actresses of some accomplishment who, for one reason or another, had gained so much weight that they were finding it virtually impossible to get parts; they saw Andre's scheme as a way to diet themselves back into the business. For those who passed the audition, there were fees for all personal appearances and a bonus of $50 for every pound lost after the first fifteen. For a regular on the "Today" show this could amount to a rather handsome income, and one of Andre's most popular "average housewives" later reported earning $17,701.00 over a period of slightly more than a year.

What she also reported, when the Regimen scandal broke and Andre's recruits began to talk, was that she and the others had been carefully schooled before their public appearances, lest they attribute too much of their weight loss to Regimen or blurt out the truth about their actual regimen. They were coached to praise Regimen, attest that it made them *want* to eat less than they had previously eaten . . . and allow the viewer to make the inference. They were never to say that they were not dieting, but they were also never to mention that they were on a severely restricted low-calorie diet.

Interestingly enough, Andre himself never prescribed any sort of diet for his recruits. The cash inducements that he offered, in combination with the implicit understanding that failure to lose twenty pounds during the first month of the diet would mean termination of their contracts and an end to the lucrative television appearances, was the only inducement that any of these women needed to put themselves on near-starvation diets of the most dramatic and debilitating sort.

At first it was rather easy for Andre's housewives to show a weight loss each week, but as the diet wore on, each woman drawing nearer and nearer to her ideal weight, the task became more difficult. Andre's charges developed short tempers and chronic depression, common features of all extreme diets, and several developed edema—or water retention and swelling in the lower legs and ankles. They took phenobarbital for their nerves and diuretics to hasten the dehydration process. And when nothing else would work, they simply starved.

The pills that were part of the Regimen program came in three colors—green, pink, and yellow—each with a different chemical content and a different specific function. A ten-day supply cost approximately eighteen cents to manufacture and retailed for three dollars—a mark-up of 1,600 per cent.

The principal ingredient of the green Regimen pills was benzocaine, supplemented by various vitamins. Accompanying literature described the green pills as appetite suppressants that worked by dulling taste sensation in the salivary glands. As we will learn in the next chapter, vitamins in any combination and at any dosage have no impact whatsoever on overweight, and benzocaine is nothing more than a mild topical anesthetic. Whether benzocaine in such small doses—7.5 mg. per tablet—could have a numbing effect on the salivary glands is arguable; it is also quite beside the point, for the salivary glands are a part of the mouth and the pills were in the stomach.

The pink Regimen pills contained an ingredient guaranteed to remove "the excess bloatlike fluid that accounts for up to 70% of your fatty tissue." This ingredient was ammonium chloride, a mild diuretic, and in sufficient doses it would indeed cause a drop in total body weight through dehydration. But, as consultants from the American Medical Association were to tell the National Better Business Bureau, that water loss would come from extracellular, rather than fatty, tissue—and in any case the body's adipose tissue is at most 20 per cent fluid, and not 70 per cent as the Regimen ads claimed. What is more, water loss is simply water loss, as the A.M.A.'s experts were quick to point out. It is never converted to fat loss, and it is regained as soon as diuretics are abandoned and normal drinking and eating habits are resumed.

The A.M.A. delegation was equally dubious about the efficacy of the yellow Regimen pills, which were billed as potent appetite suppressants. These last tablets contained phenylpropanolamine hydrochloride, a central nervous system stimulant that had previously demonstrated some effectiveness as an appetite inhibitor—but only in dosages twice as powerful as those contained in the Regimen pills. At best the drug's impact on appetite was "slight," in the experts' opinion, and certainly its effectiveness was of limited duration. Dosages as small as those permissible in over-the-counter diet aids such as Regimen were deemed worthless, the experts said, adding for the record that propanol, as the drug was also known, had been largely abandoned by the medical profession after nearly four decades of ineffective experimentation.

As it turned out, the essential ingredient of the Regimen program was contained not in the colored pills, but in the literature that accompanied them. It contained a "recommended" low-calorie diet and a familiar admonition: "It's a medically accepted fact, if normally healthy, to reduce you must restrict your caloric intake. To weigh less you must eat less . . ." So there it was. Take away the professional endorsements, take away the television weigh-ins, take away the hype—even take away the little green, pink, and yellow pills—and what remained was a nutritionally balanced low-calorie diet, exactly the regimen that your family doctor had been telling you for years was the only proven means of achieving weight loss. What Andre counted on—correctly—was that millions of overweight Americans would read the boldface of the ads ("NO-DIET REDUCING With New Wonder Drug") and skip the small print in the booklet that came with the pills.

It took years for the Post Office and the Better Business Bureau to strip the Regimen program down to its essentials, however. Not until 1964, six full years after the Federal Trade Commission first filed a complaint against Regimen for false advertising, did the government succeed in putting John Andreadis out of the reducing racket, and by that time overweight Americans had invested some $16 million in his sensible little diet and utterly superfluous pills.

Regimen may have been the most audaciously marketed diet aid of all time, but the so-called "diet candies" known as Ayds have certainly been the most durable. Billed as an appetite suppressant in pleasant-tasting candy form, they have been sold over the counter for almost four decades. Neither the product nor the method of advertising—full-page testimonials familiar to the readers of any of the major women's magazines—has changed much over the years, and with good reason. In 1939, the year Ayds were introduced, sales approached $800,000; they now top $7 million annually and may account for half the over-the-counter diet products sold in the United States. The Campana Corporation, which manufactures Ayds, plainly appreciates that both its formulas have been perfected. The candies—which are nothing more than dextrose (a form of sugar), minerals, and vitamins—come in four flavors and sell for $3.79 for a month's supply. And the testimonials, which always include before-and-after photographs of the featured dieters, cost Campana a mere $250 per story.

In these testimonials triumphant dieters tout the miraculous powers of Ayds ("I was a 325-pound creampuff until I met Ayds"), which are said to contain no harmful drugs, laxatives, or thyroid stimulants. The Ayds campaign also has its Hollywood connection. Its ad copy once boasted:

> Today's screen stars now eat candy. Oh, not ordinary candy, but a special low-calorie, vitamin-and-mineral enriched candy, called Ayds. Taken as directed before meals, it curbs the appetite, so you automatically eat less and lose weight naturally.

If even two of today's screen stars are eating Ayds before meals, then the above statement is two-thirds true, for Ayds are indeed a candy. Originally developed for diabetics, they contain less dextrose and more cream than most candies. They also contain 25 calories per piece. Their purported value, when ingested just before a meal, is that they "stimulate the blood-sugar apparatus which helps control our appetite." Medical authorities flatly dispute this contention, insisting that Ayds' actual impact on blood sugar levels is too small to be accurately measured, and that if they have any value at all it is purely psychological. Ayds work, if and when they work, because desperate dieters want to believe that they work.

Like John Andreadis, the Campana Corporation markets a

small pamphlet along with its product; and like the Regimen literature, the Ayds handout urges the buyer to follow the enclosed diet plan for "even quicker" results. The recommended diet in this case is a 1,400-calorie-per-day regimen, from which the Ayds user must remember to subtract 25 calories for each of the six pieces of "diet candy" that he or she consumes during the day. What remains is a 1,250-calorie daily diet—on which even the most chronic sort of obesity will eventually submit to reduction.

As long ago as 1945 the Federal Trade Commission attempted to force Ayds to change the thrust of its advertising campaign to place greater emphasis on the diet that was an integral part of the Ayds program. The manufacturer, understanding full well that the only real difference between its product and, say, Hershey's bars was that Ayds were being bought almost exclusively by the very people who had sworn off candy bars—rightly saw the F.T.C.'s complaint action as a threat to Ayds' continued existence and fought back in court. To the government's considerable surprise and the manufacturer's unending delight, the court ruled that the eating of candy—presumably any candy, not just Ayds—before a meal did act to curb one's appetite enough to reduce weight, which meant that Ayds could continue to be offered as a therapeutic remedy for overweight.

The court's ruling proved to be a disastrous setback for those governmental agencies assigned to policing food faddists and health hucksters, and it accounts in large measure for the seemingly laggard manner in which John Andre's multiple frauds were brought to a halt. Unlike the manufacturers of ethical drugs, the promoters of diet aids were under no obligation to prove the safety or efficacy of their products; the burden of proof lay with the government, which found itself hard-pressed to keep abreast of a burgeoning market in new "wonder drugs," old wonder drugs with new labels, older patent medicines applied as cures to new ills, and the like.

It took years, for instance, for the Post Office to halt production and distribution of Enerjol, a capsule compounded of royal jelly (the substance that worker bees create to feed their queen), vitamins, iron, and oyster concentrate. (Owen Laboratories, the makers of Enerjol, claimed that their product would cure impotency, restore "youthful functions" to menopausal women, treat Parkinson's disease and various heart ailments, reverse baldness, and treat low blood pressure and nervousness.) Several years later the F.D.A. fared somewhat better with Pure Pacific Sea Kelp, a tablet that its makers claimed would prevent tuberculosis and harden bones while ridding the user of excess weight. In the latter case, the claims—but not the product—were withdrawn, and kelp in various forms remains a staple item in health food stores, where it is still touted as a cure-all for countless human ills.

It is this same formula—a combination of a nutritionally sound low-calorie diet and a nutritionally inconsequential but heavily promoted placebo—that underlies the hormone treatment scheme devised in the late 1950's by Dr. A.T.W. Simeons, a British-born endocrinologist then practicing at Rome's Salvator Mundi International Hospital. It was distinguished from other weight-reduction schemes only by its high cost—up to $500 for a series of injections—and the severity of its accompanying diet.

Simeons offered his patients the comforting counsel, familiar to victims of Taller's safflower-oil diet, that "calories don't count"—and then proceeded to put them on a near-starvation diet of no more than 500 calories per day. He reassured them that "obesity is a very definite metabolic disorder"—a dietary "fact" discounted by all reputable authorities on obesity and disproved by medical evidence—because he appreciated how eager the overweight are to be absolved of the sin of overeating. (It has long been the aim of the promoters of diet aids to find a culprit for the problem of obesity. Glands, underactive thyroid, mineral imbalance, vitamin deficiency, hormonal irregularity—any cause except the only cause, which is overeating.) And, finally, Simeons promised results: "Within a few days the excess craving for food from which overweight patients suffer vanishes, because now their blood is continually saturated with nourishment"—presumably as a result of the hormone injections they were receiving.

As we know, the loss of appetite that Simeons promised was due to ketosis induced by his Banting-type diet, and the loss of body weight that followed was due to the severe caloric deficit that he imposed on his patients. The injections themselves, derived from human chorionic gonadotropin (HCG), a hormone produced in the placenta during pregnancy and used since the 1940's to treat young boys with undescended testicles, have no proven therapeutic value whatsoever in treating obesity, although the excessively high cost of the treatments may itself have been an inducement to compliance with Simeons's diet plan.

Equally encouraging—and equally suspect—were Simeons's claims for his treatment program, which boasted impressive results chiefly because Simeons eliminated from his program—and therefore from his statistics—all patients who could not adhere to his near-starvation diet. He insisted that dieters could lose up to a full pound a day on his diet without ill effects, a statement that the *Journal of the American Medical Association* flatly contradicted: "Continued adherence to such a drastic regimen is potentially more hazardous to the patient's health than continued obesity." He also insisted that it was possible, through his treatment program, to reduce a woman's hips by as much as ten inches without altering the total weight of her body—to which preposterous statement he appended the astounding observation that, in any case, "it is always and only the unwanted fat that goes."

Medical authorities have not concerned themselves with the most patently absurd of Simeons's claims, but studies have been done to test the merits of HCG. One of the more elaborate was conducted by Dr. Barry W. Frank in 1964, seven years after Simeons first introduced his diet in Rome. Using forty-eight volunteers in an elaborate "double-blind" experiment (so constructed that even Dr. Frank did not know which of his patients were receiving HCG and which a placebo) he discovered that the two groups lost almost precisely the same amount of weight. Based on such findings, the American Medical Association declared that its department of drugs found "no scientific evidence from controlled experiments to justify the use of human chorionic gonadotropin in the treatment of obesity." "Proof is lacking," says Dr. Gastineau, "that this scheme of treatment is effective in any way other than through caloric restriction and facilitation of adherence to diet by means of elaborate ritual."

The most recent "solution" to the puzzle of obesity is called "cellulite therapy." Like Simeons's HCG treatments, it is a foreign import—French, this time, rather than Anglo-Italian—and this automatically confers a certain authority on the program. One of the durable fictions concerning health and beauty care, at least to Americans, is that Europeans know more than we do about preventive medicine and the preservation of personal beauty. Why this is so, analysts are at a loss to explain; but neither can they adequately explain why the addition of lemon juice to almost any skin- or hair-care product will boost the sales of that product. Neither phenomenon submits to reason, and consequently no amount of evidence to the contrary will disabuse Americans of the notion that European health programs and beauty products are inherently superior.

Cellulite therapy had this positive prejudice working in its favor when the concept was first introduced to the United States in 1972. Also in its favor was that it combined the salient features of John Andre's promotional techniques and A.T.W. Simeons's right-sounding physiological claptrap while avoiding the excesses peculiar to each. "Cellulite," a French neologism, refers to a puckering and dimpling of fat that occurs most frequently on the buttocks and thighs of overweight middle-aged women. In actual fact this dimpling is a result of aging rather than overindulgence. It manifests itself when the subdermal connective tissue that forms a sort of honeycomb around the body's adipose cells begins to lose its elasticity and shrinks with age. When this happens, the overlying skin also contracts—and if the encased fat cells cannot shrink, they cannot help but pucker.

It is often said of these fatty pockets that they are first to take up excess calories and the last to give them up, and this is too often true. It is true in the first place because excess calories are primarily stored in adipose tissue, which means that the effects of systematic overeating—or even of a protracted eating binge—will soon be reflected in rounder hips and rounder cheeks. And it is true secondly because most popular diets, and all "quick weight-loss" diets, result in water loss and the loss of lean body mass—neither of which is fat. As we have already noted, it is only by adhering to a balanced, low-calorie diet that the overweight individual is able to reduce those pockets of stubborn fat.

The promoters of cellulite therapy would have you believe otherwise, and with good reason: their weight-reduction package—which includes ionization machines, paraffin wraps, air hoses, and deep massage as well as a series of ten injections of "cellulite-diffusing enzymes"—costs $550. The enzyme involved is identified by its promoters as thiomucase. It is not listed in Food and Drug Administration files, nor is its use approved by the F.D.A. or any other governmental regulatory agency. If it is indeed an enzyme, it clearly does no immediate harm to those who are injected with it, as evidenced by the fact that there have been no reported fatalities connected to its administration.

But neither is there any evidence that it benefits the overweight beyond the placebo effect we have previously associated with Ayds, HCG, and other purported diet aids. A true enzyme would indeed cause tissue around the injection site to "diffuse," but what would diffuse is the tissue, not the fat it contains and this action would leave a hole behind. There is, in addition, the very real danger of a possible allergic reaction to the supposed enzyme involved, as medical authorities have warned.

The same experts have even less to say in favor of the "cellulite machine," which appears to be identical to the Diapulse machine, first marketed in the 1950's as a form of short-wave therapy for "treating" a wide variety of afflictions, overweight not among them. Since January of 1974 an F.D.A.-obtained restraining order has barred interstate shipment of the Diapulse machine on the grounds that it is ineffective and mislabeled. It remains to be seen whether the machine will find a new market in its newest incarnation, but the suspicion is that it will. "Spot-reducing" devices similar to the Diapulse have been on the market for decades, all of them operating on the physiological "principle" that a low current, passed through the body by means of electric contact pads, causes involuntary muscular contractions that tone up the body while breaking down adipose tissue. Reputable medical men are in agreement that only exercise tones flabby muscles, and only diet reduces fatty tissue.

As for the other aspects of cellulite therapy, the best that can be said of them is that they do the body no enduring harm. The paraffin applications, for example, involve wrapping the hips and thighs in cheesecloth soaked in paraffin, the theory being that this combination of binding and heat will cause excessive perspiration—which it does—and that this, in turn, will cause the breakdown and reabsorption of "fatty globules" of cellulite—which it does not. What it does do, in some instances, is aggravate an already poor circulatory system. The air hoses, applied for essentially the same reason, can be even more dangerous. Far from breaking down subcutaneous fat, they often break up surface blood vessels, causing bruising and hemorrhaging. And if massage were of any real help in breaking up the adipose tissue gathered on the hips, buttocks, and thighs, we would all have svelte upper legs and trim fannies—for no part of the body is more frequently massaged by sedentary Americans than the part they sit on.

At this point it should come as no surprise to learn that cellulite therapy includes a diet component, in this case a zero-carbohydrate diet that induces ketosis and encourages dehydration. On this diet, of course, victims of cellulite (as they have learned to call their excess poundage) lose weight everywhere—from the bust they admire as well as the hips they abhor. At great cost, some discomfort, and no small risk to their health, they are participating in a Banting-type diet program, all but invisible beneath a panoply of space-age machines.

What they will have learned, when the paraffin wraps are peeled away, the injections discontinued, the Diapulse disconnected, and the air hoses stowed, is that this solution to the puzzle of obesity is no solution either. For as the American Medical Association has repeatedly observed, there is no drug preparation currently available on a nonprescription basis that will cure exogenous obesity—not Regimen pills, not Ayds, not HCG, not "cellulite-diffusing enzymes." "Don't throw away your money on 'medicated' caramels, chewing gum, and cigarettes, fad diets, tonics, and other over-the-counter nonsense," the A.M.A. warns—and millions of overweight Americans fail to heed. Hearing the siren call of the promoter, whose tune is full of promise, they ignore the somber voice of medical reason.

In saying that the currently available over-the-counter diet aids are worthless in treating obesity, the A.M.A. has not specifically ruled out *prescription* drugs as a means of weight control, and indeed for a time in the early 1960's it appeared that the puzzle of what to *add* to the diet in order to achieve weight loss had at last been solved. For generations the only prescription for weight loss was to eat less, but that was before the advent of the diet pill. Such eminent authorities of diet and nutrition as Harvard's Fredrick Stare have called these pills nothing more nor less than "twentieth-century charlatanism," but they have become Big Business nonetheless, and a new breed of medical man has evolved to dispense them. Dispense is indeed the operative word here, for many of these "fat doctors" have dispensed with all but the most rudimentary sort of work-up on their new patients, the better to dispense pills to scores of overweight patients every day.

In general, what these doctors are prescribing is a combination of several medications that is known as a "rainbow package." (John Andre took shrewd advantage of this practice when he launched Regimen. "Doctors know what's good for you," the ad copy ran. "They know all the different methods to reduce—the scientific way to attack excessive weight. They normally prescribe—not one—but a careful combination of drugs, which is the basis of Regimen Tablets . . .") How careful this combination actually is has been hotly debated in recent years, not only among members of the medical profession but by members of Congress in open hearings on the diet-pill industry.

The standard diet "package" differs from ethical drug manufacturer to manufacturer, and the dosage from doctor to doctor, but the fundamental ingredient does not. It is some form of amphetamine, a powerful drug first used in the 1930's as a means of treating certain types of psychological disorders, particularly acute depression. Noting that the drug also had a powerful anorexic effect, medical men began using it to treat emotionally stable but overweight patients. What they soon discovered was that amphetamines alone produced highly undesirable side effects in these obese patients. Many became agitated, excitable, and highly nervous—and a few suffered from paranoid delusions and hallucinations.

To ameliorate this situation, chemists began adding phenobarbital to diet pills, a refinement that reduced but did not completely eliminate the nervous agitation caused by the amphetamines. It had been evident from the outset that medicine had found, in amphetamines, the strong anorexic for which it had long been searching, a magic elixir that acted on the satiety center of the hypothalamus and produced a pharmacological sense of fullness in the absence of real food. It was now evident that the power in amphetamines was almost impossible to control and direct. It successfully suppressed the appetite, but in doing so it often produced both vascular and gastrointestinal disturbances, insomnia, nausea, and hypertension.

To many medical men, these adverse side effects seemed too high a price to pay for any sort of short-term weight reduction, and they cautioned against the use of diet pills in any form. "A fake cure," Dr. Hilde Bruch of Baylor University called them, noting that she had personally treated a number of cases of psychosis that had resulted from indiscriminate use of diet pills. Moreover, as she and others were quick to point out, the pills were no long-term remedy anyway. They were certainly habit-forming, if not addictive, and they were of strictly limited usefulness. For reasons no one could fully explain, they lost their effectiveness after six to eight weeks. What lingered thereafter was the body's dependence on the pills, and it remained as the dieter inexorably regained the weight he had recently lost.

In order to extend the effective length of this new treatment program, it was necessary to reduce the amphetamine content of the pills and add other ingredients. Among these were thyroid hormone to increase metabolism; the heart stimulant digitalis—given for no discernible medical reason; and a diuretic to promote rapid water loss. According to most experts, thyroid has no place whatsoever in any weight-reduction program. (It is required in cases of myxedema, but that uncommon thyroid condition requires lifelong treatment whether the patient is overweight or not.) Most obese individuals are already hypermetabolic, in comparison with people of the same age, sex, and height but normal weight, so administering thyroxin to such people serves no purpose. Moreover, the consumption of thyroid hormone in greater than physiologic amounts can cause degradation of lean body mass. In some instances the presence of superfluous thyroid hormone is thought to aggravate certain types of cardiac disease—and in *all* instances the presence of excessive thyroid in the body causes nervousness, an increased heart rate, and an abnormal elevation of body metabolism. In no instance is it recommended for weight loss.

Jean Mayer describes the inclusion of digitalis in diet pills as "absolutely worthless," and there is evidence that this drug is likewise inimical to the health and general well-being of the overweight individual. Digitalis is normally prescribed as a heart stimulant for patients suffering from a variety of cardiovascular diseases. One of its common side effects is a feeling of mild nausea, and it is this aspect of the drug's overall effect on the body that manufacturers of diet pills have seized upon—for nausea, even mild nausea, is a natural inhibitor of appetite.

Where diet pills are concerned, however, the actual risk to the dieter's health comes not from any one of these supplemental drugs alone, but from all of them in combination. Thyroid can irritate the heart, and when diuretics are used in combination with thyroid hormone, the body's store of potassium is depleted—with potentially lethal implications, as we noted in discussing the protein-sparing diet. Add to these digitalis, another shock to the heart, and the possibility of drug-induced arrhythmia becomes very real indeed.

Why, then, do patients crowd the waiting rooms of the "fat

doctors," many of whom have been so overwhelmed by the success of their diet-pill "filling stations" that they have been obliged to franchise part of their practices to younger colleagues? Because, like Banting-type diets, this method of weight reduction works, however temporarily. At least it works for some of the people, some of the time. Roughly a third of the dieters who tried the pills during their heyday responded well to them. Another third experienced a distinct loss of appetite but were unable, in controlled tests, to distinguish the pills from a placebo—indicating that here, too, autosuggestion plays a significant role. The final third failed to respond at all. It is noteworthy that those who did respond were, by and large, young and only moderately overweight—the very patients who respond well to any diet program.

What is often overlooked in assessing the merits of any new anorexic agent—from human chorionic gonadotropin to amphetamines—is the fact that most overweight people tend to lose weight on *any* new treatment or during the first weeks of their association with any new physician. Nevertheless, the efficacy of diet pills cannot be entirely discounted. One young woman from Boston, for example, managed to lose more than fifty pounds on her rainbow package, which included thirteen pills a day. That she later regained all fifty pounds—plus twenty she had not been carrying before she began her ill-advised diet—is tragic testimony to the net effect of any diet that does not insist on a fundamental restructuring of existing eating habits and sound nutritional reeducation.

Dieting, as one leading nutritionist says, is not a question of drugs; it is a question of will power, and that has not yet been offered in capsule form. Until it is, until someone finally produces an effortless solution to the puzzle of obesity, there will doubtless be a ready market for "medicated" caramels, fad diets, hormone injections, and pills, pills, pills. "I have a skinny body and a fat spirit," declared one frequent user of diet pills, who then added, somewhat ruefully, "I know the minute I stop taking the pills I'll put on every ounce of weight I've lost." Surely there is a better way.

5

Vitamins and Vita-Hoax

"But wait a bit," the Oysters cried,
"Before we have our chat;
For some of us are out of breath,
And all of us are fat!"
Lewis Carroll

You do not have to be told that something is wrong with our national diet; you have only to look around you. Some 79 million Americans are overweight, and 98 per cent of them have tooth decay. According to one estimate, we pay a national health bill of $30 billion annually for illnesses attributable to faulty nutrition, and George Briggs, a nutrition expert at the University of California, Berkeley, has suggested that more than one-third of all chronic illnesses—which account for 83 per cent of all adult male deaths—are diet related. The statistics are appalling, the need for remedial action acute, and the outlook grim indeed. Under the best of circumstances it would be difficult to get America's headstrong gourmands and heedless dieters to voluntarily submit to a new national regimen, and as long as the experts differ on the question of what constitutes the most sensible contemporary diet, the prospects for mass conversion are practically nil.

It is, in short, a piece with a thousand villains and not a single hero. The former, as identified by qualified nutritionists or by self-styled "authorities" on nutrition, have included refined sugar (too much), fiber (too little), an excess of saturated fats, a dearth of minerals, too much cholesterol, too little vitamin C. And it may well be that both the experts and the "experts" are right, although not necessarily for the right reasons. Ours is indeed a diet of "too much" and "too little," consumed on the run by haphazard, nutritionally ignorant dieters whose notion of weight control is to wolf down the 1,200-calorie sirloin and leave behind the 150-calorie baked potato. It is, for the most part, a diet deficient in both fresh and dried fruits, vegetables, and whole-grain products. The admonitions of the health-food hucksters notwithstanding, it is also a diet almost ridiculously overfortified with essential minerals and vitamins. In many ways it is the most nutritious diet that has ever been widely available; in other ways it is the most pernicious, for it encourages patterns of food consumption that can ultimately be highly detrimental to the dieter's well-being.

Consider sugar, often cited as the foremost nutritional villain. Our per capita consumption of sugar has risen steadily for as long as records have been kept—40 per cent in seven decades. More disturbing, from the nutritionist's point of view, is the fact that this growth has been exponential. In a four-year period during the 1960's, for example, the amount of sugar being added to processed food increased by half. It is hardly surprising to find large amounts of refined sugar being used in the canning of fruits, which are traditionally packed in a thin fruit syrup, or to find like quantities being used in the preparation of frozen fruits. It is somewhat more disturbing to discover that sugar is a principal ingredient in such diverse products as cereal and salad dressings, catsup and peanut butter, salami and canned corn. One way or another, Americans consume two and a half pounds of sugar apiece every week. And because each pound of sugar contains 1,800 nutrient-free calories, this means that nearly a quarter of our total caloric intake is, except for calories, nutritionally valueless.

Our national sweet tooth, nurtured by a plethora of sugar-saturated convenience foods and encouraged by the estimated 5,000 television commercials that the average American child sees in a year, contributes heavily to our $5 billion annual dental bill. (There is a particular irony in the phrase "sweet tooth," for close to 20 million adult Americans have lost half their teeth to decay caused by the consumption of vast quantities of refined sugar.) Small wonder, under the circumstances, that refined sugar should so often be identified as the principal culprit in the nutritional debacle that surrounds us, for as Jean Mayer has noted, sugar is valueless in the diet except as a flavor enhancer, and it does play havoc with the very sweet tooth it satisfies.

The popular belief that excessively high levels of sugar consumption are a leading cause of poor health in general and obesity in particular has led to the development of thousands of sugar-free food products, from low-calorie chocolates to dietetic marshmallows, many of them manufactured and marketed by the very companies that first introduced sugar-saturated foods and drinks to the grocer's shelf. James Goddard, former commissioner of the Food and Drug Administration, has estimated that Americans waste $500 million a year on vitamins and health foods that they do not need. How much larger this figure would be if it were revised upward to include the money spent on the sugar-free foods that a proper national diet would obviate is impossible to guess—and depressing to contemplate. Hilde Bruch scorns the mass ingestion of sugar-free foods as "fake asceticism," atonement for the consumption of foods that are high in sugar content through the consumption of foods that only *taste* like foods that are high in sugar content.

Watch an overweight diner finish off an elaborate French meal with black coffee and saccharin and you understand what Dr. Bruch is talking about: the escargot, veal Orloff, timbale of spinach, foie gras salad, and chocolate mousse may have contained 3,800 calories, but the coffee contained none. You also understand why sugar-free foods and artificial sweeteners are here to stay: they permit ill-disciplined dieters to cut their daily caloric intake slightly while continuing to satisfy a craving for sugar that in some instances can only be described as addictive. Indeed, the steady consumption of artificially sweetened low-calorie drinks may actually encourage sugar addiction by sensitizing the palate to excessive amounts of "sugar" in artificial forms. In any case, the advent of sugar-free foods and drinks has had no impact on our per capita consumption of refined sugar, suggesting that the wide availability of these products has only made us more relaxed about the quantities of sweeteners that we do consume.

The dimensions of the boom in the production of sugar-free foods is best illustrated by the growth of the diet soft-drink market. In 1962, the year before the major manufacturers of soft drinks entered the market, companies producing sugar-free drinks, principally an imitation ginger ale, did $21 million worth of business, up an impressive $6 million in six years. Two years later the producers of diet soft drinks did $200 million worth of business—a *ten-fold* increase. The cost of launching these new products had been enormous—Coca-Cola spent a million dollars in New York City alone when it introduced Tab—but then so was the market. Diet soft drinks now account for fully half of all soft-drink sales, and low-calorie beer is making steady inroads in its market—although confirmed beer drinkers insist that the reason for drinking a beer with two-thirds the calories of regular beer is to be able to drink one-third again as much.

It was perhaps inevitable that the rush to stake out a share of the diet-food market would produce its own brand of bunkum. The "diet" bread that had fewer calories in each slice than regular bread only because those slices were marginally thinner. Or the dry-roasted nuts that were advertised as "low-calorie"—which of course they were, but only in relation to other processed nuts, nuts being one of the most caloric of all foods. And New Yorkers in particular will remember the "Skinny Shake" scandal of 1968. Weight-conscious Midtown secretaries and their thick-waisted bosses lunched all that spring on a milkshake they thought contained a mere 88 calories. In fact it contained 377 calories, roughly 100 less than a normal milk-shake, because it was made with "88-calorie diet-approved skim milk," as the distributor insisted he had been saying from the beginning. That thousands of eager customers did not read the label that way was hardly his fault.

By this time the search for a solution to the puzzle of obesity had led researchers in a full circle. Having tried with only limited success to curb overweight by taking foods *out* of the diet, and having tried with even less success to reduce adipose tissue by adding something *to* the diet, they turned again to the question of what to remove. Only this time they tried taking the food value out of the food, rather than taking the food itself out of the diet. The problem here was that the simple solutions, the elegant answers, did not work in practice. Feed laboratory rats on a diet of cellulose, which has no calories and all the bulk in the world, and what happens? What happens is that the rats grow sated not when their stomachs are full to bursting with cellulose but when they have eaten enough to supply their daily calorie requirement, even when that means eating virtually nonstop. The solution to the puzzle of obesity, if there proved to be one, would clearly take some searching for.

For one thing, the notion of using cellulose as a source of bulk without calories shortly proved unworkable. It was simple enough to concoct a white goo out of cellulose powder and water, and it was possible to persuade rats to eat the stuff. What it was not possible to do was to make the goo palatable to human beings. Texture was sometimes a problem, and flavor was almost always a problem. You could produce a synthetic butter, for instance, that looked a good deal like butter. But it did not cook like butter and it tasted precisely like what it was, a chemically flavored compound consisting of 5 per cent cellulose powder and 95 per cent water. To make matters worse, this starch substitute was expensive to produce—55 cents per pound versus 7 cents per pound for most natural starches—and it passed very quickly out of the stomach. So quickly, in fact, that it was impossible to tell if it did indeed reduce stomach contractions and hunger pangs. Researchers working with cellulose goo realized that they would have to look elsewhere for an answer.

The search soon led to saturated fats and, more specifically, to cholesterol. There were several reasons for this beyond the obvious—that fat in the diet has a way of becoming fat in the body. The first, and certainly the most important, is that cholesterol has been linked to the dramatic increase in atherosclerosis and coronary diseases that afflict Western man. In support of this contention Ancel Keys, the University of Minnesota physiologist who developed K (for Keys) rations in World War II, liked to cite statistics from his study of native Japanese, Japanese residents in the Hawaiian Islands, and second-generation Japanese living on the West Coast of the United States. The first group, Keys noted, derive a mere 13 per cent of their calories from saturated fats; the second group, 32 per cent; the third, 45 per cent. And, as Keys discovered, their cholesterol levels rise accordingly. What did not always rise accordingly was the rate of actual coronary disease, but this did not prevent Keys, an especially vehement foe of cholesterol, from mounting a campaign against the fatty yellow substance found in the cardiovascular systems of so many men with serious coronary problems.

Cholesterol is a lipid or "saturated fat," a technical term referring to the proportion of hydrogen present in a compound; it is found in every cell of the body, but particularly in the liver and the brain. It is the main component of adrenocortical hormones and so vital to bodily function that some tissues actually synthesize it from acetates and phosphates. As it happens, we get 60 per cent of our cholesterol from egg yolks, which fact provides us with a splendidly simple solution to the conjoined problems of obesity and coronary disease—if a surfeit of cholesterol in the blood is indeed the cause of those problems. Eliminate eggs and you are more than halfway to a solution—which is exactly what Keys proposed. "People should know the facts," he said. "Then if they want to eat themselves to death, let them."

In putting the "facts" before the American people, Keys and those who, like him, favored a drastic reduction in national cholesterol levels succeeded in frightening the public more thoroughly than the opponents of "sugar mania" ever had—and as a result the consumption of dairy products in the United States dropped 3 *billion* pounds in a single year. It did little good for the dairy industry to argue that the consumption of saturated fats was a desirable thing, even for the overweight. They pointed to growth studies conducted with rats which showed that a diet containing 20 to 40 per cent fat by weight had the highest nutritional value—but to no avail. They noted for the public record that fats serve as a source of essential fatty acids and, under certain conditions, of fat-soluble vitamins. They mentioned that fats also contribute significantly to the tastiness of any diet. All to no avail. Opponents of high-cholesterol foods urged Americans to switch over from saturated animal fats to polyunsaturated vegetable oils, and what was an unmitigated catastrophe for the dairy and poultry industries became a boon to corn growers.

Depending on whose studies you studied, the argument against cholesterol could look very solid or rather shaky. A number of Keys's adversaries suggested that it was possible to find "a correlation as good or better" between coronary disease and smog. And such noted authorities as Jean Mayer opined that many other factors besides cholesterol had to be taken into account where atherosclerosis was concerned, among them the correlations between coronary disease and both emotional stress and physical inactivity.

And there must be other factors as well, experts reasoned, for neither lack of exercise nor stress could account for the fact that Finns living in bucolic North Karelia, a region on Finland's common border with the Soviet Union, should have a heart attack rate nearly double that of the capital, Helsinki—and ten times the rate in Sofia, Bulgaria, which has the lowest coronary disease incidence of any major city in the world. What might explain the fearsome death rate in North Karelia is a combination of factors, among them a diet high not only in cholesterol and saturated fats but protein and dairy products. In North Karelia women fry most foods in butter, and they spread their sandwiches with lard. Both sexes also smoke heavily, and they consume very few vegetables. All of which makes it difficult to single out high cholesterol levels as the chief agent of coronary disease in that particular region—or, indeed, in any region.

Advertising joined forces with Keys and his colleagues in 1957, although the marriage was strictly one of convenience. Members of the anticholesterol crusade were pleased by the national attention that their campaign was receiving and the heightened awareness of the dangers of high cholesterol levels that had developed. And the advertisers, for their part, were pleased to exploit the national "cholesterol scare" to promote, first, unsaturated fats and, later, cholesterol substitutes. Of one of these, a yolkless egg, it has been said that the color is perfect, the consistency when scrambled is correct, and even the texture is passable. The problem is that the product doesn't happen to taste much like a scrambled egg. And unlike eggs, which contain only whites and yolks, these yolkless eggs contain, in addition to egg white: corn oil, nonfat dry milk, a number of emulsifiers, cellulose and xanthan gums, trisodium and triethyl citrate, artificial flavor, aluminum sulfate, iron phosphate, artificial color, thiamin, riboflavin, calcium, and vitamins A and D. The dieter might wonder which poses the greater risk to his health.

In time, of course, it was the advertising industry and not the medical profession that became the guardian of the flame, and because the cholesterol scare sold products, advertisers continued to fan the flame long after medical science had taken a long, hard look at the question of cholesterol and come to a rather different conclusion. "Medical science knows of no reason why normal healthy people should try to reduce their cholesterol level," one expert declared, but it seemed altogether possible that his revisionist stance had come too late. Like diet soft drinks, unsaturated fats had become a fixture in the American diet, and their assiduous promotion, as Philip L. White, director of the A.M.A.'s Department of Foods and Nutrition, observed, "was frustrating the physician's efforts to treat heart patients."

It seems increasingly likely that the cholesterol level in the blood, long thought to be a direct reflection of cholesterol in the diet, is actually determined by the body's own synthesizing activities, but this news has had little impact on Madison

Avenue, much to the chagrin of the Council of Better Business Bureaus. Faced with the same sort of inflated claims that characterized the promotion of diet aids in an earlier era, and hampered as before by legal technicalities and a ponderous bureaucracy, the bureau recently resorted to issuing this stern warning to the makers of cholesterol-free products:

> It is the belief of this Bureau, based on a review of literature published by responsible medical groups, that no advertiser should claim at this time that the substitution or addition of a particular food item in the usual diets of consumers will lower blood cholesterol and help prevent heart disease, unless or until the advertiser has competent clinical data establishing that the food item will, in fact, produce such results.

The bureau based its opinion on the fact that no study has ever proven that reducing the body's cholesterol level reduces the risk of heart disease. And in the absence of "competent clinical data," the bureau's experts indicated, no advertiser should claim that product would help prevent heart disease. A quick survey of your supermarket shelves will suggest how bound both manufacturers and advertisers have felt by this restriction.

The question here is not who will win the consumer dollar—dairymen or corn farmers—or how much each will win, but rather how much the consumer is likely to lose in the process. For just as our per capita consumption of sugar has increased steadily despite nutritionists' warnings about "empty calories" and despite the proliferation in recent years of sugar-free foods and drinks, so our per capita intake of fats has risen despite the cholesterol scare and the introduction of polyunsaturates. Our national diet is 40–60 per cent fat, significantly above the ideal, which is no more than 25–30 per cent fat, and it hardly matters whether that fat is saturated or unsaturated; in such quantities it is dangerous to the cardiovascular system and anathema to weight control. One good way to take the burden off one's heart and hips is not to cut out cholesterol but to cut down on all fat-saturated foods and increase one's intake of fresh and cooked fruits, and vegetables, as well as whole-grain products.

What fruits, vegetables, and whole grains contain, as every schoolchild now knows, are vitamins. Vitamins cannot be manufactured by the body, and they are essential to its proper functioning. Until rather recently vitamins could be obtained only from the foodstuffs in which they occurred naturally, and as a consequence vitamin deficiencies were endemic in certain parts of the country where, for example, green leafy vegetables—a potent source of vitamin A—could not be obtained on a regular basis. Abetted by Bell Laboratories' first synthesis of vitamin B1 in 1936, it has become possible to correct any known vitamin deficiency simply by prescribing a tablet containing that vitamin in synthetic form, and as a result it has been possible to eliminate vitamin-deficiency diseases even in these areas. What have not been eliminated along the way are a number of extremely hardy myths concerning vitamins and vitamin deficiencies, and they have given rise to two multimillion-dollar industries, one specializing in vitamin supplements, the other in health foods.

It is the opinion of Ralph Lee Smith, author of *The Health Hucksters,* that "no normal person who is eating properly has to take any supplementary vitamins or minerals." "In fact," Smith goes on, "the American food supply is so abundant and diversified and so many staple foods have been fortified with supplementary vitamins and minerals that it is actually difficult to avoid getting enough." Few reputable nutritionists and medical men would take exception to Smith's remarks, and their unanimity on the subject is reflected in the relatively modest annual sales of prescription vitamin supplements, which totalled only $29 million last year.

But nutritionally ignorant consumers respond to old myths rather than modern medicine, and to promoters' blandishments rather than physicians' suggestions; and so they spent an additional $500 million on over-the-counter vitamin supplements last year. Many of them did so out of their conviction—shared by three-fourths of the adult Americans polled in a recent survey—that vitamin supplements are a source of energy, which simply is not the case. A smaller number did so because they believe, or have been led to believe, that a number of serious degenerative diseases, among them arthritis and cancer, are caused by vitamin deficiencies and can therefore be cured by "megavitamin therapy."

Converts to megavitamin therapy claim that its curative powers are legion, and they back up their claims with heartfelt testimonials from doubtlessly sincere fellow converts who attribute their restored vitality, or improved vision, or cancer remission to massive doses of vitamin A, or C, or E. (This last, late in discovery and elusive in function, has been offered as a cure-all for such a wide range of afflictions that one expert has dubbed it "a cure in search of a disease.") Skeptics note that these claims, like those made for Laetrile, the purported cancer cure derived from apricot pits, are supported exclusively by the testimony of laymen, rather than by scientific evidence and objectively documented cures. As a matter of fact, the evidence at hand seems anything but conclusive. In a recent Canadian study, for example, it was the patients receiving the placebo, rather than those getting the vitamin C, currently fashionable as a means of preventing colds, who got fewer stuffy noses.

To point up the degree of public confusion regarding the role of vitamins in nutrition, clinicians asked a random sample of interviewees to identify the following statements as true or false:

> Manmade vitamins are just as good as natural vitamins.
>
> There is no difference in the food value between food grown in poor worn-out soil and food grown in rich soil.
>
> Food grown with chemical fertilizers is just as healthful as food grown with natural fertilizers.

All three statements are true, but fully 68 per cent of the people interviewed judged them to be false, including 55 per cent of the college graduates questioned and fully 83 per cent of those who identified themselves as "confirmed health-food users." Old dietary notions, it seems, die hard.

Among the most persistent of these myths, as the respondents' choices indicate, is the belief that we are, for the most part, eating food that has been raised in played-out soil, and that we need vitamins to replace what has been lost from the soil over the decades and cannot be imparted to crops grown in it. In actual fact there is only one disease that is known to result from soil deficiency. It is simple goiter, which is due to lack of iodine in the soil and/or the water in certain areas, and it can be readily remedied by the addition of iodized salt to the menu.

An equally durable and equally troublesome myth concerns what promoters of vitamin supplements call "subclinical" vitamin deficiencies, by which they mean alleged vitamin deficiencies, especially in the aged and infirm, that cannot be detected by conventional clinical procedures but which health hucksters insist can nonetheless be diagnosed. These purported deficiencies go by many nontechnical names, of which perhaps the most common is "tired blood." Quite often they correspond in outward manifestation to genuine physical complaints, but only in very rare instances are they due to actual vitamin deficiencies.

The octogenarian who complains of "tired blood" almost certainly does not need Geritol. His feeling of listlessness and fatigue is real enough, but it is most likely a function of inactivity and old age—and not the result of iron-deficiency anemia or vitamin deficiency. In actuality, men and women over the age of sixty-five need less of certain vitamins such as thiamin than do people under twenty-five, yet the elderly are the principal buyers of multivitamin tablets. False or misleading advertising has led them to believe that these pills alone are going to cause their cataracts to vanish, their gaits to steady, their firm grips to return, their prostate cancers to abate, their bridge games to sharpen up. The sad truth is that vitamins are no panacea. *They only cure vitamin deficiencies,* for all the additional claims their manufacturers and distributors may make for them. And they are so abundant in our vitamin-enriched diet that Smith is right in declaring that "it is actually difficult to avoid getting enough."

This was not always true, of course. But it has been the case at least since 1936, when the A.M.A.'s Committee on Food came up with the concept of fortifying staple foods with synthetic

What You Need to Know About Vitamins

Vitamins are certainly the most confusing component of our daily diet, and they may well be the most abused. Vitamins are, quite simply, organic molecules that the body requires—in very small amounts—in order to function properly. The so-called water-soluble vitamins (vitamin C and those of the B complex) act as organic catalysts in metabolism; the four fat-soluble vitamins (A, D, E and K) have somewhat more complex functions. Vitamins serve *only* these limited functions, however. They do not, in any amounts, prevent or cure colds, stave off baldness or tooth decay, restore sexual potency or rejuvenate wrinkled skin, cause cancer to go into remission, or promote general vitality. Indeed, in doses exceeding the minimum daily adult requirements, they are of no value whatsoever, and in excessive dosages they can even be harmful, as the chart on the following pages shows.

vitamins. The Great Depression was full upon the country at the time, and as a result vitamin deficiencies were rampant. The notion of eradicating pellagra through the addition of vitamin B and niacin to bread dough was appealing to the medical community on two grounds: it was a scientifically elegant solution to a widespread problem and it was broadly humanitarian. And so, by World War II, vitamin B was being added to bread and vitamin D to milk. Vitamins prescribed as a drug were subject to prior approval by governmental agencies, but those sold as additives or food supplements were initially subject to little or no restriction, and as soon as manufacturers discovered the selling power in the phrase "vitamin fortified," the wholesale addition of vitamins to processed foods began.

Imagine how galling it was, under the circumstances, that the very foodstuffs first fortified to prevent vitamin-deficiency-related diseases were the ones most frequently attacked for nutritional inadequacy by the first of the food faddists and health-food promoters. In those days commercial white bread and pasteurized milk often seemed to be the whipping boys of

What You Need to Know About Vitamins

Vitamin	*Dietary sources*	*Deficiency*	*Excess*
		Fat-soluble	
Vitamin A (Retinol)	Green vegetables, dairy products	Night blindness, permanent blindness	Headache, vomiting, anorexia, sloughing of skin, swelling of long bones, liver disease
Vitamin D	Eggs, dairy products, cod-liver oil	Rickets (bone deformities)	Vomiting, diarrhea, weight loss, kidney damage
Vitamin E (Tocopherol)	Leafy green vegetables, seeds, shortenings margarines	Possible anemia	Relatively nontoxic
Vitamin K (Phylloquinone)	Green vegetables, cereals, fruits	Severe bleeding, internal hemorrhages	Synthetic forms cause jaundice at high doses
		Water-soluble	
Vitamin B-1 (Thiamine)	Pork, organ meats, whole grains, legumes	Beriberi (edema, heart failure, peripheral nerve changes)	None reported
Vitamin B-2 (Riboflavin)	Widely available in foods	Reddened lips, cracks at corners of mouth, lesions of the eye	None reported

Niacin	Liver, lean meats, grains, legumes	Pellagra (lesions of skin and gastrointestinal tract, mental disorders)	Flushing, burning and tingling around the neck, face, and hands
Vitamin B-6	Meats, vegetables, whole-grain cereals	Irritability, convulsions, kidney stones	None reported
Pantothenic Acid	Widely available in foods	Fatigue, sleep disturbances, impaired coordination	None reported
Folacin	Green vegetables, whole-wheat products	Anemia, diarrhea, gastro-intestinal disturbances	None reported
Vitamin B-12	Eggs, dairy products and muscle meats	Pernicious anemia, neurological disorders	None reported
Biotin	Vegetables and meats	Fatigue, depression, nausea, skin disorders, muscle pains	None reported
Choline	Egg yolk, liver, legumes, grains	Not reported	None reported
Vitamin C	Citrus fruits, green peppers, tomatoes salad greens	Scurvy (degeneration of skin, teeth and blood vessels)	Crystals in urine, possible kidney stones; may block utilization of B-12; causes diuresis in adults and diarrhea in children

the entire health-food movement, but they were scarcely the only targets of the food faddists' ire. "Almost every food we eat has been tinkered with in one way or another," declared Adelle Davis, the doyenne of the health-food movement. "The majority of children today, especially those living in cities," she continued, "have never once tasted truly high quality and nutritious fruits, vegetables, milk, or bread. Our foods are grown on depleted soils and are covered with poison sprays which fall on the ground and are carried with soil moisture into the heart of the food itself."

Adelle Davis was long a force to reckon with in the field of nutrition. Her four books—*Let's Eat Right to Keep Fit, Let's Get Well, Let's Cook It Right*, and *Let's Have Healthy Children*—sold an aggregate of 2.5 million hardback and 7 million paperback copies, and her followers were both numerous and loyal. Where her views on diet and nutrition were sound and reasonable, she was a considerable force for good, and many experts credit her with having created public awareness of the function of vitamins and the necessity of balance in the diet. But too often her views were neither sound nor reasonable despite her advanced degree in biochemistry. She claimed, for example, that an acquaintance was cured of tuberculosis by following her personal diet, which consisted of fruit, homegrown vegetables, raw milk, eggs and cheese, and homemade cereal—all supplemented with vitamin tablets. And she insisted that no one who drank a quart of raw milk every day would ever get cancer—until she herself died of cancer in 1974.

Edward Rynearson, an emeritus member of the Mayo Clinic staff and himself a noted nutritionist, has issued a condemnation of *Let's Get Well* that is couched in the strongest possible terms: "Any physician or dietician will find the book larded with inaccuracies, misquotation, and unsubstantiated statements." And Russell Randall, former chief of the Division of Renal Disease at the Medical College of Virginia, has found Davis's chapter on the kidneys to be, in his opinion, "fraught with errors and inaccurate statements that are extremely dangerous and even potentially lethal."

In Rynearson's judgment Davis is guilty of subscribing to every one of the nutritional fallacies that support the health-food industry—and are without support in scientific fact. Foremost among these is the belief that depleted soil and the use of chemical fertilizers cause malnutrition: "Our foods are grown on depleted soils and are covered with poison sprays . . ." The U.S. Department of Agriculture, the Office of Consumer Affairs, and dozens of eminent nutritionists disagree. Foods raised in depleted soils that have been properly enriched with chemical nutrients and fertilizers, they say, are every bit as nutritious as those raised in rich soil that has been treated with organic fertilizers. Harvard's Fredrick Stare declares flatly: "We know of no further research that has demonstrated any slight nutritional advantage of organically fertilized food over food grown with chemical fertilizers."

Growing plants use only the chemicals in fertilizers anyway, and no plant is capable of distinguishing between nutrients derived from organic compounds and those derived from inorganic compounds. What really distinguishes so-called "organic foods" from ordinary produce—which is, of course, every bit as organic—is that they cost substantially more, often twice as much as regular foodstuffs.

The foundation of the health-food industry, which generates close to $500 million in annual sales now and may reach a gross of $3 billion by the early 1980's, is not the innate nutritional superiority of "natural" and "organic" foods, but rather their symbolic value. Stone-ground flours, Victory Garden vegetables, homemade cobblers—all are reminiscent of an earlier, less troubled age. They recall a time of greater national cohesion and optimism, of rising rather than falling expectations, of economic and territorial expansion rather than domestic stagnation, and of more certain values more securely held. The simple meals of a simpler life. What they lack in vitamin supplements and nutritional value they more than make up for in their special emotional appeal.

The appeal of health foods is not strictly limited to taste, appearance, and the old-fashioned values associated with homegrown, homemade foods. As we have already noted, they are touted by their promoters as antidotes for everything from generalized fatigue to terminal cancer. Adelle Davis equated faulty nutrition and crime, for instance, and made public note of the fact that the Manson family consumed countless candy bars in the days prior to the Tate-LaBianca murders. And J.I. Rodale, who is often referred to as the father of "organic" gardening, went so far as to write a play on this theme. Called *The Goose* and produced off-Broadway in the 1960's, it records the efforts of a young social worker to reform a juvenile delinquent by putting him on a strict low-sugar regimen. A Coca-Cola binge almost undoes the social worker's achievements, but human decency and human nature triumph over Demon Sugar in the end.

Rodale, an indefatigable propagandist for organically grown foods, subsequently became convinced that the aluminum in much modern cookware imparted poisons into foods cooked in it; he wrote *Poison in Your Pots and Pans* to outline his case against this type of cooking utensil. What Rodale could not account for, and therefore chose to omit from his book, was the fact that aluminum is one of the most abundant elements in nature, with traces to be found in most foods and drinking water. If the metal was indeed poisonous, why hadn't it killed us all already? Such inconsistencies apparently didn't trouble Rodale, who saw them as hobgoblins of smaller minds and who built a prosperous health-food business on the principle of ignoring the contradictions inherent in the diet he espoused and the journal he edited. "One M.D. in California," he informed his subscribers, "has cured four cancer cases by putting them on a 100 per cent organic diet." Once again, testimonials in lieu of evidence, but then Rodale was preaching to the converted, and all they asked for was reassurance, not lab reports.

Indeed, such high-handedness in the face of seemingly solid—and strongly contradictory—scientific evidence has been a consistent feature of health-food hucksterism. Adelle Davis urged her readers to drink raw rather than pasteurized milk, for example, even though clinicians agree that the pasteurizing process results in minimal nutritional loss while affording the drinker protection against undulant fever and tuberculosis, both of which can be contracted by drinking raw milk.

Davis was just as enthusiastic about the benefits of vitamin C, which she claimed would cure colds and "every form of injury" and also reduce anxiety. In actual fact, vitamins are prescriptive rather than descriptive—and in abnormally large doses they can even be harmful (see "What You Need to Know About Vitamins," pages 107–09). Massive overdoses of vitamin A, for example—usually resulting from the misguided use of high-potency vitamin pills—can lead to thickening of the skin, headaches, increased susceptibility to illness—and, more rarely, to fatal liver disease. Excessive amounts of vitamin D can cause kidney damage—a phenomenon that used to occur with greater frequency at a time when vitamin D, rather than C, was the fashionable remedy for preventing colds. And C, the vitamin so favored by Davis and others, can, in sufficient quantities, cause crystals to form in the urine. It also induces diuresis in adults and diarrhea in children—and some experts even think that large doses of vitamin C actually destroy vitamin B12. Finally—and certainly worst of all where overweight is concerned—it has been demonstrated that in laboratory animals, at least, vitamins actually act as an appetite *stimulant*.

The immense popularity of vitamin supplements, then, must be attributed in large part to assiduous promotion by the health hucksters. Vitamin E, to cite but one example, has become a small industry in itself. Its function in the body is to inhibit the oxidation of unsaturated fatty acid—which has made it a natural target for promoters of diet aids. Not content with pushing vitamin E as a key to rapid weight reduction, its advocates have lauded its near-mystical powers as a healing agent and general restorative. It has even been promoted as a means of restoring graying hair to its original color and luster. According to the current edition of *Principles of Internal Medicine*, "Reliable evidence is lacking that supplementary vitamin E, in whatever dose, can favorably affect physical endurance, cardiac status, potency, fertility, or longevity." Nor, to complete the list, can it favorably affect obesity.

But promotion alone cannot account for the popularity of multivitamins; what one expert has called our "national neurosis" over the state of our health must account for the rest. Some 79 million of us are obese, and all of us have bad teeth. We suffer from persistent headaches, aching feet, low-back pain, acid indigestion, insomnia, listlessness, and "tired blood." So many ill-defined complaints, so many small-scale assaults on our well-being, so much that does not register clinically but does register with us, every waking hour of every day. And so we buy vitamin supplements and iron tablets and rejuvenating tonics and curative elixirs because our problems are "subclinical"—even if clinicians refuse to acknowledge the term—and because someone is promising something as a treatment for what ails us.

In the realm of health-food hucksterism, hyperbole seems to know no bounds. Adelle Davis cures tuberculosis with vitamin C; Adolphus Hohensee cures cataracts and cancer with honey and ulcers with cabbage juice; and Bruce MacDonald, president of one of the country's major producers of health foods, cures the soul: "Organic foods can give a person new insights into the order of the universe." Such hype moves products. Health foods are Big Business, according to *The Wall Street Journal,* which estimates that food quacks may be bilking the public of half a billion to a billion dollars every year. Ironically, anywhere from 50 to 70 per cent of the foods that are labeled "organic" are in fact no different from similar items being sold in supermarkets.

The phrase that Dr. Russell Randall applied to Adelle Davis's *Let's Get Well*—"extremely dangerous and even potentially lethal"—might well be applied to the more extreme health-food regimens, and the more accurately the more extreme the diet. Interestingly enough, it is often possible for overweight individuals to lose weight on these regimens, not because they are designed to that end—food faddists promote well-being, and it is understood that fitness and obesity are incompatible—but because they are low in calories and nutritionally unbalanced.

The purest of these diets, and consequently the most dangerous, is the Zen macrobiotic diet developed by George Ohsawa and promoted as a universal cure-all for everything from dandruff to cancer. Cereals, principally brown rice, are at the heart of the Zen macrobiotic diet, which initially includes small amounts of vegetables and occasional bits of fish, meat, dairy products, and fruit, but moves toward the gradual elimination of everything but rice from the diet. A clinical study of men and women participating in this regimen revealed that the group was getting less than half its recommended daily energy requirement, and anywhere from two-thirds to three-quarters of its protein requirement. As a matter of fact, only the daily intake of vitamins A and C was at or above normal allowances. Readers who recollect the experience of American prisoners of war in Japanese internment camps—where the diet was also rice and water—will have no difficulty understanding how some disciples of the Ohsawa diet have starved themselves to death.

Something has gone fundamentally wrong with the whole concept of diet and nutrition when people begin starving themselves to death in the pursuit of better health. What has gone wrong, in simplest form, is that our "national neurosis" has evolved into full-blown paranoia. We can no longer trust the foods we eat, convinced as we are that at least one of the 10,000 chemical additives that the Government permits manufacturers to add to our food is killing us. And we have lost faith in modern medicine, which warns us that fad diets are folly and reminds us that the body requires specific nutrients, not specific foods.

We choose instead to become our own diagnosticians and physicians, to heal ourselves. And so we eschew processed foods, rich in added vitamins, for "natural" foods, which contain only natural vitamins—and, almost inevitably, hundreds of those chemical additives, leached out of the soil or taken in with the rainwater. We are poorer for our efforts but otherwise no better off than before. We still have bad teeth, tired blood, queasy stomachs, nagging back pain, and tension headaches. And, like the Oysters in *Through the Looking-Glass,* "Some of us are out of breath, And all of us are fat!"

6

Exercise, The Great Variable

Better to be eaten to death with rust than to be scoured by perpetual motion.
William Shakespeare

It is said that Socrates danced every morning to keep trim, and it is known that the ancient Spartans ostracized the overweight members of their society. The hapless outcasts of Sparta might have been spared their fate had they taken a lesson from the wisest of the Athenians, who obviously appreciated the central role that exercise plays in weight control. Steady, sustained exercise of any sort, whether it be dancing, running, swimming, or even walking, can effect a net loss in total body weight even in the absence of a calorically restricted diet, and it can often double the effectiveness of a medically sound low-calorie regimen. The opposite is also true, of course: any significant reduction in an individual's activity level will eventually result in weight gain, even at what is, theoretically, a maintenance level of caloric intake.

For the chronically obese, particularly those who have been overweight since early childhood, exercise rarely figures in weight control. As Jean Mayer has observed, the obese have a remarkable ability to conserve energy, and many of them preserve their adipose tissue by leading lives of marked inactivity. For all the rest of us, however, a sedentary life and overweight have a very definite correlation. Females, whether fat or lean, become less physically active after the onset of the menstrual cycle, and males begin to exercise less once they graduate from school, if not sooner. The nature of modern society, which is highly mechanized and rigidly specialized, casts most of us in sedentary roles in adult life, regardless of our temperament or inclination.

Today's office worker has little in common with the clerk described in Herr Voit's turn-of-the-century study. That supposedly sedentary type, introduced in Chapter 1, rose at dawn, spent an hour laying in a supply of fuel, walked an hour to work, labored at a stand-up desk for ten hours, and then walked back home, where evening chores awaited him. Today's workingman, by contrast, has few household chores to perform before he rides to work, and he spends his office hours—generally far fewer than ten—sitting rather than standing. On the weekends he is likely to be found sitting again, this time in front of the television set, rather than leading his family on a cross-country hike.

Small wonder, then, that millions of American men and women find themselves gaining weight, slowly but inexorably, after they marry and "settle down." It is the settling down that does it, rather than any radical change in eating habits. The tendency, of course, is to attack this problem from the wrong end—by dieting. Reducing caloric intake does lead to weight loss, but it puts particularly harsh demands upon the dieter who may never have needed to diet before and who therefore feels the caloric restriction most acutely. "In obesity," as the British medical journal *Lancet* so neatly puts it, "sloth may be more important than gluttony." And where this is so, exercise is a more effective solution to the puzzle of obesity than diet.

Unhappily for the millions of Americans who should be considering it as a solution to their weight problems, exercise is both the most widely misunderstood and the most neglected component of weight reduction. Vigorous exercise is too often shunned by the very individuals who would benefit most from increased activity, on the mistaken belief that it only stimulates the appetite. This is not the case, as we shall see. Nor is it true that exercise is valueless as a form of weight control because it burns such a modest number of calories for the effort involved. A frequently cited example of the supposed "inefficiency" of exercise as a means of weight control is that an overweight person must walk two hours a day for an entire week to shed a single pound of unwanted fat. This statement is true, strictly speaking, but it exaggerates the effort involved and minimizes the benefits that can be derived.

What is also true, where exercise is concerned, is that America's overweight millions have so fixed on the notion of dramatic weight loss—of the sort promised, and temporarily delivered, by a succession of voguish ketogenic diets—that they can no longer contemplate the idea of modest, long-term weight reduction. They want to lose eight pounds in a single week, twenty pounds in three—even if it means losing, regaining, and relosing those same twenty pounds at more or less regular intervals throughout their adult lives. They speak of dieting and mean starvation, either partial or total. They speak of diet and mean a radically imbalanced regimen that cannot be sustained for more than a month at a time without having a deleterious effect on the dieter's health. What they have lost sight of is the fact that diet actually refers to *all* the food an individual consumes, and dieting to the way in which he or she approaches *every* meal.

Were the nation's overweight not so fixed on this season's diet "revolution," offering familiar blandishments and well-worn weight-loss schemes in a new package, they would perceive the true value of exercise in *any* weight reduction program. They would appreciate, for instance, that two hours of walking is more than most obese Americans can incorporate into their day, but half an hour is not. And walking at a steady pace for thirty minutes each day will produce a net loss of *thirteen pounds* in a single year. Every ounce of that will be fat—not water, not lean body mass—and the only requirement for losing that weight is walking. Eating the same high-calorie meals that made him overweight in the first place, a man can literally walk off fifty pounds of excess adipose tissue in four years—far more weight than all but a small percentage of the country's obese need to lose—and he can do so, if he insists, without sacrificing a single dessert.

In a very real sense it is not the walking that matters, but the development of new eating and exercise habits. Four years of daily constitutionals—and of modest but steady weight loss resulting from those walks—is not a dietary plan or an exercise program, it is a new lifetime regimen. It implies what one expert calls the "mobilizing of the individual's self-interest," the missing factor in most "quick weight-loss" programs. Unlike most fad diets, which are essentially passive, exercise by its very nature actively involves the dieter in his own redemption from what Shakespeare's Falstaff called the "rust" of inactivity. Here the thin man, instead of merely signaling wildly, is forcing the bars—with results that frequently surprise even the most reluctant convert to a simple exercise program.

For one thing, exercise of any sort tends to promote a general sense of heightened well-being. Muscle tone and posture improve with increased activity, and they improve steadily as long as the activity is sustained. This in itself may be the best sort of encouragement for the obese individual, who is frequently moved to do something about his condition out of sheer vanity and who is consequently spurred to redoubled effort by any material improvement in his outward appearance. Physical changes, as one Mayo Clinic physician is fond of saying, have a way of producing emotional changes, and emotional changes of producing physical changes. It is hardly surprising, then, to find that physical fitness is frequently associated with a balanced emotional outlook. Looking good almost cannot help but make you feel good, and feeling good about how you look is one catalyst to mobilizing self-interest. It is not only in charm school brochures that poise and vitality are associated with slimness.

Looking bad, on the other hand, almost cannot help but make

you feel bad. The strong causal relationship between physical changes and emotional changes works in reverse as well, and it has been noted that many formerly obese people continue to think of themselves as overweight, ungainly, and therefore unattractive even after they have successfully lost weight. They carry with them long and bitter personal histories—of awkwardness on the athletic field and gracelessness on the dance floor—that often stretch back into earliest childhood. So strong are these mental images, and so repugnant the memories aroused by them, that some formerly fat people never completely rid themselves of the incubus of overweight, even after they have liberated the thin man who signaled so wildly to be let out. In these instances physical changes have failed to produce emotional changes—and hence a balanced emotional outlook.

Although many Americans are overweight, few suffer from obesity so physically and emotionally disfiguring as permanently to alter their self-perception. For all the rest of us, excess poundage is a difficult but not insoluble dilemma. Its resolution lies, first, in mobilizing our self-interest and, second, in choosing the most effective method of weight reduction. On the face of it, exercise would seem to be the long-sought solution to the puzzle of obesity. In regular doses it achieves what neither fad diets, health foods, amphetamines, nor vitamins ever do—namely steady weight loss with minimized risk of regression, no serious side effects, and generally revivified spirits. As a bonus it stimulates the entire cardiovascular system, thereby reducing the threat that overweight and inactivity pose to the heart and great vessels. Why, then, are we not jogging regularly on every city street and country lane in the country, achieving for free the weight loss we pay so dearly to achieve by other means? Why does exercise remain the most widely misunderstood and the most neglected variable in weight reduction? And why is so little stress put on the role exercise can play in any diet, especially when the solution to the puzzle of obesity seems to be at hand?

The answer, if there really is one, has to do with the complex interaction between exercise and overweight that apparently begins shortly after birth. Here, too, the word from *Lancet* is anything but encouraging: "A reduction in the amount of specific movement has been observed in the infants of obese families." What this observation strongly suggests is that the same potent combination—of genetic makeup, environmental stimuli, parental attitudes, and infant feeding and socialization patterns—that encourages obesity in newborn babies (see Chapter 2) *also* acts to discourage physical activity. We know that fat babies generally grow up to be fat adults. It now appears that, for many of the same reasons, inactive children grow up to be sedentary adults. Sloth and gluttony work in tandem throughout an overweight individual's life, and they work *against* the luckless thin man's efforts to step free of the fat that imprisons him.

It is relatively easy to document the relationship between obesity and inactivity in childhood—and it is nearly impossible successfully to interrupt this self-perpetuating cycle once it has been established. Adults have the option of a calorically restricted diet as a means of regulating their body weight; children and young adults do not really have that choice, for their bodies are still growing and almost any diet sufficiently rigorous to induce weight loss will also stunt growth. Dr. Jean Mayer's pioneering studies with obese children and adolescents suggest that exercise is the only reasonable option for physicians determined to help their overweight younger patients.

According to Mayer, most obese children eat no more than normal youngsters, and some actually eat less—which means that there is little or no caloric surfeit to trim away. Impose any sort of low-calorie regimen on such a child and you automatically deprive his still-growing body not only of excess calories, which he does not need, but of the minerals essential to bone formation, which he does. Happily, exercise may be the only choice in such cases but it is also the logical choice, for Mayer's studies found obese children to be extraordinarily inactive. Many, he was shocked to learn, spend only a third as much time engaged in physical activity as their leaner classmates.

To obtain his results Mayer set up still cameras in the activity areas of two Cape Cod summer camps. There, over the course of several weeks, he took some 30,000 photographs at three-second intervals. What Mayer and his colleagues found was that the fat children involved in the study—and, by extension, all fat children—were almost uncanny in their ability to conserve energy. In the course of a typical tennis match, for instance, the slim players stood still only 15 per cent of the time; the fat ones managed to remain motionless 65 per cent of the time. The same was true with volleyball, except that here the figures were 30 per cent and 80 per cent, respectively. The most astonishing results of all were recorded in the swimming area, where Mayer's team discovered that during an hour of supervised "swimming" the lean campers actually swam an average of thirty-five minutes, the overweight campers a total of only seven.

"All these youngsters," Mayer concluded, "seem to be terribly affected by their obesity in a way that tends to perpetuate that obesity." They were, among other things, markedly passive by nature, as if conditioned from an early age to anticipate failure and to expect derision and rejection. This was particularly evident in the fat children's responses to a picture that Mayer showed them. It was of a group of girls, with one girl standing slightly outside the circle, and when it was shown to girls of average weight they habitually interpreted it to mean that a straggler was hurrying to join up with a group of her friends. Fat girls, on the other hand, always saw the straggler as an outsider, wanting to join in but unable to do so.

Self-image, which can be such a positive force and source of encouragement to those who *do* exercise, can also be a powerful inhibitor to those who do not, it would seem. Fat and cumbersome through no perceivable fault of his own, the obese child must learn to endure being taunted on the playground and lampooned in the lunchroom. Increasingly, he sees himself as an outsider, and slowly his desire to join in group activities is extinguished. The less he joins in, of course, the less he is teased and humiliated. But the less he joins in, the less he exercises and the more weight he gains—even if he does not while away the hours he might be spending on the football field or baseball diamond snacking in front of the television.

With graduation from grammar school, the fat child loses even more ground in his already losing battle against the combined forces of sloth and gluttony, for hereafter organized athletics will take the form of team sports—and because he lacks the overall coordination, the specific skills, and the necessary motivation, he will be excluded from these. Under the circumstances he may actually greet graduation from high school with relief, for the physical-education system in this country is so closely tied to the school system that most people, lean and fat alike, stop exercising the day they graduate. This is a matter of no small concern to all young adults as they begin to "settle down" into adult activity patterns, but it is a particular problem for the overweight, who have developed neither the inclination for, nor the habit of, regular exercise. For them the skills are nonexistent, the associations are mostly negative, and the stress involved in any sort of physical exertion is prodigious.

As it happens, the caloric expenditure in exercise increases rapidly with the intensity with which the activity is performed. It also increases proportionally with weight, which means that an overweight person burns *more* calories when he exercises than do his thin friends, even though their exercise programs are identical. This alone should be sufficient inducement to get all overweight Americans to adopt some sort of modest exercise program, cheered on by the knowledge that they can exert precisely the same amount of energy as their trimmer neighbors and burn more fat in the process. But there is one additional factor involved in exercise that especially recommends it to the obese as a means of weight control, and it may be an even more compelling reason for incorporating an element of exercise into your new diet plan.

In considering the whole question of exercise and its bearing on metabolism, Dr. Mayer devised a laboratory experiment to test the actual correlation between diet and exercise. He began by giving a group of rats one full hour of vigorous exercise every day, and he noted that these well-exercised rats ate precisely what they needed to maintain their body weight. He then sharply reduced the amount of exercise these laboratory animals were getting. What Mayer observed was that his exercise-starved rats *gained* weight. It was apparent that they had lost the ability to regulate their own diet, to match food intake and energy output with their former precision. At very low levels of physical activity, it seemed, the brain's "glucostat" simply ceased to register hunger or satiety with accuracy.

If this is true for human beings as well—and Mayer seems to feel that it is—then increased exercise may be imperative, rather than merely recommended, in all serious attempts at weight regulation. One of the very real problems that researchers face in dealing with the puzzle of obesity is that almost no one eats a truly balanced diet, which makes it next to impossible to establish what "normal" eating habits and weight ranges actually are. The question of whether cholesterol is a genuine threat to the cardiovascular system, for example, is complicated by the fact that most of us eat excessive amounts of cholesterol in the first place, making it difficult to gauge the impact that a "normal" amount of dietary cholesterol might have on the heart and great vessels.

Mayer's theory about exercise is that almost no one gets enough of it to promote the effective functioning of the brain's "glucostat," or hunger monitor. As a result, we respond almost exclusively to external rather than internal hunger cues, which is why only one adult in four actually feels "full" after a large meal. The rest of us feel "hungry" because it is mealtime, or because we smell food being prepared, or because we see food being served. And we feel "full," if we feel full at all, only because the plate is empty or the table cleared. This pattern of conditioned response can be observed in all adults, and nowhere more clearly than in overweight adults, whose hunger pangs are a function of environmental stimuli—the noon whistle, roadside billboards, glossy magazine advertisements, radio jingles, and "golden arches"—rather than physiological needs.

There may well be upper as well as lower limits to the glucostat's regulatory capacity, but few of us are ever likely to test this end of the so-called hunger center's functional range. Less than half of all adult Americans perform any sort of regular activity that can be described as pure exercise, and consequently most of us fail to stimulate effective glucostatic function at the lower end of the scale. Only a handful—professional athletes, field hands, miners, and the like—work hard enough to develop a physiological rather than a psychological sense of hunger, and only a tiny minority of these exert as much energy on a daily basis as Herr Voit's "active" man of 1890. Our collective problem is one of enforced inactivity rather than obligatory exertion, and what occurs when we severely overtax our bodies is therefore a matter of purely academic concern.

Academics, in this case, can teach us a practical lesson, however. "When a person is physically overworked to the limits of his endurance," Dr. Mayer states, "he *loses* appetite, eats less, and loses weight." There is, it appears, a fairly well-defined caloric threshold above which there is no significant loss of weight, even when caloric output—in the form of strenuous exercise—is substantially above caloric intake—in the form of eating. There is also a glucostatic threshold above which appetite does not increase with caloric output. What this means, for those of us who view exercise as an effective means of weight control but who cannot imagine overworking ourselves to the limits of our endurance to achieve that end, is that two popular misconceptions about exercise can be laid to rest.

The first of these is that exercise so stimulates the appetite that the two effectively cancel each other out—and effectively eliminate exercise as a component in weight control. In its most distorted and most durable form this myth has it that vigorous exercise produces unquenchable thirst and uncontrollable hunger, prompting us to greater attacks of gluttony than ever before. (The suspicion among professional nutritionists is that this myth is kept alive by gluttony's lifelong partner, sloth. It is easier not to exercise, and it is still easier not to exercise if one can justify not doing so on quasi-scientific grounds.) What professional nutritionists know is that appetite—true appetite as opposed to psychological "hunger"—*does* increase with exercise, but it never increases enough to overcompensate for the exercise itself. And as Mayer has shown, strenuous exercise, physical overwork to the limits of endurance, actually inhibits appetite.

The second myth that we can dispose of is the one that suggests that *only* strenuous exercise of the sort that pushes the body to the limits of endurance has any impact on adiposity. Except for that handful of adult Americans who exercise as part of their jobs—on the playing field, in the cornfield, or in the coalfield—few of us have the time, resources, or energy for such exercise. The alternative, we have been taught, is to accept obesity, poor muscle tone, shortness of breath, inadequate circulation, and a host of minor physical complaints such as low back pain, aching feet, and "tired blood," as our fate. But this too is a misconception sustained by the slothful. The truth is that exercise of almost any sort is valuable—and where weight loss is the objective, strenuous activity may be the *least* valuable form of exercise. Above the body's "caloric threshold," exercise does not result in significant weight loss—which is why swimming, which consumes 400-500 calories per hour, is a recommended form of exercise, while athletic competition, which burns *three times* as many calories, is not.

As the chart on pages 128–29 makes abundantly clear, the energy range and the actual benefits derived from various forms of exercise vary widely, and those that call for a high level of exertion are not necessarily the best. Skiing, for example, and tennis—both highly popular recreational activities—tend to promote skill, not endurance, and although any sort of vigorous exercise will consume calories, the most beneficial forms of exercise for the overweight are those that are least taxing. The number of calories your body burns is related to the total amount of weight that is supported or moved by the muscles. This means that standing consumes more calories than sitting, for more total weight is being supported by the muscles when you stand, even if you stand perfectly motionless. It also means that walking for an hour consumes more calories than running full-out for ten minutes, for the total number of pounds being moved in that hour is far greater, and the rate of exertion is not sufficiently different to compensate the runner for his greater output of energy.

Standing would hardly seem to qualify as a form of exercise,

The Value of Exercise

Activity	*Calories burned per hour*	*Benefits derived*
Sitting	72-84	Of no value
Strolling (1-2 mph)	120-150	Of value only if you are extremely sedentary and your exercise capacity is very low
Housework (mopping floors, vacuuming)	240-300	Far more taxing than walking (see below), and of the same value
Walking (3 mph)	240-300	Good dynamic exercise for those of advanced age or marked inactivity
Heavy housework (scrubbing floors)	300-360	Good dynamic exercise, although rarely sustained for long enough to be of real value
Walking (3.5 mph)	300-360	Unusually good dynamic exercise for people of all ages, and far less taxing for sustained periods of time than other forms of activity of equivalent value in terms of calories burned per hour
Badminton, volleyball, golf (carrying clubs)	300-360	Of value only if played continuously; obese individuals must compensate for their natural tendency to conserve energy by moving as little as possible while engaged in any sort of team play
Tennis (doubles)	300-360	Not beneficial unless play is sustained for 2–3 minutes at a time; otherwise only promotes the development of skills

Activity	*Calories burned per hour*	*Benfits derived*
Calisthenics, ballet barre	300-360	Of far greater value in promoting agility, coordination, and strength than in encouraging weight loss
Walking (4 mph)	360-420	Superior exercise for weight loss if pace is maintained for at least thirty minutes and exercise is regular
Ice skating, cycling	360-420 (10 mph)	These require equipment, but they are pleasurable variations on the brisk walk (above) and of equivalent value if done continuously
Walking, jogging (5 mph)	420-480	At this pace—easily gauged with an inexpensive pedometer—it is possible to increase the benefits achieved by walking briskly
Skiing, paddleball, water skiing	420-480	Of no value; promote skill only, and water skiing involves some cardiovascular risk for the overweight
Running (5.5 mph)	600-660	Excellent for conditioning but not recommended for those with a severe weight problem
Swimming	*	Very good form of exercise if done continuously; especially recommended for those overweight individuals with joint diseases who cannot tolerate weight-bearing exercise

* Calories burned per hour will vary widely depending on such factors as water temperature, strength and direction of current, skill of swimmer and stroke used.

but it does have its merits. According to the *Journal of the American Medical Association*, "There is a difference of almost nine calories an hour between sitting quietly and standing quietly." And those people who cannot stand quietly, who pace and fidget and tap their feet, burn an additional sixty-six calories an hour. In seventy hours of restlessness they burn the equivalent of a full pound of body weight more than their more relaxed companions, and they manage this without "moving" or "exercising" in any way. The value of standing is underscored by the results obtained from a survey of passengers and personnel conducted by the London Transport System. That survey revealed a higher incidence of heart attacks among the passengers, who sit from point to point, than among the conductors, who stand throughout the day.

Doing anything, it would seem, is an improvement on doing nothing; no activity is so inconsequential that it fails to benefit the body in some way. If you combine whittling and watching televison, for instance, and if you whittle in front of you set at least one hour a day, you will lose weight—a total of three pounds in a year—as surely as you pile up wood shavings. Knitting, tatting, crocheting, fly-tieing and a wide range of similar sedentary hobbies will produce the same effect.

If doing next to nothing can result in measurable weight loss, it follows that doing *more* should result in *more* weight loss, and this is entirely true, at least until the dieter approaches his or her ideal weight. To do more the overweight individual need only do more of what we all do as a matter of course every day of our lives—walk. We are not accustomed to thinking of walking as a form of exercise, but walking at even a mildly brisk pace (see chart, page 131) is "unusually good dynamic exercise for people of all ages." It is, in addition, a skill that all of us have already acquired. It takes no special conditioning, training, equipment, conditions, or preparation. It knows no social class; no age, sex, or race barriers; and no seasons. It is also free.

From the dieter's point of view, however, the very best thing about walking is that it does not *seem* like exercise. It can be readily incorporated into anyone's daily routine without produc-

Walking Off Weight

Walking, the only form of exercise that is universally available, entirely practical, and absolutely free, enhances the effectiveness of any diet, from the most modest to the most severe. As this chart indicates, it is possible to lose as much as twenty-five pounds in slightly more than two months by combining a calorically restricted diet with a brisk, thirty-minute daily walk.

Reduction Of Calories	*Days to lose 5 lbs.*	*Days to lose 10 lbs.*	*Days to lose 15 lbs.*	*Days to lose 20 lbs.*	*Days to lose 25 lbs.*
Mild (400 calories per day)	27*	54	81	108	135
Modest (700 calories per day)	18	36	56	72	90
Severe (1,000 calories per day)	13	26	39	52	65

*Calculated on the basis of a thirty-minute walk at 3.5-4.0 mph.

ing a noticeable dislocation in that routine. Thus disguised, walking for exercise is indistinguishable from walking to work, and many overweight individuals are able to overcome sloth—without wholly abandoning gluttony—simply by walking places they used to reach by train, bus, subway, or automobile. For a large number of obese Americans, particularly middle-aged women, walking may be the only form of exercise that makes sense. Walking is easily accommodated into the most hectic and unpredictable schedule; it is easily regulated, for the walker establishes both the pace and the duration of each walk; and it is easily accomplished, for it uses the largest, strongest, and best-conditioned muscles in the body.

Because walking does not seem like exercise, because it can be incorporated into almost any daily routine, and because it is not enervating in the way that most recreational activities inevitably are, it is an all but ideal solution to the puzzle of obesity. It is not a complete solution, but in combination with proper diet it is the exercise form that "makes sense" for the vast majority of people who need to lose weight. As a result, the specific recommendations contained in Phase I of the Master Plan for Weight Loss (see pages 183–88) all involve walking in one form or another.

What those specific recommendations recognize is something that too many physicians fail to recognize or at least to acknowledge—that few overweight people are willing to follow even the most modest and undemanding sort of exercise program, just as few are willing to follow a modestly demanding low-calorie diet, even when their lives depend upon it. A Mayo Clinic physician illustrates this point by citing the case of a grossly obese patient who was told that he had a slow-growing cancer of the colon that would have to be operated on, but that surgery was out of the question until he lost 100 of his 430 pounds. The patient was given a nutritionally balanced, low-calorie diet plan to follow, and he was released with a stern warning that his life depended upon his ability to lose the necessary weight. In the course of the next year the patient evidently decided that life without the calories to which he had grown accustomed was not worth living, for he returned to the clinic as corpulent as before, and was sent home without the needed operation. Two years later his slothful cancer caught up with him and put an end to his heedless gluttony.

Sloth, like gluttony, has attracted its share of profiteers over the years, although the search for the effortless exercise program has taken a distinct second place to the search for the effortless diet. In the opinion of Mayo Clinic consultant Gordon M. Martin, the term "effortless exercise" is as meaningless as the term "foodless meal." Exercise is synonymous with physical exertion, but this seemingly elementary fact has somehow escaped both the manufacturers and the purchasers of supposedly "effortless" exercise devices. The phrase "effortless exercise" apparently exerts a special pull on the imagination in much the same way that "calories don't count" does; hearing it, otherwise sensible adults set aside what they know of physics and natural law and send in their checks and money orders.

Typical of the products the overweight squander their money on was the Relax-A-Cizor, a phenomenon of the 1960's. Like many of its competitors, the Relax-A-Cizor promised effortless exercise of the muscles through low-voltage stimulation. Readers who recollect what Chapter 4 had to say about "cellulite" therapy (see pages 87–90) will recognize the Relax-A-Cizor as nothing more than the Diapulse machine in a previous incarnation. Both operate on the "principle" that passing a low current through the body by means of electric contact pads produces involuntary muscular contractions that tone up the body. Scientists can find no evidence to substantiate these claims, but that did not stop the manufacturers of the Relax-A-Cizor from selling 350,000 of their machines at a brisk $325 per unit—a gross profit in excess of $100 million.

Perhaps the most regrettable thing about the commercial success of the Relax-A-Cizor and its equally valueless brethren has been the souring of the overweight consumer's attitude toward legitimate exercise products. Having fallen for the huckster's line—that it is possible to exercise without effort, and to lose weight while doing so—the gullible glutton invests his $325. What he soon discovers is that those low-voltage impulses are no match for his high-power appetite—and so, still slothful and now somewhat sheepish, he sets the infernal machine aside. Too often he also sets aside his belief that exercise can effect weight loss—and in so doing he denies himself a chance to profit from the exercise industry.

This is unfortunate, for the industry has lost few opportunities to profit from him and millions like him. In addition to membership fees in gymnasiums and saunas, health spas and recreation centers, this multimillion-dollar-a-year business markets indoor jogging machines, vapor baths, special exercise equipment, belt massagers, stationary bicycles, and scores of other items. These range in price from $1 for a grip strengthener to $1,200 for a variable-speed treadmill—and like all good exercise devices, they are designed primarily to build muscle and endurance, not to promote weight loss. It makes little sense, then, for an overweight adult whose primary interest is in losing weight to invest in any sort of exercise device, and it makes no sense whatever for him to invest as much as a penny in any product purported to provide an effortless mode of exercise.

The value of so-called diet ranches, known to most of their customers as well as to their detractors as "fat farms," is more open to debate. Many of these health spa-gymnasium-luxury resort combinations do achieve commendable results; the overweight matrons who frequent such places have no choice but to submit to the resort's program of strenuous exercise and restricted diet, and most do lose weight. The cost of this weight loss is exceedingly high—roughly $1,500 per week at the better-known resorts—and the loss itself is highly vulnerable. When not combined with a carry-over regimen and exercise program, it can be erased as rapidly as it was achieved.

A much sounder investment, dollar for dollar, is the cost of membership in a gymnasium. Exercise is by its very nature repetitious and uninspiring when its sole objective is to build muscle or burn off fat, and no form of exercise is duller or more monotonous than calisthenics (see Recommendation No. 1 under Phase I of the Master Plan, page 185). Much of the tedium of an exercise routine is alleviated by congenial surroundings, and they need not be as congenial as Elizabeth Arden's Maine Chance or the Golden Door to make a fitness program easier to abide by. In the end, however, it still takes exercising to achieve the benefits of exercise, and no amount of time spent lounging in the sauna or lolling in the belt massager will produce the sort of steady weight loss that can be derived from adding a brisk half-hour walk to your daily routine.

Jack La Lanne, who may well be the nation's best-known pitchman for fitness thanks to his syndicated television program of calisthenics and dietary advice, is an unabashed exponent of exercise. According to the "Billy Graham of muscles," as he has been dubbed, "Exercise is the great tranquilizer. It doesn't stimulate appetite, it normalizes appetite. I'd rather have them exercise vigorously and eat poorly." Nutritionists might even agree with La Lanne, but for millions of overweight Americans who cannot or will not exercise vigorously, the solution to the puzzle of obesity must lie elsewhere. One potential answer is to reverse La Lanne's priorities: forego exercise and eat right.

7

The Necessity of Diet

I have lived temperately, eating little animal food, and not as an aliment so much as a condiment for the vegetables which constitute my principal diet.

Thomas Jefferson

It is somehow entirely logical that Thomas Jefferson should have applied his restless intellect and quicksilver mind to the question of proper nutrition, and equally unsurprising that he should have reached the proper conclusions with regard to diet—a full two centuries ahead of most of his countrymen. His personal regimen, high in complex carbohydrates and vegetable fiber and low in refined sugar and saturated fats, is virtually identical to the diet that Senator George McGovern's Select Committee on Nutrition and Human Needs recently recommended for all adult Americans. Indeed, the only real difference between the two is that Jefferson's diet is historical fact, a general description of what the Virginia statesman actually ate throughout his adult life, whereas the McGovern committee's diet is hypothetical, a model of the way we *should* eat rather than a reflection of the way we *do* eat.

For all his sagacity where diet is concerned, Thomas Jefferson hardly qualifies as the founding father of the nutrition movement. Genuine concern about the nutritional value of the foods we eat is at least as old as written history—and from what that history tells us, nutrition has always been something of an occult science, a curious blend of common sense and complete superstition, provable fact and pure hypothesis. And so it is that we have the ancient Egyptians believing garlic to be a food with miraculous powers and feeding it to the workers who built the pyramids—while the ancient Greeks, detesting the pungent cloves, fed them to convicted criminals to "purify" their spirits. The long history of gastronomy and nutrition is replete with such amusing contradictions, and the misinformation that spawned these notions is itself fascinating and revealing. One wonders, for instance, if the lowly tomato, introduced to Western Europe in a less chivalrous age than the sixteenth century, would have been dubbed the "love apple" and consumed for its purported aphrodisiacal powers.

As historical footnotes, such anecdotes make amusing reading. As evidence of ongoing dietary folly, on the other hand, they are distinctly disturbing. Garlic is both as lauded and as vilified today as it was three millennia ago—now, as then, by people wholly ignorant of its nutritional properties—and garlic is not alone. Bemused readers of tomorrow's diet books will look with very different eyes upon the mercury-poisoning scare of the early 1970's, but no one is laughing today. Harvard University's Dr. Fredrick Stare insists "there is absolutely no evidence of anyone in the United States ever having been made ill by mercury in food," but his pronouncement has done little to reassure a public convinced by the popular press that seafoods in general and swordfish in particular are mercury-tainted and therefore dangerous to consume.

What future generations will doubtless regard with less levity is the growing conviction that we have poisoned our food supply with noxious chemicals—and now it is poisoning us. Mercury may pose no threat to our ultimate well-being, but DDT and other water-soluble pesticides certainly do. The list of known or suspected carcinogens in our food and water supplies seems to grow at a daily rate, and with it grow our suspicions regarding all foods and all food additives.

Indeed, the very term "food additives" has become commercial poison, and manufacturers who once touted the "stay-fresh flavor" of their preservative-laden products now advertise that their new lines contain "absolutely no additives." What this turnabout demonstrates, above all else, is the cynicism of the marketplace, for nutritionally speaking these new lines differ very little from the old. The principal difference is the sales pitch, which appeals to this year's dietary folly by setting it against last year's. Under it all, the popular conception of what constitutes proper nutrition remains a blend of common sense and complete superstition, provable fact and pure hypothesis.

To appreciate the degree to which emotional considerations have colored your own judgment with regard to what you eat, ask yourself whether you would willingly drink a mixture of trimethyl xanthine and chlorogenic acid. Then ask yourself how you would feel about the same potion if you were told that it was nothing other than fresh coffee. What concerns us, in the most general sense, is the fear that we have lost the ability to exercise control over the purity of our food and water, that we are ingesting poisons with every mouthful and downing carcinogens with every swallow. We fear trimethyl xanthine and chlorogenic acid because they, like other chemicals in our foods, are unfamiliar to us. Unfamiliar, and therefore dangerous.

It is this fear, as we have previously noted, that has spurred the growth of the health-food industry, with its promises of "organically grown" produce, free of pesticides, preservatives, and artificial flavorings and colorings. Yet in a survey conducted by the New York State Department of Agriculture in 1972, it was the organically grown foods, not those commercially produced, that contained the highest levels of pesticide residues. The special irony in all this is that only one food additive, out of the thousands licensed by the government, is known to be toxic under common conditions of use—and that additive could hardly be described as unfamiliar. It is salt.

If you did not know this about salt, you are hardly alone. Only sugar, the most widely used of our food additives, is more thoroughly misunderstood, and ignorance about the true natures of all additives is only one aspect of our greater ignorance about what we eat. The degree to which popular misconceptions and current conventions dictate our diet is revealed by the fact that the Golden Delicious apple, recently introduced to Europe and now very much in vogue simply because it is exotic and foreign, accounts for two-thirds of all apple production in France. This despite the fact that the Golden Delicious is lower in vitamin C, natural sugar, and fruit acids than indigenous strains.

Or, to choose an example closer to home, there is the sad fate of the lowly spud. Many factors undoubtedly account for the potato's dramatic decline in popularity since the turn of the century, when Americans consumed twice as many potatoes per capita as they do today. But one reason for this trend has got to be the potato's unwarranted reputation as one of the highest of high-caloric foodstuffs. In actuality, the much-maligned potato is 80 per cent water, and an ounce of potato contains no more calories than an ounce of apple—and fewer than an ounce of rice.

So firmly entrenched are our misconceptions about the nutritional values of certain foods, especially the so-called "starchy" foods, that we have voluntarily placed ourselves on a national diet that is not only nutritionally unbalanced, at least from the point of view of optimal health, but also more caloric than it need be. To prove this point, nutritionists at Harvard offered test subjects a choice of two plates, one containing a six-ounce steak, the other a heaping mound of spaghetti liberally covered with tomato sauce. Participants, asked to choose the least caloric of the two meals, invariably selected the steak, which contained 700 calories, rather than the pasta, which contained only 200 calories.

More fascinating to scientists—and more helpful to us as we consider how we *should* eat—is not man's ignorance about some of the foods he eats but his sagacity about certain others. A degree of nutritional sophistication is evident in even the most primitive societies, and something approaching prescience is exhibited by some. American Indians, for instance, treated migraine headaches with an infusion brewed from the leaves of the sassafras tree. They did not need to know that those leaves were exceptionally high in acetylsalicylic acid—the principal ingredient in aspirin—to know that the remedy worked. Neither, for that matter, did the ancient Egyptians need to understand the intricacies of body chemistry to appreciate the value of liver in treating night blindness. Trial and error had taught them that lesson as early as 1500 B.C., according to the Ebers Papyrus.

Trial and error is an inefficient and often dangerous way of determining the value of a particular food in treating a particular illness, however, especially when those trials are conducted on human beings and the errors cost lives. For this reason the rapid expansion of our knowledge about diet and nutrition waited until the eighteenth century and the development of modern methods of scientific inquiry. The founding father of nutrition is Antoine Lavoisier, a French chemist of the Revolutionary period who was the first to perceive food as a fuel and to correlate its intake with energy expenditure in the form of exercise.

By the nineteenth century Lavoisier's followers had succeeded in determining the fat, carbohydrate, protein, and mineral content of most foodstuffs and of body tissue as well. The next phase of the new science's growth was to occur in this country following the establishment of U.S. land-grant colleges and experimental stations in 1862. Heretofore nutritionists had concerned themselves principally with the dietary needs of farm animals; now they would shift their attention to human needs.

A century after Lavoisier and Jefferson, an American scientist working at an experimental station in Storrs, Connecticut, would make the breakthrough that earned him the unofficial title of founding father of American nutrition. The scientist was W.O. Atwater, and his discovery was that each category of foodstuffs had a different and specific physiological food value. With Atwater's experiments was born the concept of the caloric value of foods that is the foundation of modern nutrition and the basis of any medically sound diet. Deeply impressed by Atwater's achievement, Congress appropriated funds in 1894 to establish the U.S. Department of Agriculture. With Atwater at its head, the department extended its investigations to all aspects of human and animal nutrition, and in time it published the first set of dietary standards for the American people.

The Department of Agriculture still publishes dietary standards, and one cannot help but wonder what Dr. Atwater would make of them. Each seems more pessimistic than the last, suggesting that it is nutrition, not economics, that should properly be called the dismal science. The department estimates, for example, that adherence to its guidelines would save the nation close to $30 billion a year in medical bills—slightly less than one-third of our total annual health bill. Heart disease alone could be reduced by 25 per cent, the department reckons. The savings there would be $7 billion, with a more modest $21 million saved from the yearly cost of treating diet-related respiratory and infectious diseases. The infant mortality rate could be cut in half if expectant mothers would eat more sensibly, and 3 million childbirth defects could be prevented. Dental care would cost us half as much, and our chances of surviving until the age of sixty-five would rise from 65 to 90 per cent. All this and more through the simple expedient of eating a Jeffersonian rather than a junk-food diet.

As elected officials since Jefferson have pointed out, and as the McGovern committee stated without equivocation, there is a right way and a wrong way to eat, and too many of us are choosing the latter course. And we *are* choosing, for malnutrition in this country is no longer a function of poverty, just as corpulence is no longer the caste mark of the upper class. A nationwide survey conducted several years ago found that fully one-third of all American families with incomes over $10,000 per year were eating nutritionally inadequate diets. They did so, it seemed, not out of penury but out of ignorance, carelessness, or simply convenience. Such self-indulgence can be expensive, not only at the check-out counter but at the waistline as well: A hamburger, French fries, and a chocolate shake "to go" contain 1,100 calories, roughly the number that a serious dieter should be consuming in an *entire day*.

If you did not know this about fast food, you are again not alone. The purveyors of convenience foods have saturated the airwaves with their enticements, and we find we cannot keep from humming the jingles to ourselves, even when the radio is silent. (Is there an American over the age of four who cannot complete the phrase "Two all-beef patties . . ."?) This media barrage is a very nearly irresistible force, and we, in our uncertainty about how we should eat, are anything but immovable objects. We have very little in the way of solid nutritional information to resist *with,* and this is hardly surprising when you consider that our annual budget for the National Institute for Arthritis, Metabolism and Digestive Diseases is roughly $10 million—$475 million *less* than we spend each year on cancer research. Atwater would certainly say that our priorities were wrong, especially in the face of mounting evidence that a number of cancers, among them those of the breast, stomach, colon, and rectum, are diet related.

But even if our annual spending on nutrition research were equal to what we invest each year in cancer research, that amount would still be inconsequential when compared with the massive sums spent each year to advertise nutritionally worthless foods. The Department of Agriculture, with its pamphlets and press releases, cannot hope to compete with television, the American people's principal source of nutritional "information." (It is television, not the Department of Agriculture, after all, that tells us what we want to hear. We want to hear that our breakfast cereals are "vitamin enriched," as the spot ads tell us, and not that they are 55 per cent refined sugar, as the department says, and so we tune the one in and the other out.) The result is that we eat less well than we did even a decade or two ago. "Information" has replaced information, just as fats have replaced carbohydrates, milled flours have replaced whole grains, protein has replaced fiber, and refined sugars have replaced the natural sugars found in fruits.

What we have at one end of the scale—Jefferson's end—are fresh fruits and vegetables, which are produced by thousands of small growers across the country and marketed locally under regional brand names, where brand names are used at all. At the other end of the scale are the highly processed, often calorie-rich products that are marketed under nationally known brand names by a relatively small number of corporations. The former have only nutritional value; the latter also have lavish advertising budgets, and anyone familiar with the contemporary marketplace appreciates why it is that processed foods now account for 60 per cent of the average American's diet and franchised fast food for 35 per cent of *all* meals.

Fast foods are a fact of contemporary life, and no one save the most ardent of health-food enthusiasts is suggesting that America should revert to eating patterns a century old. What the experts do recommend is gradually readjusting the relative proportions of sugar, fat, protein, and carbohydrates in our national diet. This is a feasible objective, and one that recognizes the human as well as the clinical aspects of nutrition. It is not enough to say, as medical men so often do, that the human body requires specific nutrients rather than specific foods—and that nutrition is nothing more than supplying the living organism with the carbon compounds and essential minerals that maintain its integrity and allow it to function. As Jean Mayer so rightly notes, any practicable diet must also be palatable—which is why no one chooses to live on forty-five nutrient-rich "spacebars" a day, although those bars, developed as supplemental nourishment for U.S. astronauts, would provide one with a full complement of vitamins, minerals, and calories. Appetite is an extremely complex mechanism in human beings, as we know, and mere feeding—particularly where the foodstuffs involved are ill-prepared, overage, underseasoned, or otherwise unappealing—does not automatically curb one's desire for food.

Any sensible diet must also be readily available, from the viewpoint of economics as well as convenience. A nutritionally balanced diet that cannot be implemented is every bit as worthless as the junk food it is designed to replace—and what nutritionists sometimes forget is that a regimen which recommends substituting fish for beef three times a week, although eminently reasonable in the abstract, is of no use to the Iowa farmer who has a considerable supply of his own slaughtered beef at hand and who rarely sees fish in the local supermarket.

The same is true of any diet program that fails to take into account the fact that while nutritionists and food faddists may eat to live, most of the rest of us live to eat. Meals are respites from the day's labors and rewards for tasks accomplished; they are times for reconciliation, seduction, reunion, camaraderie, and banter. We enjoy meals as occasions, and we like good food, which fairly represents the fruits of our labors even when someone else has done the harvesting, milling, canning, and freezing. The problem is that few of us possess all those skills today, and fewer still have the time to employ them.

Half the mothers of school-age children in this country hold steady jobs, and after their duties are satisfied in the home and at the office they have little energy, enthusiasm, or time left over for baking bread or simmering soup stocks. Whatever enjoyment they once derived from the preparation of meals has likely been dimmed, after years of marriage, by the unending task of planning and preparing regular meals and irregular snacks for an unenthusiastic husband or unreceptive children.

Moreover, many American women themselves are likely to be on some sort of calorically restricted diet, the price too many of them pay for their week-in, week-out association with food. In such circumstances, the nutritional value of foodstuffs has a way of taking second place to their convenience. It is so much easier to plop a plastic pouch of creamed vegetables into boiling water for fifteen minutes than it is to wash, pick over, trim, scrape, and steam fresh vegetables. And on the table the two do look very much the same.

The question that most concerns nutritionists is not whether there is a significant difference in the food value of frozen as opposed to fresh vegetables. In most cases the principal difference is one of flavor, not calorie or vitamin content, and sensible clinicians recognize that, for many of us, frozen and canned vegetables are the only alternative to a monotonous diet of carrots, celery, and iceberg lettuce, the only fresh produce that is universally available during the winter months.

The question that most concerns nutritionists, then, centers on how we *should* eat rather than how we *do* eat. Their chief interest lies in determining whether there are benefits to be derived from eating *more* of one type of foodstuff, like fresh or frozen vegetables, and *less* of something else, like saturated fats. It is known, for example, that practicing vegetarians are, on the average, less obese than nonvegetarians and only half as susceptible to heart attacks. They also tend to live longer, and they are less prone to develop cancers of the breast and colon.

The McGovern Select Committee on Nutrition and Human Needs certainly had these statistics in mind when it issued "Dietary Goals for the United States," a seventy-nine-page report calling for major modifications in our national diet. Foremost among these was the recommendation that we reduce our intake of all fats from 42 to 30 per cent and simultaneously increase our intake of carbohydrates from 46 to 58 per cent (see diagrams, pages 158–59). The committee also suggested that Americans reduce their consumption of cholesterol, salt, and sugar, replacing these with fruits and vegetables of high fiber content.

The senators had strong reasons for each of their recommendations, as we shall see, and they framed their proposal in unusually strong language. Predictably, each recommendation met with vigorous opposition from the special-interest group most directly affected by it. As predictably, those groups, speaking through powerful, well-financed, Washington-based lobbies, objected only to the recommendations that might potentially hurt their sales, and not to the committee's proposal as a whole.

Cattlemen were unhappy with the committee's suggestion that *all* adult Americans would do well to decrease their consumption of saturated fats, and that such a dietary shift was imperative for overweight, beef-eating, middle-aged males. Sugar growers were incensed by the recommendation that Americans of both sexes and all ages cut their intake of refined sugar by 40 per cent. The National Canners Association was displeased by the emphasis on fresh produce. The egg industry, still suffering from the aftereffects of the cholesterol scare of the

1950's, took exception to the committee's directive that adult males avoid eggs as a way of keeping their cholesterol levels in line. Even the august American Medical Association cautioned that there was little solid evidence to back up some of the senators' recommendations, and the A.M.A.'s cautionary note was seconded by a number of university-based nutritionists with no industry connections.

Interestingly enough, no one came forward to champion the cause of salt, the oldest of all condiments and the first known food additive, yet it was salt that came in for the roughest treatment at the committee's hands. Noting that salt can prove toxic to otherwise healthy individuals under conditions of normal use, that it predisposes heavy users to hypertension, and that its overuse has been connected with increases in the incidence of migraine headaches, heart disease, and stomach cancer, the senators urged that salt be virtually eliminated as a table seasoning.

Indeed, they went so far as to recommend an astounding 85 per cent cutback in salt consumption, which would mean eliminating all salt from cooking and canning, eating salt-free bread with salt-free butter, and drinking dialysed milk. This represents *twice* the salt restriction the Mayo Clinic imposes on its own cardiac patients—an impossible goal—and it comes as no surprise that the committee recently revised its recommendations. A more reasonable objective would be the gradual elimination of all *table* salt.

The real problem with salt is that it has lost its usefulness to man, but men have not outgrown their preference for heavily salted foods. In ancient times salt was the only means of preserving foods, and because salt-cured meats and fish were a tribe's only hedge against the protein deprivation of long winters and rainless summers, it was a highly valued commodity. Bar salt was the universal currency of the day, and salt traders were welcomed by every settled community. (Significantly, the oldest permanent settlement in Europe is thought to be the Austrian city of Hallstatt, which means "Salt City," and Hallstatt lies just south and east of Salzburg, which means the same thing.)

Salt is still used in the preparation of most foodstuffs, from bacon and ham to gherkins and peanuts, and it is still the most widely available of all seasonings. The habit of salting food—to kill dangerous bacteria or mask rancidity—persists, but the rationale for doing so no longer exists. Other means of preservation are available today, and so are other seasonings. Unlike fat and protein, salt is not a physiological necessity, except in minute amounts, and those are more than satisfied by the traces of salt found in almost all commercially prepared foods.

Salt is but one member of what Jean Mayer has called nutrition's "deadly trinity." The others are sugar and cholesterol, and it should come as no surprise that both came under fresh scrutiny during the McGovern committee hearings. It was pointed out to the legislators, for example, that the recently released results of a twenty-five-year study of 5,000 residents of Framingham, Massachusetts, indicate that people with cholesterol levels in excess of 250 milligrams suffer *three times* as many heart attacks as those with levels below 200 milligrams.

On its face this would seem to reinforce Ancel Keys's disputed theories about the inherent dangers of high cholesterol levels, but there are other factors to consider. Among them is the fact that to date no one has been able to produce proof that a reduction in blood cholesterol levels reduces the likelihood of coronary disease. Also, any researcher can produce subjects who have very high blood cholesterol levels and no cardiovascular problems whatsoever. As a matter of fact, Dr. E.H. Ahrens, Jr., who was one of the originators of the theory that excessively high cholesterol levels correlated with coronary problems, has revised his original hypothesis considerably. "It is not proven," he concedes, "that dietary modification can prevent arteriosclerotic heart disease in man." And closer inspection of the data assembled in the Framingham study reveals *no* relationship between dietary habits and high cholesterol levels.

What this suggests is that the real impact of the barrage of dietary propaganda that has assaulted the American people since 1950 has been on the market, not on mortality rates. The chief beneficiaries of our shift from saturated to polyunsaturated fats appear to be the manufacturers of the latter, not the American public. If adjustment is made for recent improvements in the care of coronary victims, and for our easier access to equipment for detecting coronary heart disease, there has actually been no change in the incidence of heart attacks in the past three decades despite all those eggless breakfasts.

Writing about the diet-heart question in a recent issue of the *New England Journal of Medicine,* Dr. George V. Mann chose the word "disarray" to describe the confused conclusion of the decades-long debate over cholesterol. The word is well chosen, for the field is being abandoned without a victor's being declared. The evidence is nothing if not contradictory, and as Mann himself points out it is the consumption of *polyunsaturates* that has doubled since the turn of the century. "This period," he notes, "covers the rise of the epidemic of coronary heart disease" in this country. And during this period our intake of both saturated fats and cholesterol has remained virtually unchanged—indeed, it may actually have fallen.

It may be that we have been focusing our attention on the wrong suspect all along. What many experts now feel is that it is not the *level* of cholesterol in the blood that matters, but rather its *composition.* Cholesterol consists of both high- and low-density lipoproteins. The latter seem to contribute to the build-up of plaque in the body's major arteries, a condition that leads to coronaries and strokes; the former appear to serve the opposite function, scouring away at existing plaque and reaming out the arteries in the process. As Dr. Mann observes, measuring the cholesterol in high-density lipoproteins is *several times* more accurate in predicting the possibility for coronory disease. Medicine now has a new yardstick. Whether it will prove a more accurate means of measurement remains to be seen.

Sugar, the last member of Mayer's trinity, has been so often condemned by professional nutritionists and health faddists alike that the McGovern committee found it had little new to say on the subject. Most attempts to justify our high levels of sugar consumption cite refined sugar as the body's readiest source of pure energy, and most condemnations of refined sugar lay all the ills associated with faulty nutrition at its door. The truth is that most of us consume too much of everything except fruits and vegetables, and this includes too much sugar as well as too much fat, protein, and salt. A more sensible regimen, whether it be the one recommended by Jefferson or the McGovern committee, will naturally include less sugar, and anyone subscribing to such a diet will stand a reasonable chance of losing weight and feeling better. But the difference in fitness and frame of mind cannot be—and should not be—attributed exclusively to shaking off the "sugar blues."

Many other factors will have contributed to the dieter's new sense of well-being, for one thing; and, for another, the actual reduction in sugar intake may be very nominal, since much of the sugar we eat is "hidden" in fruits and starches. The ubiquity of sugar in our diet—in everything from catsup to peanut butter—makes it all but impossible to accurately regulate sugar intake, and eliminating table sugar altogether would not eliminate the dietary threat that sugar poses. As it happens, our annual per capita intake of refined sugar has remained more or less constant for the last half-century; it is the use of sugar as a food additive in processing that has steadily increased in the same period.

We blame sugar for tooth decay, when we should perhaps be blaming our dental problems on the lack of vegetable fiber in our diet, for it is fiber that scours the teeth and keeps them free of tartar and plaque. (Also, of course, it is vegetables that contain the vitamins necessary for maintaining and repairing gum tissue.) We also blame sugar for obesity, when starch is equally at fault in this regard and fat is worse than either. So emotional is our prejudice against sugar, in fact, that we frequently fail to recognize that sugar is not an essential nutrient but an additive, over which we have—at least in theory—absolute control. The human body can readily manufacture all the sugar it needs from starches, cereals, proteins—even from fats; in an adequately balanced diet there is actually no need for refined sugar. Like salt, sugar is an acquired taste, and the taste we have acquired vastly outstrips our physiological need. The blame lies not with sugar itself, then, but with our "sweet tooth."

Protein, the one item that remains constant in the diagrams on pages 158–59, means red meat to most Americans. To the McGovern committee, and to all professional nutritionists, however, protein means fish or poultry as a frequent substitute for beef, and alternate sources of protein such as nuts and beans as a substitute for meat of any kind. Perhaps because foods that are high in sugars or starches are thought of as "forbidden" foods for the weight-conscious, high in calories and low in nutritional value, protein enjoys a popular reputation that vastly exceeds its actual food value. As we have already seen, diets high in protein and low in both simple and complex carbohydrates (sugar and starches, respectively) produce ketosis, and ketosis in turn promotes rapid water-weight loss.

The immense popularity of "quick weight-loss" diets, all of them ketogenic, has established protein, particularly poultry and lean meat, as *the* diet food. As a result, we eat too much of both and too little of the "forbidden" foods that would balance our diet and possibly lead to long-term weight loss. In the last three decades our annual consumption of beef has risen from 55 pounds per person to 116 pounds, and our consumption of poultry from 16 pounds to 50. This increase is foolhardy on several grounds, one of which is the sheer inefficiency of meeting the current levels of demand. It takes *one ton* of grain to raise 140 pounds of edible beef, and it is the whole grains that we need in our diet, not the beef. As it is we consume twice as much protein every day as our bodies need, and whenever we take in more calories than we expend, the excess is converted into stored fat.

Any diet that includes such enormous quantities of animal protein also includes huge amounts of fat, the most concentrated source of calories in our entire diet, and it is certainly foolhardy for weight-conscious Americans to ingest so much fat along with their protein. The dry weight of a T-bone steak, for instance, contains 20 per cent protein—and 80 per cent fat. Chicken actually contains more protein per ounce, and it has the advantage of being half as fatty and less than half as caloric. Neither can begin to compete with fillet of sole, which is 80 per cent protein and a mere 10 per cent fat—and none can rival skim milk, which is 40 per cent protein and 60 per cent carbohydrates. Like all alternate sources of protein it contains little or no fat, which makes it a valuable part of any diet that calls for unchanged protein consumption and a reduction in fat intake.

And, finally, it is foolhardy for any adult, fat or lean, to eat excessive amounts of protein from a purely physiological point of view. Any unbalanced diet, whether it is low in fats or in carbohydrates, forces the body to burn protein for energy—thus depriving the system of precious protein more urgently needed to form new tissues and replace old ones.

The word protein, coined a century and a half ago by a Dutch chemist, is derived from ancient Greek words meaning "to take first place," and in nutritional terms it certainly does. Half the dry weight of the human body is protein, which is a component of every cell. It is protein that enables the muscles to contract and to hold water, and it is protein that keeps the major blood vessels elastic. Protein provides the framework of bones and teeth, and it is also found in the nails, skin, and hair. All enzymes and most hormones are exclusively protein, and only bile and urine are normally devoid of it.

Protein takes first place among the nutrients not only because it is vital but because it is fragile and contrary. Unlike fats and carbohydrates, which can be derived from one another if either is missing from the diet, protein in the body can *only* be derived from dietary protein. In addition, the human body does not conserve protein well. For these reasons protein should be consumed daily—ideally, six times a day for optimal bodily function, although few of us manage three real meals a day, let alone twice as many smaller ones.

When you eat, dietary protein is broken down into its basic building blocks, known as amino acids. These are absorbed into the blood, distributed to the cells, and there dismantled and reassembled into new proteins according to each cell's specific needs. Of the roughly twenty amino acids found in nature, all but eight or nine can be manufactured by the body out of carbohydrates and nitrogen, the principal component of all amino acids.

The Perils of Protein

Over the past decade the terms "high protein" and "quick weight loss" have become virtually synonymous in the minds of most dieters—and protein has become synonymous with skinned poultry and lean red meat. The problem with protein in this form, as the chart on the following pages indicates, is that it contains a significant amount of fat—which is more than twice as caloric as pure protein. To obtain the protein your body needs—and avoid the fatty "baggage" that is a component of all animal proteins—you will want to make vegetable proteins a part of your daily diet.

These eight or nine are known as the essential amino acids, and they *must* be supplied in the diet.

Only animal proteins contain all of the essential amino acids in ideal ratios; vegetable proteins may be deficient in one or more of these basic building blocks. This does not mean that vegetable proteins are in any other way nutritionally deficient, only that they must be eaten in combination to ensure proper nutrition. Many of these combinations already exist in natural liaison in our diet, and without knowing it you have been consuming complementary pairings of vegetable proteins whenever you ate macaroni and cheese, or rice and beans, or peanut butter and whole wheat bread, or cereal and milk.

At present most Americans derive from 60 to 80 per cent of their protein from animal sources. The McGovern committee's guidelines call for reducing that figure to 35 per cent and making up the deficit from other sources. A diet that recommends a reduction in overall fat intake and a marked increase in the consumption of fruits and vegetables will naturally entail such a shift. The important thing to remember is that the change will prove beneficial rather than harmful, your prejudices about the "first place" of animal protein notwithstanding. Pregnant women are an exception to the rule, but in general adults need roughly the same amount of protein at age twenty as they did at

The Perils of Protein

	Food	*Amount*	*Total calories*	*Calories of fat*	*Calories of carbohydrates*
Above 75% fat	Ham	3 ounces	290	216	4
	Roast, lean and fat	3-ounce serving	390	324	0
	Cheddar cheese	3 ounces	140	108	Trace
	Peanut butter	3 tablespoons	280	216	38
Above 50% fat	Hamburger	3-ounce patty	245	153	0
	Roast, trimmed serving	3-ounce	240	126	0
	Pork chop, lean and fat	1 chop	260	189	0
	Luncheon meat	2 slices	170	116	0
	Egg, poached or boiled	3 large	240	161	0
	Milk, whole	1 cup	165	90	48
	Bean curd	3 ounces	72	40	10

Above 25% fat	Sirloin	3 ounces	330	122	0
	Pork chop, trimmed	1 chop	130	63	0
	Frankfurters	2	310	116	4
	Chicken	3 ounces	185	89	0
	Tuna in oil, drained	3 ounces	170	63	0
	Bluefish	3 ounces	135	36	0
	Fishsticks, breaded and frozen	10 sticks	400	180	60
	Sardines in oil, drained	3 ounces	180	89	4
	Swordfish, broiled in butter	3 ounces	150	45	0
	Cottage cheese	1 cup	240	91	28
Below 25% fat	Clams	3 ounces	70	9	12
	Milk, skim	1 cup	90	Trace	52
	Brown rice	2/3 cup	237	12	204
	Macaroni, cooked	1 cup	148	5	120
	Whole wheat bread	2 slices	109	13	84

age eight, and their actual needs decline steadily thereafter. As the chart on pages 154–55 indicates, vegetables can provide a nutritious, fat-free, alternative source of protein in any diet plan, and animal protein can be relegated, as it is in Oriental cuisines, to a distinctly subordinate role.

The last of the committee's recommendations, that all Americans boost their carbohydrate consumption by almost 100 per cent, would doubtless have pleased Jefferson most of all. It also pleases advocates of high-fiber diets, for they are convinced that a number of physiological disorders ranging from appendicitis to rectal cancer can be attributed to our fiber-deficient diet. Until quite recently medicine has been inclined to focus on the roles that the essential nutrients play in human nutrition, and the notion that something was needed *in addition* to these nutrients, something critical to the digestive process but calorically and nutritionally valueless, is a relatively new one.

Much of the current enthusiasm for returning fiber to the diet stems from observations made by British medical personnel assigned to groups of rural Africans. It was noted that these people were rarely bothered by heart disease, hernias, appendicitis, diverticulitis, polyps, and colo-rectal cancer. It was also noted that urban blacks, who had abandoned their tribal foods for more civilized European fare, manifested these disorders with as much frequency as the Europeans who had introduced the new cuisine. The principal difference between the two diets, rural and urban, was that the unassimilated tribesmen in the bush consumed far higher amounts of "roughage," or dietary fiber, than their citified brothers.

The function of fiber in the large bowel is to absorb water, which makes the stools larger, softer, and heavier. As a result they pass more quickly through the digestive tract. This much no one contests; the rest is hypothesis. According to Dr. Denis Burkitt, an English physician and early advocate of the high-fiber diet, the swift passage of stools through the colon reduces the length of time that the large intestine is exposed to the carcinogenic bile acids that are released in the presence of food. The shorter the period of exposure, Burkitt figures, the less likely the possibility of cancer of the colon or rectum. Dr. Albert I. Mendeloff, discussing the role of dietary fiber in human health in a recent issue of *The New England Journal of Medicine*, concluded that fiber was valuable if only because "chewing vegetables slows ingestion and protects against dental caries." As for fiber's role in preventing colon cancer, Mendeloff said simply: "The hypothesis is concise and consistent. It has yet to be tested."

One of the inevitable problems of discussing how we *should* eat in terms of a new national diet is that such a formula makes no provision for individual dietary needs. It does not account for the changes that are a function of the aging process, for instance, nor does it account for the changes that are a function of sex. As a woman ages, her daily caloric need falls steadily—from, say, 2,100 calories per day at age twenty-five if she weighs roughly 130 pounds, to 1,600 calories at age sixty-five if her weight remains constant. This phenomenon applies to men as well, of course, but a woman's nutritional problems are compounded by the fact that one-third to one-half of all females develop iron deficiency by the time they reach the age of fifty. In addition, osteoporosis, which is a gradual weakening of the bones that makes old people much more susceptible to fractures, is four times more common in women as in men.

In any case, a national diet is of value only as it can be applied meaningfully to each individual's nutritional needs. What every reader should know is that the recommendations of the McGovern committee, as set forth in the graph on page 159, are guidelines, not hard-and-fast rules. And what every overweight person should know is that they contain two built-in components for weight reduction. First, the suggested regimen is lower in actual caloric content than our existing national diet. The shift from fats and refined sugars to complex carbohydrates implies a drop in calories, and the consumption of increased amounts of fruits and vegetables militates against weight gain because it obliges the dieter to consume far more bulk in order to ingest the same number of calories.

Second, the new diet is better balanced from a nutritionist's

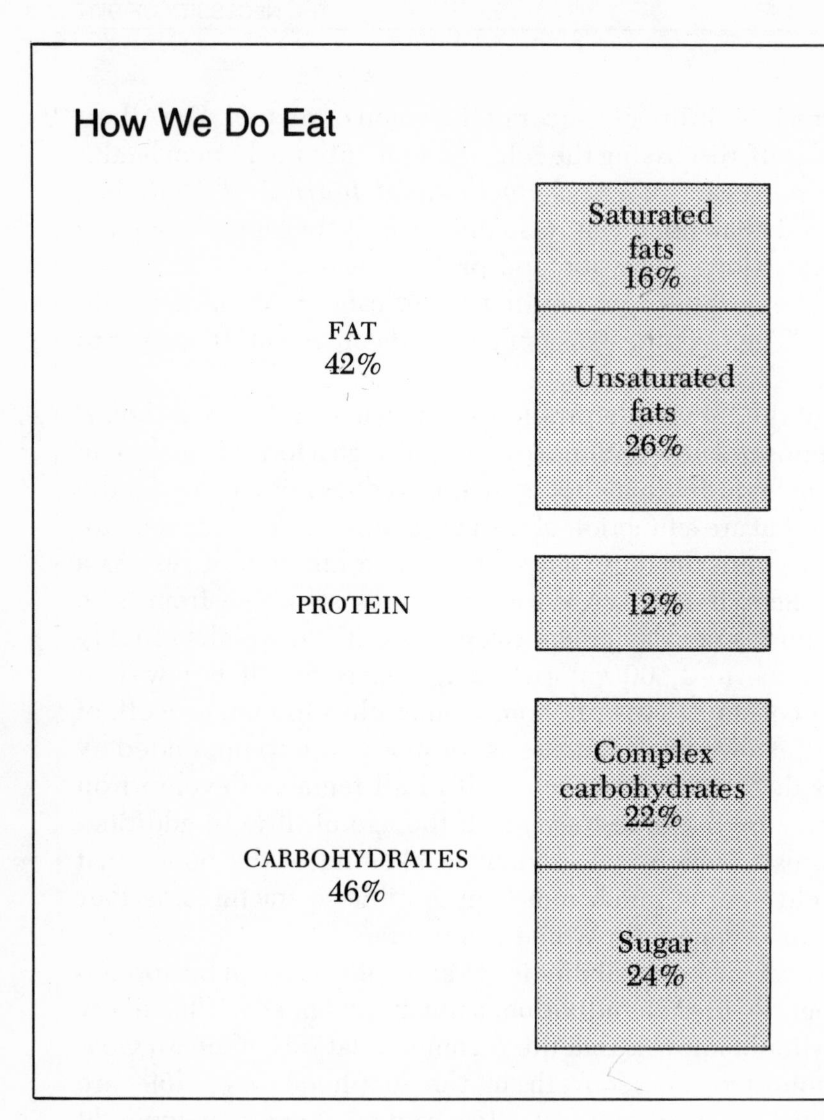

standpoint, and the advantage of a genuine balanced diet is that it works two ways to suppress hunger. First, the sweet or starchy elements in the meal work rapidly on the brain's satiety center, so that the diner soon *feels* full. Second, the protein and fat elements in the meal linger in the stomach—the fats lingering longest of all—and this slows down the digestive process so that the diner *continues* to feel full. The result is a rapid restoration of satiety and a postponement of the next round of hunger pangs.

In short, eating better may well be the key to consuming fewer

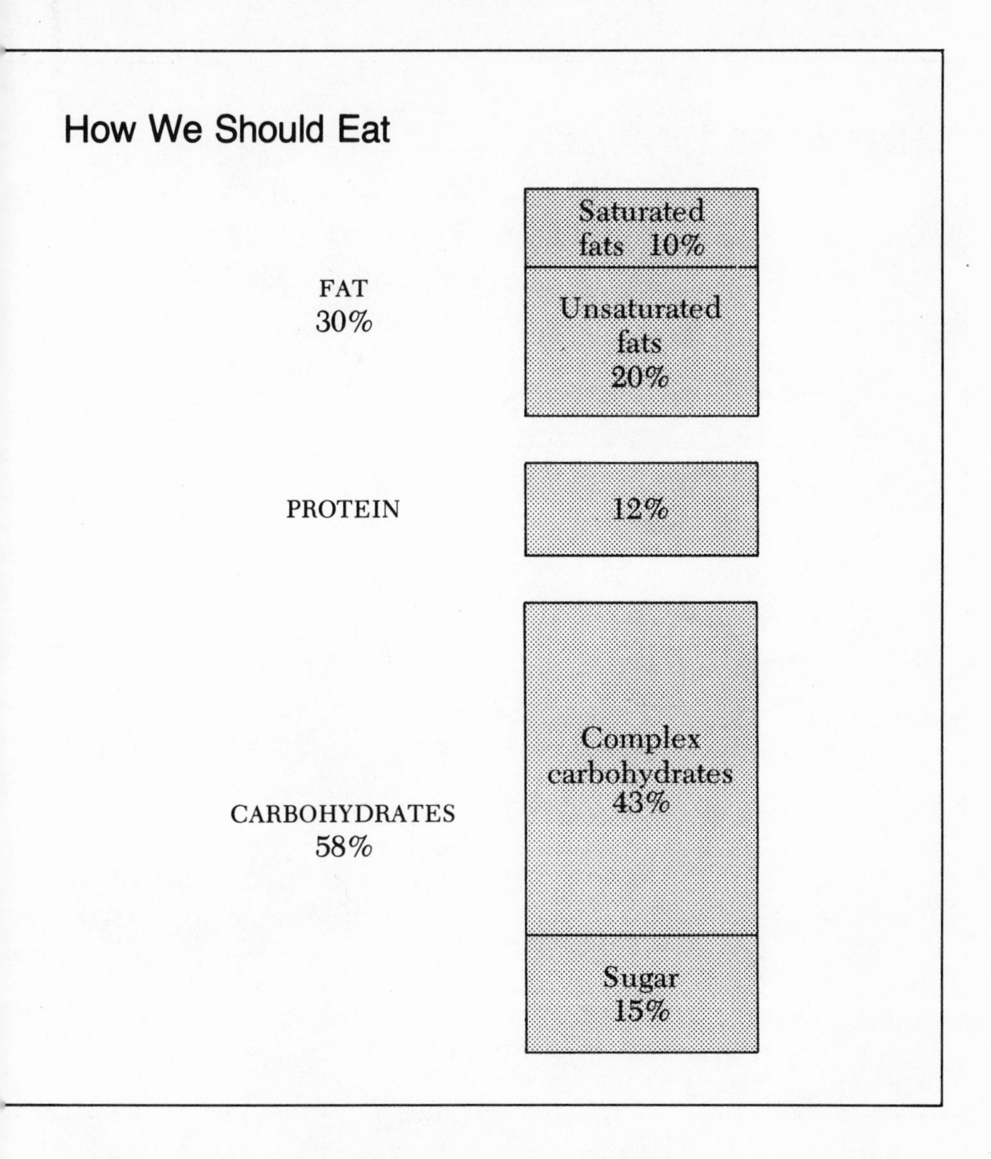

calories. This is true not only because what we *should* eat is better balanced and lower in caloric content than what we *do* eat, but because heightened awareness of what we are eating often produces voluntary and highly beneficial changes in eating habits. What has been changed in that case is the *way* we eat, rather than *what* we are eating. This is but one instance of a process known as behavior modification, a new approach to the puzzle of obesity that has already proven itself to be twice as effective as conventional methods of weight reduction.

8

Changing How You Eat

Fill me with sassafras, nurse,
And juniper juice!
Let me see if I'm still any use!
For I want to be young
And to sing again,
Sing again, sing again!
Middle age is a curse!
Don Marquis

Ask a hundred middle-aged housewives to list the reasons why they think of middle age as a curse and you will get a hundred highly individual responses—with one common denominator. Of the one hundred women, almost half will have put obesity on their list, for no age group in our society is more frequently cursed with weight problems than the middle-aged, and that curse falls more heavily on married women than anyone else. By and large their obesity is late in onset, aggravated by lack of exercise, and resistant to standard diets. What they need, having bought the books and taken the pills and eaten the salads and worn the sauna pants, is a miracle. And it may just be that medicine has finally produced that miracle, for them and for all other overweight individuals whose obesity is not compounded by severe personality disorders.

It is an admittedly modest sort of miracle, but it has proved almost twice as effective as conventional means of weight reduction, even in its infancy, and its advocates make strong claims for its potential value in the treatment of moderate obesity. It is known as behavior modification (BM), and it is based on the belief that the way to achieve weight loss is to change *how* we eat rather than *what* we eat.

According to Stanford University's Albert J. Stunkard, one of the nation's foremost authorities on weight control, "The distinctive feature of the various methods of behavior modification is the belief that behavior disorders of the most divergent types are learned responses and that modern theories of learning have much to teach us regarding both the acquisition and the extinction of these responses." Overeating is certainly a behavior disorder; and although our desire for sustenance is present at birth, our responses to specific foods are indeed learned responses. This being the case, modern theories of learning may indeed help to explain how we acquired these responses—and show us how to extinguish undesirable responses.

Proponents of behavior modification are convinced that this is the case, and Stunkard admires them for "their willingness to put their results on the line for comparison with other forms of treatment." In this if nothing else the advocates of BM are distinguished from Drs. Atkins, Stillman, and Linn, who have made broad claims for the efficacy of their diet programs without offering statistics to substantiate those claims. Advocates of BM are further distinguished by the explicitness of their methodology, which focuses exclusively on *behavior* modification rather than *dietary* change—on the apparently correct assumption that if they can succeed in altering how we eat, weight loss will follow automatically.

By limiting their therapeutic focus in this manner—by zeroing in on specific, easily defined "bad habits"—BM advocates have succeeded where others have routinely failed. The secret of their success is almost embarrassingly simple: instead of attacking the problem of overweight in the traditional fashion, with a comprehensive program of diet and exercise, they have chosen to think of the monolithic dilemma of obesity as many small problems to be solved one by one. By refusing to accept the conventional wisdom—that "of low-calorie diets, there are many; of patients who have solved the problem of obesity, there are few"—they have engendered a new spirit of optimism in their patients. And by applying so much skill, attention, and determination to the solution of relatively small problems, they have dramatically increased the probability of solving them—and, by solving them, of solving the puzzle of obesity itself.

Specific programs of behavior modification naturally differ from practitioner to practitioner, but four general principles remain constant throughout. The first of these is a detailed description of the subject's eating habits, without which an effective, individually tailored BM program cannot be devised. The subject must undertake this task with absolute candor if the program is to succeed, and this means overcoming what the Mayo Clinic's Clifford Gastineau calls the obese individual's natural tendency to "hide" calories in the form of unrecorded second helpings and unreported snacks.

The program that doctor and patient devise will depend for its success upon an accurate accounting, and it is therefore incumbent upon both to produce the truest possible behavior profile. As you will note again when you come to Phase III of the Master Plan for Weight Control (pages 200–11), this profile, if it is to be of real value, must include information that is normally omitted from diet plans—such as the dieter's mood at mealtime, the location of his seat, and the names of his companions at the table. These details have nothing to do with *what* the subject ate, but they may have influenced *how* he ate and what and when he ate next, and whether, for instance, he felt the need for a second glass of wine or a second helping of dessert. And all of these are details that translate into extra calories consumed.

In most instances, as Stunkard notes, the immediate results of this inconvenient and time-consuming procedure are "grumbling and complaints." Fortunately, the cataloging of dietary habits comes during the first few weeks of the dieter's association with his physician, at a time when optimism is at its peak. It has been noted that most obese persons adapt easily to the authoritarian doctor-dependent patient relationship, and they generally lose some weight during the initial phase of any new diet specifically to please the doctor.

Failure to deal, during this initial phase, with the environmental variables that control or condition the patient's eating habits, is what dooms most medically supervised diets, for as soon as the patient leaves the doctor's care he is subject to the influence of those variables. The particular attractiveness of behavior modification is that it capitalizes on the patient's early trust and optimism to elicit a description of those variables—and therefore his vulnerability to them is markedly lessened when he strikes off on his own.

The second phase of behavior modification involves learning simple means of controlling the environmental stimuli that govern eating habits. In broad terms this means decreasing the potency of the variables that stimulate appetite or encourage overeating. To this end, patients are urged to confine all forms of eating, including snacking, to a single place at a particular table. They are further encouraged to make any meal, no matter how small, a "pure" experience. By doing nothing but eat when they eat, patients are able to concentrate on what they are eating and how they are eating it, undistracted by televison, radio—even family squabbles at the table. And by eating at the same exact place, meal after meal and snack after snack, they are reinforcing the notion that all eating is eating and that calories cannot be hidden by being consumed elsewhere.

In more specific terms this phase of BM begins the process of supplanting pernicious old habits with beneficial new ones, chief among them the idea that eating means eating meals at a table, not gulping a glass of milk on the way out the door, or bolting a hastily made sandwich while the kids are home for lunch, or nibbling fretfully while waiting for a boyfriend to call. Until such a habit is firmly established, most overweight people fail to appreciate how many calories they consume "on the run" every day. Once it is successfully established, they begin to appreciate the roles that anger and boredom play in overeating, and they begin to curb these bad habits by confronting them at the table instead of ignoring them in front of the television.

In the third phase of behavior modification, the patient develops specific techniques designed to control the act of eating itself. A number of these are listed under Phase III of the Master Plan (pages 200–11), but they represent only a fraction of the total. It is impossible to guess how many specific techniques to control the act of eating BM specialists and cooperative dieters have developed in the past decade, but the number must be in the thousands. Taken individually, they tend to sound a bit frivolous, unworthy of serious analysis—and as we observed earlier, that may be precisely why they work. A twelve-point daily exercise program may seem overwhelming in its subtlety and complexity, but anyone can learn to place his fork on the plate after every second or third mouthful. Which may explain why most exercise programs are abandoned long before they begin to achieve their desired effect, whereas most BM recommendations, once adopted, can be sustained as long as is necessary to achieve the desired effect.

For the most part these specific techniques to control the act of eating fall into one of three general categories:

Those that slow down the meal itself. These include, in addition to returning the utensils to the plate after every other mouthful: coming late to the table; counting each bite of food as it is eaten; and deliberately interrupting the meal for a fixed length of time, generally between the main course and dessert. The function of all of these techniques is to delay the eating process sufficiently to give the brain's "hunger center" a chance to respond, with a feeling of fullness, to the food that has been introduced into the system—before *more* food has been taken in than is actually necessary to produce that sensation of satiety.

Those that reduce the temptation to snack between meals. These include: keeping all foods in opaque, unlabeled containers (dry foods on a high shelf, perishable foods in an unlit refrigerator); substituting exercise for snacking or making the one contingent upon the other; and telephoning a cooperative friend whenever the temptation to snack becomes too great. The aim here is to curtail the three most serious threats to any weight-reduction program: emotional and uncontrolled overeating, eating in isolation, and eating between meals.

Those that reduce the palatability of high-calorie foods. These include eating favorite calorically rich foods without seasonings or with inappropriate seasonings—fried chicken with sugar instead of salt, for instance. (One man reported that he had overcome a lifelong weakness for chocolate layer cake by dousing each piece with Tabasco—and then forcing himself to eat the results.) It also includes "spoiling" a heavy meal by snacking an hour in advance on some low-calorie fare such as cottage cheese or a salad. The aim in the first instance is to reduce the sensory appeal of certain calorie-laden foodstuffs; the aim in the second is to allow the hunger center of the brain to begin to register satiety *before* the diner begins his dinner.

The fourth phase of any successful program of behavior modification is the prompt reinforcement of actions that serve to delay or control eating. This is best achieved through the adoption of a personal program of punishment and reward, one that offers the dieter a meaningful, attractive incentive for adhering to his or her BM program, and that invokes a meaningful penalty for failure to do so. Many people find it easiest to translate these into monetary terms, adding one more unit to a running tally when they have successfully concluded another meal and docking themselves when they have failed to do so. But incentives of all kinds have been used with happy results—one teenage girl saved "points" toward a dress she particularly wanted, and a middle-aged man bought himself one iron toward a new set of clubs for every "perfect" week—and the only real challenge is for the individual dieter to develop a system of punishments and rewards that works for him.

Because behavior modification treats obesity as an addictive behavior disorder, akin to alcoholism or drug addiction, it is highly effective in treating cases of neurotic overeating. As Baylor University's Dr. Hilde Bruch has observed, overweight individuals with mild personality disorders do not respond well to conventional diet schemes, which appeal to the rational man's desire to improve his health and appearance but have little effect on man's sometimes irrational craving for food. They often respond better to BM, although not as well as Dr. Bruch's patients with anorexia nervosa, a form of neurotic, self-imposed fasting that in particularly severe cases can lead to starvation. For some reason obesity has proved more resistant to BM than anorexia, perhaps because the very tricks and strategems that distinguish BM are also characteristic of anorexia nervosa. Both involve an almost compulsive attention to inconsequential details, for example, which means that Dr. Bruch, in treating anorexia patients, is fighting fire with fire.

Before the development of behavior modification as a means of weight control, the accepted figures for reduction by conventional means were these: one dieter in every four would succeed in losing as much as twenty pounds, and one in twenty would lose as much as forty. Results varied slightly from doctor to doctor and study to study, but when they varied significantly it was almost axiomatic that someone was fudging the results to promote a new diet, diet book, or diet aid. It is hardly surprising, therefore, that the medical community greeted the first published reports of weight reduction through behavior modification with a certain degree of skepticism.

According to those initial reports, BM was enabling *four* out of five patients to lose twenty pounds in a single year, and one in *three* to lose at least forty. Subsequent statistics were not always quite as impressive, leading some experts to scale these stunning figures down a bit, but even the most conservative estimates show *half* of the people involved in BM programs losing at least twenty pounds, and one in *six* reaching the higher figure. What medical science had found, it seemed, was the first diet program that actually worked for most of the people most of the time—and without the serious side effects of ketogenic diets, the potential dangers of fasting, or the backsliding of both. And if that was not a genuine miracle, it was something very close to it.

The question in some minds is whether medical science should really be credited with the development of behavior modification, or whether that honor belongs to a Long Island housewife named Jean Nidetch who evolved her own response to the great curse of middle age in the early 1960's. As Mrs. Nidetch tells it, her determination to solve the puzzle of obesity dates from the day an acquaintance caught sight of her lumbering down a supermarket aisle—and asked her when she was expecting. It occurred to Mrs. Nidetch that she knew of half a dozen friends who, like her, were emphatically unpregnant and distinctly overweight. They had tried the diets she had tried and failed at them as she had failed; perhaps they might all gain by meeting once a week to discuss their common curse.

The first of these meetings was held in Mrs. Nidetch's living room. At the time she weighed 214 pounds, wore a size 44 dress, and subsisted on a steady diet of cookies, whole boxes of them at a time. Today the meetings that grew out of that first meeting are held weekly in all fifty states and fifteen foreign countries. Mrs. Nidetch weighs 142 pounds, wears a size 12 dress, eats special low-calorie foods that she markets, and presides over Weight Watchers, Inc., the largest, best-known, and most commercially successful of all the weight-reduction clubs. Mrs. Nidetch's organization, which also includes summer camps for overweight children and a monthly magazine, currently claims 5 million members and 10 million alumni.

Unlike BM, which restricts its focus to perceivable patterns of behavior and avoids all reference to hypothetical or inferred entities such as self-control, motivation, and will power, weight-reduction clubs stress diet and exercise, the components of all conventional diets. What is unconventional about such groups is the way in which they stress those components. Taking a leaf from BM, they offer a highly public system of punishments and rewards for their members, who are openly castigated for each pound gained and warmly applauded for each pound lost. The resultant mix of camaraderie and competitiveness works with great success in most cases, and professional medical men have nothing but praise for the clubs' achievements.

Referring to Weight Watchers' principal competitor, TOPS (for Take Off Pounds Sensibly), Dr. Stunkard declared that his research showed that the *average* results achieved by members of TOPS were "superior to that achieved by routine medical management" and compared favorably "with the *best* reports in the medical literature." Dr. George V. Mann, a nutritionist at Vanderbilt University, echoed Stunkard's conclusions in a recent interview in the New York *Daily News*. "Although some of the practices, including the lyrics of the TOPS songs and the modeling of ill-fitting old clothing may seem schmaltzy," Mann said, "the record of a 95 per cent follow-up study shows average weight losses of fifteen pounds or more persisting for sixteen months or more, which will match any available medical treatment."

If there is any drawback to weight-reduction clubs as a means of girth control, it lies in the fact that they have solved only one aspect of the overall puzzle of obesity—the curse of middle age. Their membership, as Dr. Bruch notes, is mostly "middle-class, middle-aged women who feel isolated"—and these women also respond well to medically supervised diets and to BM programs. Their particular problem, their peculiar curse, is that they can lose weight only so long as they remain active members of the weight-reduction club. Without the weekly reinforcement—the threat of humiliation and the prospect of felicitation—they fare no better on the diet and exercise programs promoted by their clubs than do the followers of plans sponsored by other organizations or professional groups.

What distinguishes behavior modification from all other forms of weight control, including TOPS and Weight Watchers, is that it is not dependent upon some outside agent for reinforcement. It survives the transition from supervision to self-administration because the goads and goals are built in. The scope is limited, the specific demands readily met, and the ends attainable. Here as nowhere else, the mechanism of control is in the hands of the dieter, whose task is to monitor his behavior, not his caloric intake. He need know nothing about the mechanics of fat, the effects of ketosis, the regulation of hunger and satiety, or the food value of specific nutrients to do this. Indeed, the less he thinks about such matters and the more he thinks about setting his fork down after every other bite, the better off he will be.

So convincing is the argument in favor of behavior modification as the keystone of any successful weight reduction program that all others fall before it. The Master Plan for Weight Control that follows is divided into four principal sections, each devoted to a different aspect of weight reduction. These four sections differ in specifics, but not in their underlying thesis—behavior modification is the first principle of successful weight loss.

9

The Master Plan

Like liberty, the price of leanness is eternal vigilance.
Theodore Van Itallie

Without identifying them as such, we have discussed three key elements of a master plan for permanent weight loss in the last three chapters. They are: regular exercise, sensible nutrition, and behavior modification—and, with diet, they are the principal components of any successful program of weight reduction. Each implies a change—in what we eat, in how we eat, in how much we eat—and any one of these changes will result in a decrease in total body weight. In combination, they will produce faster and more dramatic results; and all four, acting in concert, will naturally produce the most satisfying results of all.

It would seem to follow logically, then, that the best way to achieve maximum results in the minimum amount of time is to adopt the Master Plan in its entirety, and for a handful of highly motivated, well-disciplined, moderately overweight readers this may indeed be the answer to the puzzle of obesity. But for all the rest—for the more than moderately overweight, for the weak willed, and especially for those with long histories of overeating, overweight, and dietary failure—this is most emphatically *not* the answer. For them the answer to the puzzle of obesity, the solution to their personal weight problems, lies somewhere within the Master Plan. To extract the answer, to solve the puzzle for themselves, they should begin by considering each phase of the plan separately, recommendation by recommendation, choosing those elements best suited to their personal needs.

A desk-bound former athlete, whose life has become an unavoidable round of business lunches and club dinners, may find it easier to increase his energy output through exercise than to reduce his caloric intake through diet. He will want to consider *Phase I: Exercise* most carefully. A young housewife and mother, on the other hand, may find it easier to restock her refrigerator and shelves with more nutritional, less caloric foodstuffs, a move that will benefit both her and her children. She will prefer to consult *Phase II: Nutrition.* And the middle-aged matron, her children departed and her life increasingly sedentary, will probably find it easier to alter the way she eats than what she eats. For her, *Phase III: Behavior Modification* may provide the solution. For all, *Phase IV: Diet* will be of interest, for its simple charts are a refreshing reminder that dieting need not be strenuous to be successful.

In each case the critical thing to remember is that *any* change, no matter how modest, will produce some loss of adipose tissue. The long, dismal history of dieting is, almost without exception, a tale of radical changes, rapidly abandoned. The lesson to be learned here, lest those mistakes be repeated, is that the diet that works best—against the only yardstick that counts, which is *pounds shed permanently*—is that diet which asks the smallest sacrifice for the longest time. Only you know your limitations well enough, and your past history of weight reduction intimately enough, to be able to judge how much change you can tolerate, and for how long. Only you know how much of a sacrifice you can comfortably make and consistently sustain. Bite off more than you can chew, in dietary terms, and you will fail here as you have failed before. Begin *modestly*, on the other hand, and you may achieve the first *real* weight loss of your adult life—the first loss that is principally fat rather than predominantly water, the first that you can reasonably expect to keep off, forever.

In developing your personal weight-reduction program from the Master Plan it is vitally important to bear one fact in mind: It is always possible to *step up* an already successful program; it is infinitely harder to remake a failing one. And for that reason alone it is probably wisest to think of the Master Plan as a kind of dieter's smörgåsbord. The metaphor may be highly inappropriate under the circumstances, but the concept is accurate. Begin by surveying all the offerings, then pass by the table once, selecting one or two items that particularly appeal to you. Digest them, and only then return for more.

By setting your own pace, by tailoring the Master Plan to your own circumstances and needs, you will avoid the pitfalls inherent in other dietary plans, many of which are so calorically restricted as to be physically debilitating, or so ketogenic as to be potentially harmful, or so monotonous (or bizarre) as to be automatically self-limiting. Choose the recommendation or recommendations that inconvenience you *least*, and you will have chosen those that will serve you best. If the result doesn't seem like dieting to you, then that is as it should be, for the most effective form of weight loss is that which deviates least from what the individual dieter has come to think of as normal. Successful dieting is its own best inducement to further dieting, and what once seemed like a small caloric sacrifice, a small deviation from the normal, has a way of becoming normality itself when practiced long enough. The price of leanness *is* eternal vigilance, and that vigil is indisputably easier to maintain over modest changes than over major ones.

Before considering the specific recommendations of the Master Plan, it is important for each reader to assess roughly how many pounds overweight he or she is. And for many readers this may be the most important—and most revealing—task of all. In another, earlier age, that task would have been a happier one, for in the era of the hourglass figure and the "prosperous" waistline it was the lean, long-limbed ectomorph who was out of vogue; an ample figure was not only accepted, it was openly admired and actively cultivated. It was also rather easily achieved by the 85 per cent of all men and women who are not ectomorphs, who are not born with those long, tapering fingers that Jean Mayer says identify the happy few who will never, ever be fat.

It is our collective misfortune to be living instead in the age of the ectomorph. For reasons that no expert can fully explain, it is the adolescent male figure that is currently ascendant, emulated by men and women alike although it is characteristic of neither. Society has never before settled on so androgynous an ideal type, nor has it ever previously venerated such thinness—and this combination puts four out of five of us at an automatic and insurmountable disadvantage. We cannot hope to achieve such slimness, but because we perceive it as perfection we too often see ourselves as heavier than we actually are. We do not belong to Mayer's elect, to his happy tribe of ectomorphs, and the best we can reasonably hope is to achieve the ideal weight for members of our tribe, for those with our body types.

It is critical to establish at the outset just what that ideal weight really is, and you may not be your own best judge in this regard. For every seriously obese individual who has concealed fifty excess pounds from himself under a loose-fitting wardrobe and an even more effective cover of self-deception, there is at least one modestly overweight individual who is striving to transform a mesomorph's solidity into ectomorphic svelteness. It is impossible to guess how many adult Americans are told each year that they "look wonderful"—*not* when they succeed in losing ten or even fifteen pounds, but *after* they gain two or three of those pounds back—but if millions hear those words it is because they do look better at a weight that is actually somewhat higher than the one that they have learned to consider ideal. As we observed earlier, recognizing one's natural genotype may be the most important task of all, for implicit in that step is acknowledging that four out of five of us *are* heavier, by genetic default, than the current national ideal.

Your face, rather than your waistline, is probably the best

index of ideal weight, for it records not only excess poundage but also the effects of excessive dieting—to which women, in particular, are prone. Indeed, the soundest advice for many middle-aged, slightly overweight women may well be to learn to live with the weight they now carry rather than subject themselves to this year's fad diet. They might just be happier—and healthier—following the example set by seventeenth-century English poet John Dryden's Maiden Queen, who declared: "I am resolved to grow fat, and look young till forty." In Dryden's day, of course, the average woman's life expectancy was not much more than forty years, and so his Maiden Queen's resolution had more appeal. Even so there is a good case to be made for avoiding strenuous dieting for beauty's sake alone, both before forty and after. The woman who resolves to "grow fat," or at least not to deny her natural genotype, will indeed look younger till forty—and thereafter, for her face, though fuller, will be freer of wrinkles.

But if your resolve is, instead, to reduce, there are several standard methods of determining what your "ideal weight" is, and therefore how many pounds you need to lose. The first of these is the standard weight chart issued by major insurance companies such as Metropolitan Life and based upon their actuarial tables. You will find such a chart on page 177, but you should approach it with a certain amount of caution. For one thing, all such charts are derived statistically, and what they are designed to reflect is ideal weight for optimum longevity. Overweight may seem a matter of life and death to the chronically obese, but it is a far more subtle matter to all the rest of us, one influenced by personal aesthetics, prevailing fashions, and many other standards. The 1941 Green Bay Packers team, mentioned earlier, was overweight by Navy standards, but certainly not by anyone else's. Conversely, it is altogether possible to be underweight by actuarial standards and overweight by your own.

Such tables are based on national averages—which means, inevitably, that fully half of us are too heavy and no one is actually average. In a society as genetically homogeneous as,

How Much Should You Weigh?

Weight charts such as the one reproduced at right were once regarded as the readiest method of determining what an overweight individual should weigh. In recent years, however, such charts have come under attack from a number of quarters, and many specialists now encourage their obese patients to disregard the concept of "ideal weight" entirely. They argue that such charts reflect a contemporary prejudice against heavier body types, and they point out that the weights listed in these tables are based upon an inaccurate sampling of the population as a whole.

The case against weight charts is outlined on pages 175-78, and you should familiarize yourself with its salient points before consulting the chart at right. In attempting to determine your "ideal" weight, you should bear two further considerations in mind. The first of these is that weight charts are, by and large, superfluous; you do not need a chart to tell you if you are too fat. The second is that weight charts are likely to tell you that you are fatter than you actually are—particularly if you are nonwhite, female, or over forty—and this makes the task of dieting even more disheartening. Better to ignore the chart which tells you that you have thirty-four pounds to lose and go about the business of losing ten pounds. Ten pounds is a reasonable goal, whereas thirty-four is an impossibility—unless you approach that objective ten pounds at a time.

say, the Japanese, where the range of heights and weights is much narrower, such figures have considerably greater validity than they do in the United States, which encompasses virtually every national genotype and yields practically every imaginable genetic mix. It is known, for example, that Eastern Europeans are more inclined to obesity than Western Europeans, but what does that tell a young woman of Finnish-Irish ancestry about her own prospects for avoiding a weight problem?

In addition, it should be recognized that the figures found in actuarial tables reflect data gathered from those people who buy

Approximate Desirable Weights*

HEIGHT (WITHOUT SHOES)	WEIGHT IN POUNDS (WITHOUT CLOTHING)		
	MEN		
	Small frame	*Medium frame*	*Large frame*
5' 3"	118	129	141
5' 4"	122	133	145
5' 5"	126	137	149
5' 6"	130	142	155
5' 7"	134	147	161
5' 8"	139	151	166
5' 9"	143	155	170
5'10"	147	159	174
5'11"	150	163	178
6' 0"	154	167	183
6' 1"	158	171	188
6' 2"	162	175	192
6' 3"	165	178	195
	WOMEN		
5' 0"	100	109	118
5' 1"	104	112	121
5' 2"	107	115	125
5' 3"	110	118	128
5' 4"	113	122	132
5' 5"	116	125	135
5' 6"	120	129	139
5' 7"	123	132	142
5' 8"	126	136	146
5' 9"	130	140	151
5'10"	133	144	156
5'11"	137	148	161
6' 0"	141	152	166

*From U.S. Department of Agriculture.

insurance, not from the population as a whole. As a result they are most accurate for educated, middle-class white males, those with homes, cars, careers—and hence lives—to insure. They are a good deal less accurate when applied to other classes, other races, and the opposite sex.

In making her case against overreliance upon ideal-weight charts, Anne Scott Beller refers to a recent study of two ethnic groups in Providence, Rhode Island—one Italian, the other Jewish. Statistically, 72 per cent of the Jewish women surveyed were deemed overweight, meaning that they weighed anywhere from fifteen to thirty-five pounds more than their ideal weights according to the charts. It was the Italian women, however, who exhibited the highest incidence of actual obesity, where obesity was defined as being thirty-five pounds or more in excess of the ideal weight for women of like age and build. It is fair to ask how useful any chart is that identifies an entire subgroup as overweight but fails to identify real obesity in a population.

What such charts can tell you—all they can really tell you—is how much your own weight deviates from the national norms for someone of your approximate age, height, and body type. They may indicate, for example, that you weigh twelve pounds more than the average five-foot-six-inch, forty-five-year-old woman of medium build—but that is all they indicate. How heavy you actually look will depend less on national averages than on how and where you carry your "excess" weight, how much exercise you get, how good your muscle tone is, and a number of other factors. And how heavy you *feel* will depend much more on your own self-image than on any published statistics.

A more accurate means of determining whether or not you are overweight is the so-called skinfold test. Two things recommend this method of assessing overweight, the first being that it sidesteps altogether the question of average weight, the second being that it is rather easily determined. In a physician's office, this test is performed with special calipers that gauge the thickness of the body's subcutaneous fat layer with a high degree of accuracy. What the doctor is seeking to discover is whether that layer exceeds half an inch in thickness—and that is something you can measure with a fair amount of accuracy on your own, using your thumb and forefinger as calipers. To determine the thickness of your subdermal fat, choose a spot beneath your lowest rib and two to three inches in from your left side. Using either hand, lift a fold of skin and pinch it firmly. If the gap between your thumb and forefinger is greater than an inch, you are indeed overweight.

The function of such charts and tests is to tell you something you already know—which is that you need to lose weight. Very few individuals, including those with the most modest sort of weight problems, need a chart or test to tell them they are too fat; their own eyes are sufficient. A twenty-three-year-old ectomorph, suddenly sedentary after settling into his first office job after finishing school, will instinctively recognize that he is five to seven pounds over his ideal weight, even though he has a "negative" skinfold test and is actually eleven pounds underweight according to the actuarial tables. The thirty-eight-year-old housewife, on the other hand, may find that her weight has stabilized at a level that is a bit on the heavy side by statistical standards but that affords her a comfortable compromise between caloric intake and energy expenditure.

In sum, the best index of overweight is also the very simplest: *If you think that you are too heavy, you are probably right.* And if you think that you need to lose weight, you are almost certainly right again. This in itself is not much help, however. Obesity may well be the easiest disease in the world to diagnose—and the hardest to cure. Preventive medicine's greatest failure has come by its appellation honestly, and one would do well to approach any serious weight-reduction program with respect and caution. Merely knowing that you need to lose weight is not enough; it is also necessary to appreciate your own response to diets, for that, more than any other factor, will determine how much weight you can successfully lose, and how fast.

A physician can help you to make this assessment, based upon an informed evaluation of your previous dietary history. What the doctor cannot do is make you lose weight, at least not as much weight as you want to lose, or for as long as you want to lose it.

And, as you may already have discovered, the good doctors Stillman, Atkins, and Linn will serve you no better in this regard. The vigil is yours to maintain; the puzzle is yours to solve. And if the Master Plan has a particular advantage over other weight-reduction programs, it is that it affords so many solutions that one is almost certainly destined to suit you.

It is extremely risky to generalize about overweight, but there is one thing that all those with a weight problem do seem to have in common—they all set overly ambitious and therefore self-defeating goals for themselves when they diet. And when the goal is unreasonable and thus unattainable, the result is predictable: another cycle in what Jean Mayer calls "the rhythm method of girth control," the pattern of loss and gain following loss and gain. The serious dieter's first objective should therefore be to break free of that cycle. Better to lose five pounds forever than the same fifteen pounds again and again.

A Mayo Clinic physician with forty years of medical practice behind him recommends to his obese patients that they try to lose *no more than* half a pound per week, no matter how successful they have been with past diets. For the patient who is seventy-five pounds overweight, this may seem a laughably modest goal, so modest as to be virtually indistinguishable from what he thinks of as a normal diet. What the patient fails to appreciate—and the physician understands full well—is that this modest regimen will permit the patient to shed all seventy-five unwanted pounds in three years time, and that its very innocuousness will be the chief reason for its success.

If there is any single explanation for the failure of nine out of ten diets, it almost certainly lies somewhere in the yawning gulf between an overweight individual's perceived capacity for caloric sacrifice and his or her actual ability to adhere to a diet—that is, between ambition and accomplishment. And this leads us directly to a second generalization about dieting, which is that almost no dietary goal can fairly be labeled too modest.

In a business where the only true measure of success is the number of pounds lost permanently, it hardly matters whether the dieter tried—and failed—to lose ten pounds or forty. What matters, in the long run, is whether he or she managed to lose any weight at all. It is a business of magnificent failures and marginal successes, one so fraught with disaster and so marked by backsliding that a woman who actually manages to lose a single pound of excess fat every year after her fortieth birthday is something of a medical phenomenon, although it would hardly occur to her to think of herself in that way.

The Master Plan is designed to compensate for the earnest dieter's natural inclination to "overdiet" in three general ways. To begin with, it deliberately discourages excessive exercise, radical behavior modification, and severe caloric restriction. All are options long available to the overweight individual; all are of proven worth in weight reduction; and all have a way of failing the average dieter, who finds them too high a price to pay for leanness. Instead, the Master Plan offers dozens of specific suggestions for weight loss but makes no overall recommendations. This encourages the dieter to develop a workable weight-reduction program of his own, and then to amend or expand it at will, adopting a new suggestion here and discarding a less effective one there until the resultant program begins to yield the desired results. It also reinforces the idea that a truly successful weight-loss program is modest in concept, flexible in design, and workable in practice.

The Master Plan also recognizes that sheer impatience at the rate of weight loss—an all too human reaction—is the greatest single stumbling block to effective long-term weight reduction, and as a result many of the plan's specific recommendations take the form of intentional self-deception. They dissociate the dieter from the very concept of dieting—from daily weigh-ins, from counting calories, from dietary foods and measured portions, and all the other external cues that regularly reinforce the notion of dieting. Instead, the dieter is encouraged to think of his diet in the literal sense of the word—as what he eats, every meal of every day—rather than in its popular sense—as a short-term fast with a definite beginning and an identifiable conclusion.

And, finally, the Master Plan stresses practicality, on the theory that the easiest sort of vigil to maintain is that which involves the smallest alterations of old habits and the slightest accommodations to new routines. It is all well and good, for instance, for the author of a recent exposé of food fads and nutritional fallacies to catalog the potential dangers of the chemical additives found in almost all processed foods; it is quite another thing to airily suggest that the way to avoid these alleged toxins is to "Avoid products of commercial farming." The question of whether "organically grown" produce is actually any less tainted notwithstanding, the author's "solution" is in fact no solution at all for the millions of Americans who live nowhere near a source of organically grown produce, free-range eggs, and uninjected poultry—and whose budgets might not stretch to absorb the significantly higher prices of such foodstuffs if they could purchase them.

It makes no more sense, in purely practical terms, to urge overweight readers to adopt a steady diet of, say, Chinese or Japanese food—despite the fact that those national cuisines are near-perfect models of the sort of "right eating" that the McGovern committee recommended. They are nutritionally balanced, high in fiber, low in fat (particularly saturated animal fats), and they feature fresh fruits and vegetables. As significantly, neither stresses the consumption of sugar; a lavish banquet in Peking or Tokyo is as likely to conclude with a soup course as with a Western-style dessert.

Oriental food is also, as it happens, vastly impractical from the average Occidental housewife's point of view, requiring exotic and unfamiliar ingredients, many of which are unavailable outside the nation's largest cities, and a battery of specialized cooking utensils. If you happen to live in New York or San Francisco, and if you happen to have acquired a taste for Oriental cuisine, then there is much merit in such a suggestion. But if you happen to live in Beloit or Biloxi or Beaumont instead, or if you happen to have a husband who prefers a good New England boiled dinner and children who insist on pop tarts, then it is merely another intriguing dietary suggestion that does not happen to apply.

The Master Plan takes all these limitations into account—the geographical, the social, the financial, and the psychological. And if it lacks the superficial glamour of fad diets and eschews their deceptive rhetoric, it more than compensates for these seeming deficiencies in sheer effectiveness. It is meant to work, and it does. Each specific recommendation of the Master Plan has proven an effective means of weight reduction for someone—and your task is to discover which of the following suggestions work for you. When you have done that you will have solved, for yourself and on your own terms, the puzzle of obesity.

Phase I: Exercise

The particular appeal of exercise is that it permits weight loss without any alteration of basic eating habits, and for the compulsive overeater this may indeed be the only effective solution to the puzzle of obesity. In general, however, exercise is valuable as an adjunct to, rather than the mainstay of, a sensible reduction program. Ideally, it is an integral part of *any* weight-control plan, both during and after the period of weight loss.

There are two important facts to remember about exercise. The first is that the more often you engage in any sort of physical activity, the easier that activity becomes. This is true not only of recognized recreational activities, such as skiing and tennis, where the gradual acquisition of specific skills would obviously be a factor, but of such mundane activities as walking and climbing stairs. (In the elderly, it is even true of sitting and standing. Many octogenarians find that they have difficulty rising from deep chairs—in large part because they spend so much of the day sitting in such chairs and so little of the day rising from them.) Significantly, this is *not* true of dieting, which becomes more difficult with each pound lost. The closer an overweight individual comes to attaining his or her ideal weight, the more stubbornly the body's remaining fat resists being mobilized—until, in the end, dieting alone seems fruitless.

Physical conditioning, by contrast, has a uniformly salubrious impact on the body. After several weeks of regular exercise, even of the most restrained sort, positive physiological changes begin to manifest themselves. You find that you tire less readily, both when performing specific chores and during the course of the day. Your skin color, muscle tone, and posture all improve. You perform each day's tasks with greater ease and efficiency, and you sleep more soundly when they are finished. In this sense alone exercise achieves what diet seldom does—a steady, easily perceived improvement in one's appearance. Weight loss is too often ephemeral: the scale records what the eye fails to see. This is especially true in the case of ketogenic diets, of course, since even profound water loss has little impact on the all too evident packets of fat we carry on hips, thighs, jowls, and upper arms. There is nothing illusory about the physical changes that result from exercise, however. A flat stomach is undeniably flat, and well-toned muscles are exactly that.

The second thing to remember about exercise is that where weight loss rather than muscular development is the objective, it is *sustained* exercise that is most beneficial. The number of calories your body burns is based upon the total amount of body weight that is supported or moved in the course of a day. The easiest and most effective way to burn calories, therefore, is to keep your entire body in motion for long periods of time. Most of the ensuing recommendations do not even involve exercise in the popular sense of the term. What they do involve is keeping the entire body in motion for long periods of time. For people who exercise infrequently or not at all—a category that includes fully half of all adult Americans and a far greater percentage of overweight adult Americans—the easiest way to keep their bodies in motion is simply to do more of what they are already doing every day—which is standing, walking, and climbing.

Walking, like jogging and running, its more ambitious cousins, is a particularly good form of exercise for weight reduction, as the chart on pages 128–29 plainly indicates. It employs the largest and strongest muscles of the body, which means that it is less enervating than activities of a more specifically athletic nature and can, therefore, be sustained for longer periods of time.

Unlike all other forms of exercise, walking requires no special equipment, clothes, hours, conditions, or previous training. And after the first year to eighteen months of life, it does not even require conscious effort.

As we said, the ensuing recommendations do not involve exercise in the popular sense of the word. Instead they devolve from forms of daily exercise that have become so familiar we no longer recognize them by that name.

Avoid calisthenics. Contrived exercise programs of any sort are not only dull but inefficient as a means of losing weight. They will do you no harm, but they will not be particularly helpful either. A brisk half-hour walk will produce a greater caloric deficit than fifteen minutes of "spot-reducing" exercises, which generally involve only isolated parts of the body at any given time and too frequently are performed while supine. If such exercises achieve any appreciable effect beyond improving the subject's muscle tone, that effect comes from the overall caloric deficit that exercise creates. There is simply no such thing as "spot reducing."

Buy a pedometer. Wear it from the moment you get up until you go to bed at night, and keep track of the actual distance in feet that you cover each day. (If you can bring yourself to do so, keep a tally of each day's subtotals as well, recording them before every meal or snack. The more information you have, the easier you will find it to develop a personal "activity profile.") Study the chart you are keeping at weekly intervals. What does it tell you? That you cannot seem to get started in the morning? That you slow down drastically after four in the afternoon? That you scarcely move at all on Sunday? When you can answer such questions for yourself, you will be in a position to answer two far more critical questions: How does my daily activity pattern influence what I eat? How can I *make* my daily activity pattern influence what I eat? If you recognize, for example, that your peak activity period comes in the late morning—and leaves you ravenous at lunchtime—you may find it helpful to postpone some of those chores until immediately after lunch. Or you may discover that it is possible to avoid late-afternoon hunger pangs by taking a brief walk around four o'clock, a time when you are often idle.

Take the extra step. To the more distant telephone, when the nearer one would do. To the water cooler at the far end of the building, rather than the one twenty feet from your desk. To the mailbox that is three streets over, not the one on the corner. To the upstairs bathroom; to the last bank of elevators; to a wastebasket in another room. Park your car in the remotest corner of the lot. Run all of your downtown errands on foot. Drop in on a neighbor who lives five minutes away by car but twenty minutes away on foot. It hardly matters what choices you make or how consistently you make them. What matters is to push a bit further each day, to cover enough ground so that each day's pedometer reading is higher than the last.

Walk when you feel like napping. The perfect antidote for end-of-the-day fatigue is a brisk walk, not a brief nap. This is a truism that can only be verified through practice, but it does not require much practice. If you find yourself feeling run-down at the end of the day, the reason may well be psychological rather than physiological. You have been running in high gear for hours, set on accomplishing the day's tasks, and when you finish you naturally downshift, you instinctively relax. Out of long habit this emotional release has a way of translating itself into physical inertia. This is only habit, however; the body's real need at this point is for a fresh surge of activity to revitalize the spirit and tone up the muscles.

Run one superfluous errand—on foot—every day. Walk the dog one additional time. Or walk to the neighborhood newsstand rather than having the paper delivered. Or go out for your lunch every day rather than having it delivered. The key to any new form of exercise is to integrate it so thoroughly into your everyday routine that it loses its specific, alien identity. Walking six blocks out of your way two mornings a week to have your shoes polished by a particular bootblack is an artificial exercise the first twenty times you do it; after that, it is a habit.

Climb, don't ride. A Mayo Clinic physician in his early sixties makes rounds every morning in one of the largest hospitals in the world. He is well known for his compassionate bedside manner, for the degree of concern he expresses for each of his patients, and for the length of time he spends with each one. He is also well known for the efficiency with which he makes rounds. The explanation for this seeming contradiction is that he never uses the hospital's many elevator banks; he uses the stairwells, and he takes the steps two at a time. Many of the young residents on the doctor's service are overweight, but not the doctor himself, who weighs within four pounds of what he weighed when he graduated from medical school thirty-six years ago. Where there are elevators and escalators there are, by law, stairwells. Find them and use them. Climbing burns twice as many calories as walking on the level does, and climbing two steps at a time burns more still. It also improves your heart and lung capacity in a way that mere walking never does.

Don't sit when you can stand. Remember, the number of calories your body burns is based upon the total amount of body weight that is supported or moved—which means that you burn more fat when you stand, even if you stand motionless, than when you sit. It has been calculated that if you spend one additional hour each day standing—even if you do not engage in strenuous activity during that period—you will lose half a pound a month, six pounds in a year. Just by *standing*. If standing bores you, pace. In doctors' offices, while waiting at the check-out desk, while your groceries are being loaded at the supermarket, while your bags are being unloaded at the airport. You will probably work off some tension, and you will definitely work off six or more pounds each year.

Vacation where you can walk. You have just returned from a two-week vacation—during which you abandoned your diet and indulged your palate—and your caloric sins are weighing heavily upon your mind. You step on the bathroom scale . . . and to your astonishment discover that you have somehow managed to lose four pounds. The scenario is a familiar one—and the explanation is actually quite simple. You often eat more when you vacation, but you tend to exercise a great deal more—and that makes all the difference. Make a point of taking vacations where you can walk—or of walking in the places where you usually vacation.

Walk somewhere you now ride. Home from work, or from the station. Or from the hairdresser, or P.T.A. meetings, or your bridge game. Any short trip that you make regularly, preferably on the same day of the week, week in and week out, will do. The more habitual the activity—be it a Rotary luncheon, a library board session, a night-school class, or a Scout meeting—the easier you will find it to incorporate walking into that particular routine. You will soon adjust your schedule to accommodate the extra exercise, and others will soon adjust their schedules to accommodate you. Your wife will learn to expect you twenty-five minutes later for dinner on Tuesdays and Thursdays because you have chosen to walk home from work on those days. Your husband will make a point of getting home promptly on Wednesdays or Fridays so that you will have the option of walking, rather than driving, home from your den mothers' meeting.

Pick up your pace. Your body burns one-third more calories when you walk than when you amble—that is, when you pick up your pace from three to four miles per hour. This tiny differential can amount to hundreds of additional calories burned each week, thousands each month, and pounds lost every year. Having extended your daily walks to their logical limit, the next step is to make them more efficient, to cover the same distance in less time and burn a greater number of calories in the process. To achieve this objective you must set a more strenuous pace than the one that you are accustomed to, whether you are walking down the hall to the Xerox machine, across the lawn to the leaf pile, around the block with your dog, or up the hill to the neighbors' house. Consciously lengthen your stride every time you walk more than a hundred feet in any direction. The effect will be to increase your pace as well, and that will automatically increase your energy output and the amount of calories you burn. And when your feet finally tire and you run short of breath, slow down—even an amble will burn a considerable number of calories.

Phase II: Nutrition

The question of what to eat was in many ways simpler to answer 10,000 years ago. The choices were far more restricted, of course, and nature often imposed additional restrictions on what was available: fish did not bite, berries did not ripen before the frost, heavy rains flattened the wild grains, droughts scattered the great herds. But when food was in abundant supply, the choices were rather easily made. Palatability and nutritional value went more or less hand in hand, and so men ate the ripened fruit before the green and the full ear before the sere stalk. All that has changed in the last half century, changed as a result of chemical additives that make nutritionally worthless foodstuffs taste good and changed as a result of packaging and promotion that make those same products seem appealing. The choices are more numerous today, but they are not as clear as they once were. And learning to choose right is very important, especially if you are overweight. Choose the right foods and you will automatically choose foods that are less caloric. Do that, and you cannot help but lose weight.

The Mayo Clinic, in the audio-visual materials that it presents to overweight patients, stresses that "dieting begins at the supermarket," meaning that if you put the right foods in your shopping cart, you will almost certainly put the right nutrients into your system later on. Impulse buying leads to impulse snacking, and the best way to curb the latter is to curtail the former. If you do not buy the chocolate-covered doughnuts when you pass the baked goods display, you will not find yourself eating three of them when you pass through the kitchen on your way to bed. And you will not consume the caloric equivalent of another entire meal in the form of a bedtime snack.

In Chapter 7 we focused our attention upon the negative aspects of American eating habits, emphasizing the hazards of faulty nutrition as they are measured in soaring dental and medical bills; in increased dependence upon dietary supplements and reducing nostrums; and in lost teeth, reduced vitality, and increased girth. Speak of nutrition as a reflection of how we actually eat, and there is ample justification for such pessimism. The available statistics indicate that we are eating less well today than we did ten years ago—and that we will almost certainly be eating worse ten years from now. But speak of nutrition as how we *might* eat, and the outlook changes drastically. The ordinary American supermarket is the most bountiful bazaar the world has even known, and it offers all the ingredients of a diet that is nutritionally balanced, readily available, and reasonably priced. Eating right is only a matter of knowing what things to put into your shopping cart, of making the right choices.

If you make the right choices consistently, week in and week out, every time you enter your supermarket, you may well find yourself losing weight *without* consciously dieting. Choose, for example, to substitute half a cantaloupe for your usual late-afternoon snack. Even filled with a full cup of ripe, whole strawberries your choice contains fewer calories than *eight* potato chips. It is also, not incidentally, higher in fiber and in sheer bulk, a combination that speeds the digestive processes while reducing preprandial hunger pangs. To fully appreciate the wisdom of such a choice requires some understanding of the composition of foodstuffs and the complexities of human metabolism. But to *make* such a choice in your own supermarket requires nothing more than a familiarity with the following guidelines and recommendations:

Fat makes you fat faster. Any given weight of fat contains more than *twice* the calories of the same amount of carbohydrate or protein, so the first principle of sound nutrition—and an obvious answer to the question of what to eat—is to consume far less fat. The McGovern committee recommended that American adults reduce their fat intake by better than 25 per cent, with saturated animal fats accounting for most of that total and polyunsaturated fats for the rest. Any calorie chart will tell you which foods are high in natural fats and oils (pork and lamb, avocados and coconuts, sardines and swordfish, cashews and pecans) and which are low (lean beef and skinless chicken, salad greens and squashes, shrimp and sole, fruits of all kinds). It is perfectly possible to achieve a substantial reduction in your consumption of natural fats and oils by acquiring such a chart and acquainting yourself with every entry; it is also immensely complicated and time-consuming. A far easier way to reduce your intake of fats is to think in terms of the fats that are *added* to foods as they are prepared, rather than of the fats that are inherent in unprepared foodstuffs. Raw cabbage, for instance, contains only traces of oil, but cole slaw is almost 10 per cent lipids. Three simple rules will make the task of monitoring your fat consumption easier:

1. *Never order anything deep-fried when you eat out.* Nothing adds as dramatically to the caloric content of any meal as deep-frying, which can turn virtually calorie-free vegetables such as zucchini and onions into dieter's nightmares.

2. *Fry at home if you must, but choose your oils.* Remember that lard, bacon renderings, and salt pork are densest in calories, and that they are closely followed by butter. Safflower oil, on the other hand, contains only one-fifth the saturated fat of butter and one-third less saturated fat than margarine, although all are caloric. Nonstick cooking surfaces contain no saturated fats at all, of course, and meat that is pan-fried without fats or oils in a Teflon-lined skillet is every bit as palatable as meat prepared by more traditional methods.

3. *Poach the things you usually fry, and steam the things you usually sauté.* Fish, for example, and vegetables of all sorts. You will find that foods prepared in this way taste less like fat and more like themselves, having lost less of their natural color, nutritional value, and essential flavor.

Ignore the table salt. Salt is both the oldest and the most popular of all condiments, and it is employed in virtually every form of food processing, from canning to drying and from pickling to ice cream making. As a result, it is already abundant in our food supply and superfluous as a seasoning. We have no need for salt, yet we go right on salting what is put before us, habitually and reflexively. We salt salt-cured meats and salt-saturated vegetables—we even salt beer—and in the process most of us consume five or six times as much salt as our bodies actually need. In such quantities salt actually masks, rather than enhances, the flavor of what we eat. This served a very real purpose centuries ago, when much meat was rank and most fats rancid, but it defeats the purpose of eating foods at the peak of their natural flavor.

It is worth noting here that the taste of fried foods is particularly enhanced by salt, and if you can render them less appetizing by not salting them—and if, as a consequence, you eat fewer French fries, or fishsticks, or Southern-style chicken—you will be doing yourself a double favor. As an added bonus, cutting your use of table salt will produce diuresis, and although this weight loss is only water, not adipose tissue, it does come during the crucial first weeks of your new regimen and it provides encouragement during that discouraging initial phase. If you absolutely cannot live without salt, try substituting soy sauce for table salt on all meats and vegetables and in all soups. It imparts a salty taste to food but contains only one-fifth as much sodium as a pinch of salt.

Think first of vegetables when you think of food. It has been said that the real merit of a vegetarian diet lies not in the absence or near absence of meat but in the presence of quantities of vegetables. They provide natural vitamins in abundant supply, the fiber so often missing from the American diet—particularly the dieter's diet—and few calories relative to their bulk. The all too familiar caricature of the "serious" dieter—dreaming of a well-marbled T-bone and a mound of home fries while nibbling on a single stalk of celery—has given all vegetables a bad name.

Scorned by Dr. Atkins and legions of others as "rabbit food," vegetables have become the most undervalued item in the American diet. They are cooked without imagination, served without flair, and consumed without enthusiasm. In restaurants they appear as afterthoughts, in small side dishes that serve to emphasize their ancillary role; and at any table they are consumed last, perhaps out of a sense of obligation to the shade of the mother, aunt, or grandmother who first introduced them and insisted on their value. Even she, whoever she was, did not say that vegetables were good, only that they were good *for* you, and it is that notion—and that prejudice—that most of us carry into our adult lives.

Raw or cooked, vegetables need not taste like fodder. The serious dieter can concoct any number of dips and sauces for vegetables out of low-calorie products—sour cream spiked with horseradish, for example; or low-calorie mayonnaise mixed with chili sauce and a dash of Worcestershire; or yogurt, lemon juice, and dill—and although these concoctions will add a few extra calories to each snack or meal, they will also improve the flavor of each repast. Five carrot sticks, undressed and unadorned, are indeed rabbit food; but a tossed salad containing lettuce, cucumber, mushrooms, Bermuda onions, asparagus spears, carrot curls, radish roses, green pepper slices, tomato wedges, and broccoli flowerettes—topped with sliced cheese and hard-boiled eggs and tossed with three tablespoons of cream-style dressing—is a meal. And it contains fewer calories than a single slice of pecan pie—proof that it is almost impossible to devise a meal that is both high in raw vegetable content and also high in calories.

Rediscover potatoes. The potato is unquestionably the most maligned staple in the American diet, the first item abandoned by the weight-watcher and the last consumed by the gourmand. In actuality, a medium-sized baked potato contains only 90 calories, and seasoned with nothing more than a bit of salt and coarse-ground black pepper it is one of the tastiest, most nourishing, and most filling of true low-calorie snacks. It is the potato's unhappy fate to be joined, in culinary tradition, with such high-calorie condiments as butter, heavy cream, sour cream, and grated cheese. Much the same effect can be achieved by substituting yogurt or creamed cottage cheese for this caloric combination, and a far greater caloric saving can be obtained by eating potatoes boiled—hot, with lemon butter; or cold, as German-style potato salad.

Know the high price of processing. Calories—in the form of sugar—are frequently added with each additional step in the processing of food, which explains how there can be 25 calories in a cup of fresh green beans but 45 in a cup of canned beans and 60 in the same amount of frozen beans. The increase is even more dramatic in the case of processed fruits, which are often

What you thought you knew . . .

The more you exercise, the more protein you need. Protein needs correlate with total body weight, not energy expenditure, and consuming extra protein produces extra adipose tissue, not extra strength, endurance, fitness, or vitality.

The older you get, the more you need vitamin supplements. Actually, older people seem to need less of certain vitamins, and overdosing with vitamin supplements can actually be detrimental to the health of older individuals, especially women. (The notion that elderly people need less protein is also false.)

Cholesterol causes heart attacks. There does seem to be some correlation between high levels of cholesterol in the blood and cardiovascular disease, but diet has no impact on blood cholesterol levels. Whether you eat a dozen eggs a week or fewer than a dozen in a year will not change your blood cholesterol level. The real value of a cholesterol-free diet is that it reduces fat consumption, which most adult Americans should do anyway.

Yogurt is a uniquely wholesome natural food. For all its voguish favor, yogurt is no more nourishing than whole milk. Nor are its bacteria an aid to digestion under ordinary circumstances.

Well-done meat is less nutritive than rare meat. There is, in fact, no difference between the two. Vegetables are another case altogether, however; the more water they are cooked in, the more likely they are to yield their water-soluble vitamins.

You should never drink a very cold beverage when you are overheated, and vice-versa. In truth, studies conducted by the

three times as caloric when canned or frozen as when fresh. The same is true of breaded fish, vegetables in cream sauces, processed meats such as sausage and bologna, and presweetened fruit punches. With this in mind the weight-conscious shopper would do well to head directly to the fresh produce section of the supermarket. The important thing to remember is that the correct substitute for a particular fruit or vegetable, when

U.S. Army show that there is very little difference in the temperature of all ingested drinks by the time they reach the stomach. A drink that does not scald the tongue will not "shock" the intestines.

Raw vegetables are better for you than cooked vegetables. Vegetables contain starch granules, which are broken down and rendered more easily digested by moist heat. Steaming is the ideal way to break down these granules while retaining the maximum vitamin content of the vegetables.

Vitamin supplements are necessary if you don't always eat balanced meals. This myth ignores the body's resiliency and adaptability, among other things. The liver, for example, can store all the vitamin A the body needs for up to a year, and the body can function without vitamin C for five months before scurvy manifests itself. The only real need for daily vitamin supplements is a purely psychological one.

It makes a difference *when* you eat. Not so. The body's metabolism functions at a fairly steady rate, whether you are sedentary or active, awake or asleep. There are many good reasons for avoiding bedtime snacks, but the fear that those calories will stay with you longer than any others you consume during the day should not be one of them.

The body needs sugar as a source of "quick energy." The body manufactures all the sugar it needs from starches, proteins, and fats. In any adequately balanced diet there is absolutely no need for sugar as a source of instant energy. In fact, there is really no need for refined sugar at all.

that item is unavailable as fresh produce, is another high-fiber, low-calorie foodstuff, *not* the same fruit or vegetable in canned or frozen form.

Appreciate the value of air. There is more apparent bulk and less actual caloric content in anything puffed. Puffed rice, for example, can be eaten as cereal or in cracker form and contains only 55 calories in an entire cup. The same is true of unbuttered

. . . and what you ought to know

You need protein at *every* meal, including breakfast. The body does not conserve protein efficiently, and the only way to ensure a steady supply of protein is to include some form of protein, animal or vegetable, in every meal. Because four out of five adult Americans eat a nutritionally imbalanced breakfast, if they eat breakfast at all, they deprive their bodies of adequate protein supplies for up to twelve hours out of every twenty-four.

There is a vast difference in the composition of carbohydrates. Leafy vegetables, for instance, contain only 2 to 5 per cent sugar and starch, while bread is 50 per cent and dry cereal 80 per cent sugar and starch. Carbohydrates are generally spurned by dieters, but even such relatively caloric items as whole-grain breads are less fattening than fat-saturated proteins.

Vitamin C may not be a vitamin at all. With the exception of men, monkeys, and guinea pigs, all animals make their own vitamin C, and some experts speculate that what we identify as vitamin C is actually a substance that the human body once manufactured but has, through genetic adaptation, lost the capacity to metabolize.

You probably *are* iron-deficient. Particularly if you are a woman between the ages of nine and fifty-five, for females between those ages are generally *at least* one third iron-deficient. Fortunately, it is easy to regulate the amount of iron in your diet because you can "see" it. Iron is a food colorant, visible in red meats (particularly organ meats), dark whole grains, prunes, raisins, molasses, and all green, leafy vegetables.

Calories do count, but counting calories is a waste of time. Individual caloric needs and daily caloric expenditures vary

popcorn, which makes either as caloric, per cup, as four graham crackers. Rice, oatmeal, and farina all belong to this category, and one of the strongest arguments for eating cereal at breakfast—which four out of five adult Americans fail to do—is that it is an especially good source of fiber and bulk that happens to be extremely low in calories.

widely—sometimes by 1,500 calories per day—and so there is no accurate way of gauging the number of calories needed to create a given deficit on a given day. In addition, all caloric equivalency charts are based on approximations; they tell you the average number of calories found in the average apple—not in the apple you happen to be eating.

Skipping meals is the *worst* way to lose weight. The starving body burns lean mass, not fatty tissue, and the best way to ensure a steady loss of adipose tissue is to eat very small meals and snacks, as many as six per day.

Weight loss cannot always be weighed. Particularly during the second and third weeks of any low-calorie diet, the amount of water the body retains tends to exceed the amount of adipose tissue that is burned, and until that water is shed the weight loss does not register. It is important to bear this in mind during the first phase of your diet, lest you be tempted to weigh its success or failure on your bathroom scales.

Despite what you have read, the mercury found in fish will do you no harm. According to Harvard's Fredrick Stare, there is absolutely no evidence that anyone has ever been made ill by eating "mercury-contaminated" seafood.

Although fresh vegetables are indeed nutritious, unprocessed vegetables vary considerably in food value, depending on how much time elapses between when they are picked and when they are sold. The deterioration of "fresh" vegetables may therefore be greater than the losses that occur during commercial canning or freezing, where the processing is done within three or four hours of picking.

Beware of silly savings, in caloric terms. Much of what you think you know about the nutritional value and caloric content of given foodstuffs is probably wrong, based as it is upon myth and misinformation, and you would do better to rely on the nutritional facts on pages 194–97 than your own recollection where these things are concerned. There are compelling reasons to substitute poultry and fish for red meat in one's diet, for instance, but caloric savings is not one of them: a can of oil-packed tunafish contains as many calories as a lean hamburger, and a half pound of roasted chicken contains more calories than either. The same is true of many supposedly "dietetic" foods. True, 98 per cent fat-free milk does contain fewer calories than whole milk, but the difference is only 17 calories per glass. And nuts are high in natural oils, but the "diet" spread for sandwiches is nonetheless peanut butter, which is far less caloric than any of the sandwich meats or meat salads.

It helps to remember that the term "dietetic" was first used to describe sugar-free products developed for diabetics, for whom a low-sugar diet is the first priority. Quite often these dietetic foods are virtually identical in caloric value to their normal counterparts. This is true of ice creams, for instance—and where it is not true, the savings in caloric terms are hardly worth the expense in budgetary terms. If you need to lose weight you need to eat fewer cookies at 128 calories apiece, not shift to dietetic cookies at a savings of roughly 30 calories each.

Take all of the above recommendations and apply them to sugar. As it happens, they do apply. First, refined sugar does make you fat faster than many other foodstuffs, even those high in natural sugars, oils, and fats. This is so because refined sugar is the only nutritionally "pure" staple in our diet; it contains nothing *but* calories in the form of simple carbohydrates, whereas all other foods, including complex carbohydrates, contain traces of other nutrients.

Second, sugar, like salt, is an acquired taste. We consume more of it than we need, having acquired our sweet tooth at an early age and nurtured it ever after. That process begins with the introduction of solid foods, many of which are sweetened by the manufacturer to meet adult rather than infant expectations. It is compounded by our affection for sugar-laden beverages, particularly colas, which the children of Appalachia, among others, sometimes drink from the moment they are weaned, at least in part because the indigenous water supply is held to be unsafe. Habits so firmly entrenched and preferences so deeply ingrained are all but impossible to reverse in adult life, but it *is* possible for any adult to wean himself or herself from overdependence on sugar, one teaspoonful at a time.

Third, any diet that is high in vegetables and fruits will not only be low in calories, it will also be low in refined sugars. The mother, aunt, or grandmother who told you, years ago, that vegetables were good for you, but who neglected to tell you that they could be good tasting as well, probably saw no need to mention that the opposite was true of sugar. Taste alone recommended most baked goods and confections, and what you most likely heard, if you heard anything at all, was that too much of such good things could potentially be bad for you. The value of vegetables—and this includes potatoes—is that they contain natural sugars, and if you eat a diet containing sufficient quantities of complex carbohydrates you will get all the sugar your body needs without the addition of table sugar.

The chief ingredient in many stages of food processing is sugar, which is added not only to fruits but to vegetables, breads, sauces, and soup stocks. This explains how highly processed foods acquire their taste appeal, fat and sugar being nature's chief flavor enhancers. It also explains why they are likely to sabotage the unsuspecting dieter. Cooked grains, on the other hand, are a particular boon to the conscientious dieter precisely because they are processed and prepared, by and large, without the addition of refined sugar, and can be served and consumed with a minimum of additional sugar.

Finally, most nutritional quackery and dietary foolishness centers around the sugar content of cakes and cookies, candies and colas, desserts and snack foods—in short, the very items, once considered peripheral to a well-balanced meal, that have gradually displaced fruits and vegetables, whole grains and natural fiber in the national diet. Here as elsewhere our notions regarding the relative merits of such foods tend to be strongly influenced by what we have seen and read, and much of that has emanated from the manufacturers themselves in the form of print advertisements and television commercials.

As a result, we find ourselves extolling the "natural" qualities of brown sugar, unaware that it is 99 per cent refined, one step removed from the white table sugar we have learned to hold in contempt. And we find ourselves praising the virtues of honey, an "organic" sweetener that is indistinguishable from refined sugar in the body and is just as liable to promote tooth decay. We also find ourselves succumbing to the blandishments of food processors who promise us inconsequential caloric savings on favorite high-calorie foods. These savings are generally modest—several calories, even several dozen calories, out of thousands consumed every day—and in the end they are not savings at all, for they encourage the continued consumption of high-calorie foods and thereby discourage the development of sound nutritional habits. The question of what to eat, when you are overweight, is not answered by dietetic cookies, each containing a mere 100 calories; it is answered by an apple, which contains only 70 calories.

Phase III: Behavior Modification

"The most significant dietary advance in the past fifty years," Dr. Linn says of his liquid protein. If there is any single advance in the whole field of weight control that truly qualifies for the hyperbolic title "most significant," it is probably behavior modification. As we noted in the previous chapter, behavior modification does not work in all cases of obesity, but where it does work—with well-motivated, moderately overweight, middle-aged men and women—it tends to work very well indeed, in many instances producing results that appear to be twice as good as those achieved by more conventional methods of weight control.

Chances are, if you are even 15 per cent overweight, that your eating habits are largely controlled by external rather than internal stimuli. You respond to the sight, smell, or suggestion of food, rather than to the physiological sensation of hunger, and you grow progressively more ravenous as mealtimes approach, irrespective of when you last ate or how much you ate. For you, the solution to the puzzle of obesity may lie in changing *how* you eat rather than *what* you eat. Such changes can be effected only if you learn to recognize and control the external stimuli that make you feel hungry when you are actually well fed, and to do this you must keep another logbook.

This time, instead of entering the number of miles you have covered in the day, you enter everything relevant to your personal eating habits. The Mayo Clinic suggests that you make this private journal as detailed as possible, recording not only what you ate, when you ate it, and how long it took you to eat it, but what sort of mood you were in at the time, who ate with you, and the like. Here again, the more detailed the record, the more valuable it is as a means of weight control. If you are scrupulously honest about entering every single thing you eat, item by item and calorie by calorie, you may find that merely keeping the record has given you unexpected and genuinely helpful insights into how you eat and why you eat too much.

You may discover that you remain faithful to a nutritionally balanced, low-calorie diet all day long, only to undo its effectiveness with an 1,100-calorie snack just before bedtime. Or you may find yourself eating two extra snacks on days when your husband is out of town on business. Or you may find that your overeating cycles correspond to periods of financial anxiety or professional insecurity. In some cases it is sufficient simply to keep a log—an accurate record of dietary shortcomings and a yardstick for self-improvement. But for most of us, behavior modification means small but significant changes in existing eating habits. Depending on the sort of external stimuli you personally respond to, such changes might include any—or, theoretically, all—of the following:

Shop only from a prepared list. Dieting does begin at the supermarket. It is easier to resist the Danish pastries on the baked-goods counter than on your kitchen counter, and you must train yourself to do so. Consult *Phase II: Nutrition* and "Yielding to Temptation" (pages 204–05) before you set out for the grocery store. Follow the recommendations and guidelines as you make up your shopping list, and follow that list when you shop.

Shop only after eating. It is even easier to resist the Danish pastries on a full stomach. Also the "quick-sale" pork chops and the Vienna sausage samples being handed out.

Shop first for produce. A full shopping cart, like a full stomach, discourages impulse buying. As the cart fills and the total cost mounts, the desire to add spur-of-the-moment purchases to your marketing declines. Besides, it's harder to hide the Danish pastries from yourself when they're at the top of the cart.

Keep a boring refrigerator. Nothing encourages proper eating—and discourages late-night snacking—like an array of fruits and vegetables, cottage cheese and yogurt, sugar-free soft drinks and unsweetened iced tea. Discourage your gourmand's eye for the tempting tidbit, the palate-pleasing leftover, by storing all foods, particularly all high-calorie foods, in opaque plastic containers. If this proves insufficient, remove the light from the refrigerator.

Snackproof your shelves. If you must buy snack foods—and you ought to ask yourself whether you are really doing it just for the kids and the occasional guest—then transfer them immediately to old coffee cans or cookie tins, any container that renders its contents invisible. Store them on the highest shelf, so that it takes an effort to get at them. Making the effort will make you feel guilty, and when you begin to feel guilty enough you will stop making the effort.

Never skip meals, especially breakfast. One of the strongest of external stimuli is the clock. You will find it far easier to resist the odd snack than the actual meal, and most dieters who "fast" at lunchtime, making a virtue of their abstemiousness during office hours, make up for those missed calories later in the day.

Always eat in the same place. Snacks will seem more like meals and their caloric content will register more clearly when they are consumed at the table rather than at the kitchen counter or in the car. By making eating an entirely separate and distinct activity, you extract greater emotional satisfaction—and, in psychological terms, greater satiety—from what you eat, and you keep closer tabs on what you consume.

Do nothing but eat when you eat. If you read, or watch television, or sort laundry, or prepare food while you are eating, you will be

Yielding to Temptation

Snacking, often identified as the bane of the overweight, should actually be regarded as a boon to the serious dieter. There is no better way of modulating hunger pangs and curbing appetite, and any regimen that fails to recognize the potential benefits of eating *less* by eating *more often* deprives the dieter of a valuable weapon in the war of the waistline. Eating between meals is human nature; whether those meals-between-meals cause you to gain weight or help you to lose depends entirely on how and when you snack. A "snack" of two doughnuts, for example, contains more calories than a breakfast consisting of orange juice, two eggs, a strip of bacon, toast with jam, and two cups of black coffee—and it is far less nourishing to boot. As a result, doughnuts are not included in the following list of recommended snacks, all of which have been chosen because they provide a relatively high ratio of bulk to calories.

As the text indicates, snacking is an essential element of the Master Plan for Weight Control, both as a means of rewarding successful behavior modification (page 209) and as a means of curbing appetite and therefore reducing total caloric intake (page 216). Most of the suggestions contained in Phase III of the Master Plan apply with equal force to snacks and to meals, and so several of them are repeated on the following pages.

less conscious of what you are eating—and too often you will fail to take notice of how much you are eating. A large part of the pleasure of dining is circumstantial; convivial company, engrossing dinnertable conversation, and a pleasant-tasting bottle of wine can make an otherwise dull meal entirely palatable. It is when dining is reduced to feeding that we tend to overeat out of a combination of inattention and boredom.

Eat from a small plate, drink from a small glass. Skimpy portions seem even skimpier when they sit in lonely isolation on a large dinner plate; they look far less meager on a salad plate, where the visual perception of amplitude registers as a psychological sense of sufficient quantity. Extra greens—two sprigs of parsley, a

Yielding to Temptation

Eat any snack, no matter how small, off a plate. Prepare it as you would prepare a meal, eat it at your accustomed place.

Record all details regarding the snack in your log book—just as if the snack were a full-scale meal. This practice will tell you, over a period of time, what your personal "snacking profile" is. You may find you are most inclined to snack on Sunday afternoons during the pro football season, or on the mornings you do the ironing. And you may find it helpful to schedule your daily walk to coincide with these periods, as a way of reducing temptation when the flesh is weakest.

Snack before meals, never after. The right sort of low-calorie snack, consumed half an hour or more *before* a meal, tends to trip the brain's "glucostat" and reduce hunger. Any sort of snack consumed *after* a meal only adds to the day's caloric intake.

The key to snacking—as a component of diet rather than as a compromiser of diets—is choosing foods that are high in water content and bulk. These foods fall into four general categories:

Liquids. Nothing, obviously, is as watery as water itself, and the serious dieter should not neglect the option of drinking to satisfy hunger pangs. In addition to water itself, the list of recommended drinks includes tomato and grapefruit juice, both exceedingly low in sugar content; natural fruit juices such as apple, cranberry, and prune juice (as opposed to fruit drinks, which tend to be very high in sugar content); and unsweetened coffee or tea. Artificially sweetened beverages, among them diet soft drinks, are another option, recommended with the reservation that they do nothing to discourage the dieter's habituation to refined sugar. To enhance the palatability of unsweetened beverages, try seasoning them with two drops of peppermint extract, a twist of orange peel, cinnamon, or cloves.

Starches. The caloric value of starchy foods varies considerably, and those containing a high percentage of water should be included in any sensible diet. Potatoes, either baked or boiled, belong on every dieter's menu; even when seasoned with a pat of butter they contain fewer calories than the protein that is so often substituted for them. The same is true of pasta, which is caloric in combination with cream, cheese, and meat sauces but very low in calories when seasoned with tomato sauce. Cereals made with puffed wheat or rice are also low in calories, and they need not be eaten only at breakfast. Seasoned with garlic or garlic salt and a small amount of butter—and warmed in the oven until their flavors meld—they make an excellent low-calorie snack. Breads are low in water content but high in bulk, and they too make effective snacks. Try spreading them with cottage cheese or yogurt instead of butter and jam.

Fruits. The old adage "An apple a day . . ." should be reexamined by every serious dieter, for that apple is not only high in water content, it is also high in bulk. Eating an apple a day has the effect of displacing more caloric foodstuffs, and this in itself tends to promote weight loss. Nothing takes on calories during processing like fruits, which are extremely wholesome in their natural state and extremely caloric in combination with the sugar used to preserve them. For this reason only fresh or dried fruits are recommended as snack foods, and even dried fruits can be sanctioned only in combination with an unsweetened beverage of some sort—to compensate for the water that has been extracted from the fruit. One of the attractions of eating fresh fruit is that it generally requires some doing—peeling, paring, coring, or whatever—and these small operations have a way of slowing down the meal or snack and thereby decreasing caloric intake.

Vegetables. Highest in water content and lowest in calories relative to their bulk, vegetables are the ideal snack food. They are universally recommended by nutritionists—to the lean as well as the overweight—and they are as universally spurned by both groups. Our natural preference is for foods that are high in fat or sugar content, and because vegetables are deficient in the former and low in the latter they tend to rank low in palatability as well. To enhance the flavor of raw vegetables, try dipping them in natural-flavored yogurt seasoned with dill, mint, wine vinegar, or lemon juice; low-calorie mayonnaise spiked with a teaspoon of Worcestershire sauce or a tablespoon of chili sauce; or a sour cream substitute made by blending cottage cheese and skim milk. To improve the flavor of cooked vegetables, sauté them in wine and water; or baste them with soy sauce and barbeque them on a grill; or scramble them with egg whites, a low-calorie source of protein.

lettuce leaf, an additional tablespoon of vegetables—also help to fill up the plate, as does a lemon or tomato wedge.

Chew everything carefully; never gulp your food. The aim here is not better mastication, although there is no harm in that, but fuller appreciation of what you are eating. The brain's satiety center lags behind actual consumption, so that it may take a full hour for the body's glucostat to record the impact of a recent meal and damp down the hunger center in the hypothalamus. Few of us spend as long as an hour eating any meal, and as a result our total food consumption often outstrips our actual hunger. When the glucostat does catch up, what we feel is logy, not full. The trick, then, is to extend each meal as long as possible while consuming as little as possible.

Deliberately set your fork down between every other bite. Another means of protracting any meal, and for the same reason. One woman reported great success with a variation of this technique: to slow herself down she ate all her meals with chopsticks, a method that proved effective only until she became sufficiently adept with the chopsticks that she could approximate her former speed with a fork.

Come to the table last and leave last. If nothing else works, you may find it effective to give the other members of your family a slight head start. Many overeaters are also rapid eaters who bolt their first helping and then help themselves to seconds while others are still working on their original servings. By arriving at the table late you may find yourself finishing on schedule, and by lingering you may allow the full effect of what you have eaten to take hold.

Never finish what you have been served, and never, ever take a second helping of anything. The same mother, aunt, or grandmother who insisted that we finish our vegetables because they were good for us insisted that we clean our plates completely. Failing to do so was wasteful as well as discourteous. Armenians were starving. Or Chinese. Or children in another part of town. And so we ate to please the women who supervised our infant diets, and we ate to be polite, and we ate because we were fortunate enough to be able to eat, and we ate to grow strong—

and eventually we ate everything that was on our plates simply because we had been doing so for two or three decades. The concept of always leaving some portion of each meal uneaten is an important one, therefore, not because of the calories we avoid by doing so but because that uneaten portion is a tangible signal of our will to succeed in losing weight. It reminds us, at the end of each meal, of the consequences of overeating and the benefits of moderation.

Eat everything, even the tiniest snack, off a plate. Calories do count, and the calories that do not get counted are usually those that are consumed piecemeal, casually, and on the run. The most insidious kind of nibbling of all involves taking any snack food—nuts, potato chips, cookies, candies—from the container one piece at a time. It is in this fashion that entire tins of cookies and boxes of candy get consumed in an evening, often in amounts that would appall the would-be dieter if they were piled on a single small plate.

Serve plates and portions, not family style. Another way of saying take only what you want and consume only what you take. Seconds are much easier to resist if they are not sitting directly in front of you, and seasonings are much easier to control if you apply your own.

Make any change you make slowly. If you are accustomed to having a bologna sandwich on white bread with mayonnaise at lunchtime, you will find it difficult to abandon that practice outright. You will not find it nearly so difficult to tinker with that basic sandwich over a period of time, however, first halving the amount of mayonnaise you use, then eliminating one of the bread slices, then substituting less caloric fillings for the bologna, then, finally, substituting bran bread for the white bread. The important consideration here is that the change be gradual, for therein lies its effectiveness. As with exercise, the program that succeeds is the one that alters existing habits least.

Spoil any food that tempts you too strongly. Salt your desserts and sugar your potatoes. When they no longer taste as delectable as they once did, they will cease to be such a potent threat to your attempts to diet. This is especially true of favorite foods, which exert the strongest external effect upon our senses. One young man with a particular passion for instant mashed potatoes cured himself of his self-styled "addiction" by doctoring each batch with blue or green food coloring.

Drink water when you are angry. No external stimulus is as strong or as universally threatening to the serious dieter as anger. People have very different responses to sadness or elation, ranging all the way from uncontrolled gluttony to pathological anorexia, but most of us respond to irritation and ire with overeating. If you keep a detailed record of your eating habits for even three weeks you will discover that this is true. There is little that can be done to forestall life's irritants, but there is something that you can do to alter your response to them. The one response that is calorie-free and widely available is water.

Plan to fail. For reasons no psychologist can completely explain, occasional slips have a way of reinforcing newly acquired habits rather than undermining them. The mere fact that you have learned to recognize "cheating" for what it is indicates that you have learned to distinguish right eating from wrong. You know the answer to the question of what to eat, even if you choose to ignore it from time to time. You know how to choose, even when you choose wrong.

Make a point of horrifying yourself. It has long been recognized that heart-attack victims have little initial trouble in losing weight after they leave the hospital. So long as the memory of their brush with death remains vivid, they are extremely conscientious and uncomplaining, even when placed on the most bland of low-sodium, low-fat, low-calorie diets. As the memories fade, however, so does the will to diet. With this in mind it might help to remind yourself of the consequences of overindulgence. Pin old photographs of yourself alongside your dressing mirror. Tape the "before" shots of the Ayds ladies to the refrigerator door. Read all newspaper and magazine articles on overweight with special attention, and later read the pertinent sections aloud to your family.

When the coffee wagon comes, go to the bathroom instead. Retie your tie and comb your hair—or touch up your face and reapply your lipstick. In time this diversionary tactic will become a habit, and when you hear the coffee bell ring your conditioned response will be to think of primping, not of food.

When a commercial break comes, get up and walk. Walk anywhere you like *except* into the kitchen. Watching television makes many people restless, and too many of them interpret that restlessness as hunger. For them the proper response is to stretch, to move about, to stimulate the circulation—but not to nibble simply because they have become conditioned to nibbling while they watch television.

Enlist help. Weight Watchers, Inc., and similar self-help weight-reduction programs are based on the principle that the misery of overweight is easier to bear—and the pounds easier to shed—when both are done in the company of understanding friends and family members. Whether they know it or not, the other members of your immediate family have a very real stake in your well-being. So much of good health is predicated upon good eating habits that they owe it to you to assist and encourage you in achieving the weight loss you are aiming for.

Devise your own system of punishments and rewards. Weight loss is its own reward, of course, but any program of behavior modification depends for its success upon how completely pernicious, long-established eating habits can be altered—and here success is not always measured in terms of pounds lost, particularly not in the beginning. With behavior modification, the emphasis is on the habits, not the eating itself, which is why it has also proved an effective tool in treating alcoholism and drug dependence and why it enables heavy smokers to cure their pernicious, long-established habit.

The theory behind behavior modification is that if you can reduce the impact of external stimuli upon the brain's "hunger center"—and if you can reduce your conditioned responses to food, especially sugar-saturated, high-calorie food—you will inevitably reduce your total body weight. The focus, therefore, is upon trimming life of temptations rather than upon trimming your figure of unwanted adipose tissue. There are many who believe that behavior modification succeeds precisely because it deemphasizes what you eat and stresses how you eat instead.

It is vitally important, therefore, that you reinforce your own program with a system of punishments and rewards that are *in no way* associated with actual weight loss. What you are punishing or rewarding is your capacity to alter an old habit or supplant it with a new one, *not* your success in losing weight. It is entirely possible, especially during the first weeks of attempting to change how you eat, that you will lose no more than a pound or two; it is also possible to lose two or three times as much weight in the same period of time without adhering strictly to your new program of behavior modification, for many other factors can account for weight loss. The natural temptation is to think of the latter result as success and the former as failure, when, over the long run, the opposite is actually true. Habits permanently modified will produce permanent weight loss, whereas habits temporarily changed will produce nothing more than another cycle of loss and gain.

It is equally important that both the punishments and the rewards be meaningful ones to you. Deny yourself a favorite television program in a week when you have cheated once too often on your resolve not to snack between lunch and dinner—but do so only if missing that program counts as a loss to you. One middle-aged woman's answer to the question of punishment and reward is to keep two books on her bedside table—one tedious, the other engrossing. She "treats" herself with a chapter from the latter on days when she has stuck to her program, and she "castigates" herself with a complete chapter of the former when she has not. This works for her because she is a voracious reader as well as a formerly voracious eater. It will work for you only if your habits are sufficiently similar to hers.

The possibilities here are endless, limited only by the single restriction imposed above—that the punishments and rewards be in no way associated with actual weight loss—and by your own imagination. You might, for instance, choose to punish yourself by denying yourself an hour's extra sleep, or that long, soaky bubble bath before bed. One slightly overweight married woman of forty-six, combining two of the recommendations above, enlisted her husband's help in keeping her on her behavior modification program. She would not reveal the details of their conjugal system of rewards and punishments, but she insisted that it did work.

The only true test of such a system is that it does work, and devising a workable system for yourself may take some time. As with the Master Plan itself, the choice is yours to make from the listed suggestions and guidelines, and there are no set rules.

Phase IV: Diet

"To lengthen thy life, lessen thy meals," the portly Benjamin Franklin admonished the readers of *Poor Richard's Almanac*, and for the past two centuries the medical profession has been hard pressed to improve upon Dr. Franklin's advice. In stressing the importance of diet in weight control, most physicians fail to emphasize how *little* need be taken out of a diet to produce tangible weight loss over a long period of time. It is the question of the single piece of chocolate cake, mentioned in Chapter 1, but in reverse. If you can gain forty pounds in a year by eating an extra dessert every night, then you ought to be able to lose that much by giving up dessert altogether. This is not quite true, however, for most of us have already given up desserts in a futile effort to control our weight, and we may find ourselves resisting the suggestion that we give up the few desserts we permit ourselves. In our minds we are already paying too high a price for leanness, often without actually attaining the svelteness that is supposed to be the reward for constant vigilance. To be asked to forfeit what few pleasures of the table are left to us may seem a greater sacrifice than we are willing or even capable of making.

Moderation, the keynote of the first three phases of the Master Plan, is also the keynote of this final and most crucial section. Any alteration of existing eating habits that seems like a sacrifice is doomed to fail. Only a change so modest as to be virtually unnoticeable, both to oneself and to others, will succeed in establishing itself permanently—and only permanent change

Modest Sacrifices, Measurable Losses

False promise is the first premise of fad diets, which offer the dieter a potent combination of hyperbole and hope as a substitute for a reasonable regimen and sensible goals. Responsible dietary programs, which is to say those that are both medically sound and nutritionally balanced, must necessarily eschew such exaggerated claims, compensating in effectiveness for what they lack in glamour. Such diet plans recognize that fat comes only from food, and obesity results only from eating more than is required to meet the energy requirements of the body. Having acknowledged this, they cannot then blame obesity on glands, or hypoglycemia, or sluggish metabolism. Nor, for that matter, can they promise effortless weight loss, slimming without sacrifice, successful spot reduction, or rapid rejuvenation of tired flesh and "tired blood."

What any such diet *can* promise is measurable weight loss in exchange for modest caloric sacrifices. Unhappily, the promise of slow but steady weight loss has lost much of its appeal since the reintroduction of the high-protein, low-carbohydrate, "quick weight-loss" diet two decades ago. In the last twenty years we have come to equate "diet" with massive weight loss—as much as fifteen to eighteen pounds in a single month. In other words,

will produce permanent weight loss. The fastest and most effective means of lengthening your life and shortening your waistline is to lessen your meals. How little you need to actually sacrifice in a single day or week is indicated in the chart on pages 214–15. Pick any meal, pick any part of any meal. Here, as before, the choice is yours. Only you know your own habits and tastes well enough to know which item or items you can most easily do without, and the first step to successful diet is to eliminate the one item that you can most easily do without.

Before consulting the chart on pages 214–15 you should review the following recommendations regarding successful long-term weight reduction. They will prove useful guidelines no matter how you choose to employ the chart itself.

the sort of reduction that is often achieved—albeit rarely maintained—on a nutritionally unbalanced ketogenic diet. What has also been lost in the attendant confusion is a dietary fact that should prove comforting to all overweight adults—which is that you can lose weight gradually and *permanently* by making only minor modifications in your present eating habits. Give up a single pat of butter every single day, for example, and you will lose five pounds in a year without otherwise altering your daily regimen. No special exercises or foods are involved, no pills or liquid concoctions, yet steady weight loss is possible.

The chart on the folowing pages is not intended as a practical guide, for no such guide is really necessary. No one is suggesting that you give up your breakfast toast entirely, or abandon whipped cream forever. You may prefer to do without one of these "expendables" one week, another the next—or to vary your choice week to week throughout the year. It helps to pick a calorically dense foodstuff, of course; you lose weight faster if you do without French fries than if you forego cheese. But the only real guideline is to pick the item in your daily diet that you can part with most easily and eliminate it. You will miss it least, you will be much less conscious of the fact that you are dieting, and—who knows?—you may find, after six months to a year, that you do not really miss the item at all.

Never count calories. Some dieters find calorie counting a useful means of reinforcing their dietary resolve, and it is indeed diverting initially, particularly for the nutritionally ignorant. But counting calories also reinforces the notion of dieting, and the more often you are reminded of the fact that you are trying to lose weight, the less likely you are to succeed in doing so. Dieting is an artificial state for most of us, a temporary condition of unpleasant deprivation. A successful program of weight control is precisely the opposite: permanent, natural, and so unobtrusive as to seem anything but unpleasant. Consult the chart on pages 214–15 and the recommendations contained in *Phase II: Nutrition* for general guidelines on what to buy and what to eat, but do not attempt to keep a daily tally of calories consumed.

Modest Sacrifices, Measurable Losses

Item	*Amount*	*Frequency*	*Net loss in one year*
		General	
Butter	1 pat	daily	5 pounds*
Sugar	2 teaspoons	daily	4
Cream	1 teaspoon	daily	2
Cheese	2 ounces	once a week	3
Vegetable fat	2 tablespoons	weekly	3
Peanuts	½ cup	weekly	5
Pretzels	25	weekly	1½
Candy	1 piece	twice a week	3
		Beverages	
Beer	12-ounce can	4 times a week	10 pounds
Whiskey	1½ ounces	3 times a week	6
Wine	3-ounce glass	4 times a week	4
Lemonade	8-ounce glass	3 times a week	3
Carbonated beverages	8-ounce glass	4 times a week	4
		Breakfast	
Bacon	2 strips	3 times a week	5 pounds
Sweet roll	1	once a week	2
Toast	1 slice	daily	6
Doughnut	2	once a week	4
Honey	1 tablespoon	twice a week	1½
Jelly or jam	1 tablespoon	4 times a week	3
Syrup	1 tablespoon	twice a week	1½
Egg (boiled)	4	weekly	4
Egg (scrambled)	4	weekly	6
Biscuit	2	weekly	5
Waffle	2	weekly	6
Breakfast ham	1 slice	once a week	5
Pancakes	4	once a week	2½

Item	*Amount*	*Frequency*	*Net loss in one year*
		Lunch	
Bread	1 slice	daily	6 pounds
Soup (cream)	1 bowl	once a week	3
Potato chips	10	4 times a week	6
Ice cream soda	1	once a week	5
Pizza	2 slices	weekly	3
Catsup	6 tablespoons	weekly	1
Tunafish	3 ounces	once a week	3
Mayonnaise	4 tablespoons	weekly	4
Sandwich meat	1 slice	once a week	4½
Frankfurter	2	weekly	3
Hamburger	1 patty	once a week	2½
Cookies	6	weekly	6
		Dinner	
Oil and vinegar dressing	½ usual amount	daily	5 pounds
French fries	1 serving	twice a week	6
Mashed potatoes	1 serving	once a week	3½
Rice	1 cup	once a week	2
Fishsticks	1 serving	weekly	4½
Dinner rolls	3	weekly	1½
Cake	1 slice	once a week	3
Pie	1 slice	once a week	3½
Canned fruit (in heavy syrup)	1 serving	twice a week	3
Whipped cream	2 tablespoons	twice a week	2
Ice cream	1 serving	twice a week	4

*All figures approximate. Actual weight losses will depend on the subject's weight at the outset of the diet, his rate of weight loss, the consistency of his caloric sacrifice, and whether he actually drops the selected item from his diet or merely substitutes for it.

Weigh yourself no oftener than once a week. If it is true, where weight loss is concerned, that nothing succeeds like success, then it is even truer that nothing fails like failure. The principal reason why diets fail is that dieters abandon them before they have had a chance to succeed, and the principal reason for this is that most diets seem to fail at first even as they are succeeding. As the body adjusts to any new diet—and most particularly to any nutritionally balanced, low-calorie diet—fluids are retained. As a result there is frequently no apparent weight loss during the second, third, and sometimes even fourth weeks of a new diet. Adipose tissue is being burned all this time, but the impact of that loss is not registering on your bathroom scale. If you do not weigh yourself during this period, you will not be discouraged by what the scales say. In fact, the less often you listen to what the scales say, the more likely you will be to adhere to your new regimen.

Snack. This may seem the most radical suggestion of all. It may also prove the most effective. Authorities do not understand precisely why it should be so, but it happens that snacking within an hour or so of mealtimes reduces hunger during the meals themselves. The thinking is that the very act of eating, combined with even the most modest intake of calories, acts to depress the hunger center of the brain. As a result, you reach the dinner table with your glucostat artificially lowered, and you can achieve the same degree of satiety with less actual food. The chart on pages 204–05 suggests the types of foods that make appropriate snacks. If you do choose to snack before mealtimes, make this snack a regular part of your routine. Eat it at a specific time every day—say, just before going out for your afternoon walk—and use it as an excuse to serve yourself less at the ensuing meal.

What we have offered above, without identifying it as such, is an example of how the Master Plan can be applied to almost any weight problem or set of circumstances. By making the eating of that snack a part of your daily routine, by supplanting an old, pernicious pattern with a new, beneficial one, you are employing behavior modification to amend your eating habits. By choosing a snack food from the chart on pages 204–05, you are substituting a nutritious, low-calorie foodstuff for a higher calorie item—and in the process reinforcing better nutritional habits. By combining the snack—a reward—with an afternoon walk, you are making exercise a pleasurable part of your day, eagerly anticipated and cheerfully undertaken. And by using the snack as a mild form of punishment, you are denying yourself calories at dinner, and lessening your meals.

This is but one example, and admittedly a theoretical one, of how the elements of the Master Plan may be combined to produce an effective program of permanent, long-term weight reduction. The program that succeeds for you will be one that you tailor to your own circumstances, eating habits, conditioned responses, particular cravings, daily patterns, and dietary preferences. The suggestions contained in the last forty-seven pages are many, the possible successful combinations almost limitless, and the choices yours to make. You have surveyed the smörgåsbord; now return to page 183 and make your initial selection. Do not be afraid to experiment, and do not be afraid to fail. There are as many answers to the puzzle of obesity as there are people with weight problems. Somewhere in these pages lies the solution to your personal puzzle.

ACKNOWLEDGMENTS

It is the rare author who has an editorial board in the family, and I would be remiss indeed if I failed to acknowledge the contributions that my parents have made to this volume. My father, a consultant on the staff of the Mayo Clinic for thirty-six years and former editor of the *Mayo Clinic Proceedings*, is, in additon, Durling Professor of Medicine at Mayo Medical School. From the inception of this project I have relied heavily upon his decades of experience with patients, his broad medical scholarship, and his shrewd observations on human nature to guide my research and refine my approach to the subject matter.

My mother, whose first career was in publishing, also read the manuscript at every stage of production; and although her chief concern was style, not content, her contribution was no less valuable. I would like to think that the final draft reflects her conviction that it is possible to treat any subject, no matter how technical, with clarity, concision, and common sense.

I am likewise grateful to Clifford F. Gastineau, consultant in nutrition at the Mayo Clinic, former chairman of the section of Endocrine and Metabolic Disease, and Endicott Professor of Medicine at Mayo Medical School. It was he who guided me through the maze of misinformation on diet and nutrition, counseling, correcting, and cautioning along the way. From start to finish he has been generous with his time, thoughtful in his comments, and exacting in his criticism. There is no question in my mind that *The Thin Game* is a more valuable book for his efforts.

I would also like to express my very genuine gratitude to Patrick Dillon and Jill Uhlfelder for their suggested manucript revisions; to Jack D. Key and the staff of the Mayo Medical Library for expediting my initial research; to my editor, Kathleen Berger, for shepherding *The Thin Game* through production; to Roseanne Marks, for preparing the index; and to my designer, Mary Ann Joulwan, for giving the book its final form.

New York City E.B.
April, 1978

INDEX